A VAMPIRE'S VENGEANCE

DEATHLESS NIGHT SERIES #2

L. E. WILSON

EVERBLOOD
PUBLISHING

ALSO BY L.E. WILSON

Deathless Night Series (The Vampires)

A Vampire Bewitched

A Vampire's Vengeance

A Vampire Possessed

A Vampire Betrayed

A Vampire's Submission

A Vampire's Choice

Deathless Night-Into the Dark Series (The Vampires)

Night of the Vampire

Secret of the Vampire

Forsworn by the Vampire

The Kincaid Werewolves (The Werewolves)

Lone Wolf's Claim

A Wolf's Honor

The Alpha's Redemption

A Wolf's Promise

A Wolf's Treasure

The Alpha's Surrender

Southern Dragons (Dragon Shifters & Vampires)

Dance for the Dragon

Burn for the Dragon

<u>Snow Ridge Shifters (<u>Novellas</u>)</u>

A Second Chance on Snow Ridge

A Fake Fiancé on Snow Ridge

Copyright © 2015 by L.E. Wilson

All rights reserved. No part of this publication may be reproduced, distributed, or transmitted in any form or by any means, including photocopying, recording, or other electronic or mechanical methods, without the prior written permission of the publisher, except in the case of brief quotations embodied in critical reviews and certain other noncommercial uses permitted by copyright law. For permission requests, email the publisher, addressed "Attention: Permissions Coordinator," at the address below.

All characters and events in this book are fictitious. Any resemblance to actual persons – living or dead – is purely coincidental.

le@lewilsonauthor.com

ISBN: 978-1-945499-41-8

Cover Design by Coffee and Characters

This book is dedicated to my sister, Nikki. She's been my encouragement, my cheerleader, my beta reader, my idea bouncer offer, and all around person I couldn't live without. You may be my "half" sister, but I love you with my whole heart! Thank you, Coley!

1

LUUKAS

Luukas was jolted back to consciousness as a searing pain tore through his abdomen. His eyes shot open to see a long silver blade carving through the layers of skin and muscle, splitting him open like a gutted deer. Hanging by the wrists as he was, he could do nothing but watch in horror as warm blood gushed down the front of his dirty jeans, soaking through the material to stick to the bare skin beneath.

His fangs punched down in defense, a loud hiss escaping him as he threw his head back, gritting his teeth against the pain. Half a second later, fire burned through the same path as the blade before it, the stench of his own burning skin making his stomach heave. He struggled not to scream, but the hoarse sound ripped from his raw throat against his will, the agony too much for him to bear in silence. The flames sizzled inch by slow inch across his stomach, cauterizing the wound.

His dislocated shoulders jutted grotesquely through his skin as he twisted his torso back and forth, trying to escape the flames, but the silver manacles around his wrists held fast to the wall above his head. Just when he thought he was going to pass out again, it stopped, leaving behind a dull throbbing ache from his ribcage to his hip. He sagged on his chains, sucking in ragged breaths, praying to all the gods that he would pass out again.

Or better yet, that he would just die already. Die a vampire's true death.

"He's awake *now*, mistress."

At the sound of that sniveling voice, Luukas struggled to lift his heavy head. He detested that voice. Peering through the slits of his swollen eyes, he attempted to locate the source of it, and found it directly in front of him in the form of a young, dark-skinned, male vampire: young in both human *and* vampire years.

Their eyes met and held, and the young one's own grew wide at what he saw. The piece of shit stumbled backwards, the flaming torch he'd pulled off of the wall and used on Luukas falling from his hand to land with a soft thump on the dirt floor. The long, bloody knife he held in the other hand joined it with a clatter a moment later.

Maybe he was surprised that Luukas could still focus on him. Maybe he saw his imminent death in the soulless, black eyes that now had him on their radar. Whatever it was, it caused him to impatiently ask the person on his left, "May I please leave now, mistress?"

He must have been granted permission, for he hightailed it out of the room, practically running for the open door and heading towards the stone stairway across the way.

Luukas' vehement stare followed him across the room, his lip curling up in a sneer when the coward dared to peek back at him over his shoulder. He paled beneath his dark skin when he saw that Luukas was still tracking him, and he kicked it into vamp speed, disappearing up the stairs.

Luuk's eyes skittered back across the room after he was gone, coming to rest on someone else huddled in the corner, as far away from him as they could get. He winced as he blinked his raw eyes, trying to focus through the sweat running into them, but he couldn't get a clear view, there were too many shadows from the flickering light of the torches on the walls.

He had a vague feeling that he should know that cowering form, but he was so tired. His head fell forward onto his chest, only to jerk upright again almost immediately. Something pulled his attention to that corner, no matter how he tried to ignore it.

He studied the person again. He could just barely make out a small form with long, dark hair, but little else, as she kept her head down. And it was definitely a she. He could see that even through the blanket she held wrapped tightly around herself.

Did he know her? He tried to remember, but his thoughts were so disordered, jumping around randomly in his head.

He couldn't seem to concentrate on any one thing for more than a few seconds at a time.

Gradually, through the haze of his pain, he began to notice other things.

He was in a large, dimly lit room dug from the earth; a cell of sorts, with no windows. The smell of wet earth was heavy in the air, coating the back of his throat, and a consistent *drip, drip, drip* off to his right tantalized him with the promise of water. He tried to wet his cracked lips with his sandpaper tongue. He was so thirsty.

Where the fuck was he? What was he doing here? His head pounded as he tried hard to remember.

Suddenly, he sensed a darker entity in the room. He could practically feel the evil oozing through the air towards him. Tearing his eyes from the girl in the corner, he rolled his head to the other side until he was able to focus on the female slithering towards him from the opposite direction.

Her blood-red eyes flashed as she met his gaze, a pleased smile curving her lips.

"Leeha," he rasped.

Memories crashed mercilessly into his head, banging around his skull until he groaned from the impact.

He remembered now.

Seven Years Ago

. . .

He'd left his apartment in Seattle to go meet with Leeha, alone, a female vampire who'd been adopted into his colony, and who'd decided to leave of her own accord to form one of her own, after he'd rejected her amorous overtures.

She'd continued her propositions towards him even after she'd left, doing everything she could think of to try to convince him to do the unheard of - mate with another vampire. It was a ludicrous idea. Vampires couldn't sustain one another. One half of the couple always needed to be a human. There was no other acceptable match for their kind. Whenever two vampires tried to mate, the fighting and jealousy that ensued from the need to feed on others, on humans, inevitably tore them apart, often violently. Vampires were way too territorial to share their significant other, and feeding was way too intertwined with the need for sex.

They were also too possessive to share their hard-won territory, even with a prized mate.

He'd agreed to meet with her because he'd wanted to convince her once and for all that although she was free to form her own settlement if she so chose, he was never going to combine hers with his and rule alongside of her. A harsh reality she was having trouble accepting.

His brother, Nikulas, had tried to make him stay, or at least to take someone with him, but he'd stubbornly...stupidly... refused, insisting on going alone.

Driving north to the Canadian border, he'd easily "persuaded" the officials there that his passport was legit, and passed through without a problem. Less than thirty minutes later, he'd pulled off the main road towards Leeha's mountain fortress.

It'd never crossed his mind that he'd be driving into a trap, or at least not one that would ever actually work. He was one of the most powerful vampires of his time, and was, therefore, invincible.

Or so he'd believed.

Foolishly, he'd underestimated the danger he'd been in. Never in a million years would he have thought that Leeha would manage to find a way to harness *him*, a Master vampire. *Her* Master, until she'd banished herself, taking every young, besotted male in his colony along with her.

But not only had she managed to harness his power, with a little help, she'd managed to keep him in this hellhole against his will for...he had no idea how long now. Days? Months? Years?

In the beginning, she'd kept him confined to an opulent room directly next door to hers. He'd tried every mental and physical power he possessed to escape, all to no avail. It was like he'd become human again.

She'd laughed at his efforts, and tried to convince him, both with her words and her body, to see things her way. He'd refused over and over, rejecting both her ideas and her offering of herself, adamantly demanding that she release him. Even with the evidence proving otherwise, he'd arrogantly refused to believe that anyone could get the best of him. She'd responded to his stubbornness by refusing him blood to drink, starving him and debilitating him even more. He hadn't worried overmuch, even then, as he knew his brother would come looking for him when he didn't return home.

Then had come the day she'd finally lost her patience with him. Barging into his room, she'd charged over to where he sat on the floor in the corner, arms resting on his drawn-up knees, head down. She'd appeared quite remorseful, even as she'd given him one last chance to redeem himself and agree to be with her, before he forced her to take more drastic measures.

He'd slowly raked his eyes up her body, taking in her delicate high heels, her long legs and full breasts barely concealed in a black, gossamer gown, her graceful arms and long, thick, red hair. Her haunted, blood red eyes had been luminous with unshed tears, but were steady in her conviction of what she must do if he refused her.

Luukas had smiled at her warmly, and watched her expression turn to one of tentative relief.

Hope had shone from her eyes, and the corners of her full lips had turned up into a hesitant smile. Clasping her hands together in front of her with joy, she'd stepped closer, holding them out to him.

Ignoring her outstretched hands, Luukas had pushed himself up off of the floor, slowly straightening up to his full height.

As he'd towered over her, uncertainty had flashed briefly across her face before her smile reappeared full force. "Have you finally changed your mind then, my love?"

"Leeha," he'd purred, "I would sink my dick into a stinking, rotting corpse before I would fuck *you*."

The sound of her slap had echoed through the room, merging with her screech of rage. "You bastard!" Visibly fighting for control, she'd taken a deep breath. "You will regret this, Luukas Kreek. I am about to make your life so excruciatingly painful; you'll wish *you* were a rotting corpse. But have no doubts, you *will* be with me, one way or the other, even if I have to forcibly keep you here. Forever."

Luukas had smiled as she'd screamed for her freakish guards, and continued to smile as they'd lurched into the room, their putrid smell making him gag as their long, yellow claws dug into his arms and they'd dragged him from the room.

His brother would appear any moment, he was certain.

Current Day

A slithery touch on his cheek brought him reeling back to the present, his skin crawling at the contact. He jerked his face away in disgust.

"Still so stubborn," Leeha sighed. "How long must we do this, Luukas?" Her richly accented voice placed the emphasis on the last syllable of his name, as it was pronounced in her home country.

He kept his head turned away, struggling to stay conscious, refusing to speak to her, or to so much as look at her. He was so tired, the endless agony he was being forced to endure draining the life from him.

"Luukas, look at me," she demanded. "Luukas!"

Another heavy sigh escaped her when he stubbornly wouldn't heed her order; this battle of wills the only power he still had.

"Keira! Come here," she called impatiently.

Keira?

Why did that name sound so familiar? He heard a shuffling from the corner, as the girl there took a few steps forward, then stopped.

"Please," she whispered. "Don't make me do this."

Her voice...it was like that of an angel, and a wave of calmness washed over him, the blackness threatening again within the unexpected peace.

He fought it back, needing to stay alert. He wanted to hear the angel speak again.

"I said, COME!" Leeha's shrill shriek rang harshly through the small cell, making him wince.

He heard a quiet sob as the girl inched her way towards them, finally coming to stand next to Leeha. An urgent feeling of protectiveness hit him suddenly, and he frowned, confused.

"Now," Leeha ordered. "*Make* him look at me."

"I don't want to do this," the girl insisted.

Seconds ticked by. He heard the girl swallow hard, and then his head was moving against his will. He ground his teeth together and tried to keep it where it was, but nothing he did kept it from turning, until he was facing Leeha and the girl next to her.

Not the girl. The *witch*.

She stood before him, one hand raised, effortlessly directing the movement of his head. Her large, hazel eyes filled with tears as they met his.

At the sight of that lovely face, Luukas lunged forward, fangs bared in a loud hiss. Ignoring his screaming muscles, he threw himself at her, snapping his teeth within inches of her pale skin.

With a startled cry, she threw up her other hand to join the first, palms out.

Luukas let out a roar as he was slammed back into the wall by an invisible force. He desperately tried to break her hold, the sight of *her* alone succeeding at doing what the knife and torch hadn't; made him want to fight.

"Please stop!" she cried out. "You're only hurting yourself more!"

"You fucking bitch!" he bellowed.

Madness threatened as he roared at his own helplessness. *She* was the reason he was here. *She* was the one keeping him here. It was *her* fucking spells making him so weak, allowing them to starve him, beat him, slice him open…even burn him without incinerating him.

He was going to rip her apart, piece by bloody piece, if it was the last thing he ever did.

2

KEIRA

Tears rolled freely down Keira's face, her heart breaking inside her chest as she held the vampire immobile against his will. She despised her abilities, despised her magic. Hated that it enabled the evil female at her side to force her to emasculate this strong, beautiful male: this male that she now loved.

She held him there against the stones as he raged, until he finally passed out again, his blood-covered, emaciated body hanging lifeless from his chains.

Gritting her teeth and dropping her arms, she tried again to plead with the demented female standing at her side. "Please, Leeha. He's weak enough now from not feeding. It's been years. You don't need me here anymore! Please, let me go." So she could figure out a way to come back and save him.

Leeha approached her prisoner, running her hand lightly down his hard chest. Strips of his shirt fell in tatters around his lean waist from countless whippings and knifings, the waistband of his jeans and the strip around his neck the only things really holding it up. A tremor ran through him and he let out a soft groan, as though he cringed from her touch even in his unconscious state.

Keira winced at the sound, wanting to knock the bitch's hand away from him. "I won't do this anymore, Leeha. Do you hear me? I refuse to be a part of your sick plan any longer!"

"Oh, stop with all of the dramatics." Leeha scoffed. "He'll be fine, just as soon as he stops being so damn self-sacrificing." She sighed heavily. "He's only trying to protect his creations." One corner of her lips turned up in a smirk. "Little does he know, it's already too late for that."

Her eyes roved lovingly over his masculine physique, and Keira tensed, hating the possessive way she looked at him.

"I do care about him, you know." Leeha's voice was wistful. "I always have. He cares about me too," she insisted to her. "He told me so once, right after he burned my father alive. He just refuses to admit it."

She smiled strangely at Keira. It made her nervous. "Funny, how he reacts so violently to you. If I didn't know better, I'd almost be jealous." Her head jerked to the side like a bird as she eyed the other woman. "I can't quite figure it out. After all, I'm the one who brought him here. I'm the one who orders these sessions. Why do you bring out more emotion in him than I?"

She shrugged delicately, making a dismissive noise. "I'll sway him over to my side eventually."

Keira couldn't blame him for acting the way he did towards her. If it weren't for her, he wouldn't be here.

"Let me go, Leeha."

"I can't do that, witch. I need you."

"No, you don't!" Keira maintained.

Leeha smiled benignly. "Stupid, stupid girl. Did you really believe I would just let you go? Allow you to go back to your boring life? With you here, I have more power than I ever dreamed possible." She giggled with delight, gesturing to Luukas. "Even a powerful Master vampire is naught but putty in my hands."

Keira stared at her in disbelief. "You can't just keep me here forever."

Leeha bared her fangs without warning, nightmares swirling in her eyes until Keira had to look away, lest she get sucked into them, until she was as mad as her vampire. "Oh, but I can. And if you think to defy me...well, I'll just have to pay a quick visit to your home, and a certain naive little sister of yours." Sheathing her fangs, she hid a mischievous giggle behind her hand. "Well, maybe not so naive anymore."

Keira's hands fisted at her sides as her head snapped up, her eyes shooting fire at the threat to her sister. "You stay the hell away from Emma."

Leeha wagged a finger in her face. "Temper, temper, witch. Remember, I have a contingency plan. If anything happens to me, you'll never reach her in time. There won't be a thing you can do to save her."

Breathing heavily, Keira forced herself to look away, and kept her mouth shut and her magic dormant.

Leeha studied her thoughtfully for a moment. "Since you're such a bleeding heart, I think I'll just leave you in here, instead of returning you to your cell. Maybe your presence will 'comfort' him some more." She giggled again, sweeping her gown aside dramatically to leave, crossing the cell so fast she seemed to disappear and reappear in the doorway.

"What? NO! Leeha...Leeha!" Keira rushed after her, but the thick wooden door was slammed in her face. Yanking on the handle, she threw her shoulder into it and tried to knock it loose, but it wouldn't budge.

Narrowing her eyes rebelliously, she began to speak the words of an unlocking spell through gritted teeth, when Leeha called from the other side in a singsong voice, "I wouldn't do that if I were you, witch."

Keira paused mid-verse, reigning in her temper, and dropped her hands.

Tiredly closing her eyes, she listened to Leeha order one of the "normal" guards to stay there and watch the door. She pulled her threadbare blanket closer around herself, covering her bare arms and legs, unsuccessfully trying to keep the damp chill at bay. Taking a fortifying breath, she resisted the urge to cough, and tried to ignore the way the musty air burned her lungs. She didn't know if it would be enough to rouse the vampire again, but she didn't want to take the chance.

A VAMPIRE'S VENGEANCE

Quietly as she could, she shuffled back to her corner in the shadows and sank down onto the cold dirt. Her belly growled loudly and she placed a hand over it. They'd probably forget to feed her again.

Her eyes misted over. How had she gotten herself into this mess?

She missed her sister, and prayed that she was ok. The last time she'd seen Emma, they'd been leaving a carnival near their hometown. It was the first time they'd really had fun since their parents had died months before. After riding every ride and eating millions of calories worth of carnival food, they'd chased each other across the field towards their car, and had wandered into a nightmare, to find creatures of hell waiting for them.

Tall and thin, yet strangely muscular, their grey skin was rotting off of their bare bodies, yet they were alive. Blood oozed from their bulging eyes as they observed the girls, and then their leader had pushed its hairless head towards them and hissed loudly, bloody saliva dripping from its mouthful of fangs...

They'd come for *her*, one of them scooping her up onto its bony shoulder and running off into the trees. Its claws had dug into the backs of her legs to keep her still, and it had lapped at the bleeding wounds disgustingly as it carried her through the woods.

She'd screamed at her sister to "RUN!" but it was too late. As she'd watched helplessly, the remaining creatures had closed in on Emma, cutting her off from her sight. Keira had no idea what had happened to her, other than what Leeha had told her: That she was released safe and sound once Keira had been taken far enough away.

Problem was, there was no way in hell she trusted that bitch. Had they attacked her sister? Fed from her? Let her go? Was she home safe, or locked up in a dirty cell like this one? Was she even still alive, or had they killed her?

A single tear escaped her tightly closed eyes, leaving a wet trail down her dirt-streaked cheek. She wiped it away with a shaky sigh. Feeling sorry for herself wouldn't get her anywhere. What she needed to do was figure out a way to get them all out of this mess: Emma, herself, and the vampire.

As though he sensed her attention on him, she heard his chains rattle as he moaned, the pitiful sound bringing a fresh bout of tears to her eyes. Sliding one booted foot in towards himself, he tried to get his leg under him to relieve his disjointed shoulders of some of his weight, but he was too weak, and he collapsed again with a jerk and a hiss of pain as his foot slipped back out from under him. His head lolled on his chest as he, thankfully, blacked out again.

Keira let her eyes roam over him as he hung there. Even dirty, starved, and covered in his own drying blood, he was a beautiful specimen of a male.

His thick, dark hair brushed the bottom of his neck and hung in his face, hiding his broad forehead, prominent cheekbones, and strong jaw. His eyes, when open, were deep set and intense, and inexplicably, had darkened to a depthless ebony a year or so after he'd been brought down here.

What was left of his t-shirt did nothing to hide the ropes of muscle straining against the confinement of the chains. His olive-toned skin was ashen and slightly loose on his bones from the lack of feedings, but she remembered the rich coloring he'd had, and would have again, if she had anything to say about it.

Seven Years Ago

The moment she'd first caught sight of him, Keira's heart had stopped beating, only to resume pounding hard and fast in her chest a moment later.

The notorious Luukas Kreek: the Master vampire who'd crossed an entire ocean and built up his own colony of vampires in a brand new land; a risk that had been unheard of before he came along.

Her breath had caught in her throat when he'd stepped from his vehicle outside the front entrance of Leeha's main fortress and confidently strolled towards them. Wearing only jeans, combat boots, and a casual black t-shirt, he nonetheless had a commanding presence which demanded her attention.

She couldn't take her eyes off of him.

His power coiled around him like a living essence, preceding him as he strode their way. It slithered over her skin when it reached her, feeling her out. Though she'd stood behind and slightly to the left of the female vampire who'd called him there, silver-grey eyes had honed in on her immediately, shining through the inky night like beacons. He'd smiled at her, and she'd returned the smile, powerless to do otherwise, until she'd remembered the reason she was there.

He'd frowned slightly as her smile had faltered, his eyes narrowing in suspicion as he'd quickly glanced at Leeha, and then towards the thick trees on either side of the creek that flowed directly into the mountain in front of him.

He'd known then. He'd known that something was up. Pausing briefly where he was, he'd raised an eyebrow, a question in his eyes.

She'd never met him before, had only heard stories, but something inside of her had balked at being a part of what Leeha had planned. Mindful of the threat to her sister, she'd tried to warn him without drawing attention to herself, looking pointedly at his Hummer and then back at him, trying to tell him to run for it.

But he'd just cocked his head and grinned arrogantly, fearlessly. She'd known why he wasn't afraid. There weren't many threats to a Master vampire as powerful as he was. Actually, there were only two: killing all of his created children, his power draining with each death, and a witch. A powerful witch...like Keira. And she, under Leeha's orders, had been very careful to keep her magic concealed so he wouldn't sense it.

Approaching the two females, Luukas had come to a halt directly in front of Leeha, finally dragging his eyes from Keira long enough to greet her. Bending at the waist, he'd taken her proffered hand, briefly kissing the back of it before letting it drop back to her side.

"Leeha."

His voice was deep and as smooth as a fine cognac. He'd spoken in low tones, and Keira had felt chills whisper over her skin as he'd bowed again and introduced himself to her, boldly raking his eyes over her small form. "My name is Luukas Kreek, originally from Estonia."

She'd opened her mouth to tell him her name, but was interrupted by Leeha before she could say anything.

"She is not important," she'd sneered. "I trust you had no troubles finding my home?"

Luukas had stared intensely at Keira a moment longer before turning his attention back to his hostess. "No trouble at all. Shall we go in? Or are we going to do this out here?"

Leeha had smiled at him sweetly, looking up at him through lowered lashes. "Follow me." Shooting a warning look Keira's way, she'd grabbed her roughly by the arm and pushed her out in front, while she herself fell into step with Luukas.

"Do you have a new pet?" she'd heard him ask.

Leeha had chuckled. "You could say that."

"Does she not have any warmer clothes?"

Keira had still been wearing the rolled-up cargo shorts, slip-on Keds, and white, short-sleeved printed T-shirt she'd worn to the carnival.

Leeha had been silent for a moment. "I suppose I could find her something," she'd said offhandedly.

She hadn't. Keira still wore the same clothes today, but she *had* been given something of a blanket.

Following the rambling creek into the cave at the base of the mountain, Keira had felt the tiny hairs rise on the back of her neck as she felt the weight of his eyes on her. She tried to ignore him, leading them over to the tunnel that would take them into the interior. Torches lined the walls, lighting the way through the narrow space, until it gradually opened into a gaping cavern, and Luukas had whistled with appreciation as he'd taken it all in. "Wow. Quite a place you have here."

The main room they'd entered had been gouged out of the mountain interior until it resembled a great cathedral of old, including mosaic floor tiles, massive columns, and a soaring ceiling of pointed arches. At the far end of the center aisle were smooth stone steps leading up to a large platform, upon which sat an impressive throne made of the same glossy, black stone that lined the walls, with threads of glittering gold interspersed throughout. Plush red cushions covered the seat and back, completing the royal effect.

Luukas had turned in a circle, taking in the full effect. "Impressive."

Leeha had preened like a peacock under his praise. "It took my vampires a full six months to construct it to my specifications. There is no electricity, but I prefer it that way. We do have running water, however," Leeha had told him proudly. "I think they did quite well."

"Where *are* all of your little minions?" Luukas had asked.

"Oh, they're around. There are many rooms here in my home, many more than meets the eye," Leeha had alluded.

Luukas smiled. "I would expect nothing less." With another quick glance at Keira, he'd proposed, "Shall we get down to business?"

Giving him a regal nod, Leeha had glided down the aisle and climbed the stairs to take her place upon the throne, over-exaggerating the sway of her hips in her sheer gown like a canine in heat.

Keira had barely resisted the urge to roll her eyes, and placed herself over to the side of the platform as instructed beforehand.

Luukas had only looked amused at Leeha's display as he took his place on the main floor directly in front of, and below, her.

Sitting regally upon her chair, she'd indicated that he was allowed to speak.

Clasping his hands behind him, he'd presented his case, his deep voice carrying across the vast space easily. "I agreed to meet you here today to end this misunderstanding between us, once and for all. I am aware that your adopted father raised you to believe in what can only be called a fantasy, and I am truly sorry for that. But that's all it is, a fantasy. I have been lenient with you up until now, because I know it's hard for you to come to terms with the fact that he lied to you. But enough is enough. You have created your own colony by taking a group of my own vampires, and I will allow you to keep them and have your little home up here. In return, you need to stay within your boundaries, and give up this silly idea of yours. There has never been a time when two vampires have ruled together as equals and that's not going to change. Find yourself a nice, little human male to play with and make him your mate, if it pleases you."

Here he'd paused, and his eyes had begun to glow an eerie grey-green as his voice had taken on a menacing timbre. "However, if I hear anything more of you disregarding the rules and threatening our existence with your careless hunting of humans, you will have the same fate as your father. And I will come here again and carry it out myself."

Gathering the force of his power tightly around himself again, his eyes had dimmed back to grey, and he'd given her a patronizing smile. "I think I'm being more than fair about this. Other Masters would have killed you long ago for your impertinence."

Leeha's expression hadn't changed while he'd made his speech, and she'd continued to look at him impassively as she'd appeared to think on what he had just said. Finally, she'd sighed with disappointment.

"I'm afraid you still don't take me seriously, Luukas, and I'm beginning to wonder if you ever will. But you must believe that I do care about you, and I know you care about me. What do I have to do to convince you that we belong together?"

"There is *nothing* you can do," he'd asserted, "that would ever convince me. I'm sorry to be so blunt, but I don't have feelings for you Leeha. Not like that."

"But you do," she purred, "and you will come to realize this, Luukas. Eventually."

Keira had kept her eyes down and tried not to fidget as the tension in the room had grown to an uncomfortable level. It had gone on for so long that she'd nearly jumped out of her skin when Leeha had suddenly ordered, "Keira! Do it! Now!"

Keira had cast a frantic look her way. She was really going to make her do this?

Leeha had slowly stood, daggers shooting from her blood-red eyes. In a menacing tone, she'd spoken just one word: "Sister."

She'd known Luukas had been studying her, trying to figure out what was going on, but she hadn't been able to bring herself to look at him.

She'd had no choice.

Closing her eyes and lifting her arms towards him, Keira had drawn on all of the powers of the earth's energy, pulling them into herself and releasing her magic. She'd heard Luukas gasp as her spell reached towards him, swirling around him to draw on his power.

"What are you doing?!" he'd roared.

Tears filling her eyes, she'd squeezed them tight as she'd spoken the incantation that would harness the power of a Master vampire and allow him to be captured, drawing it into herself.

Her chants rose louder and louder, and she'd opened her eyes to see him fall onto his knees, his back arched and his muscles pulled taut as he'd fought the magic. But he was no match for her, and he'd collapsed onto the floor as she'd finished the spell and lowered her hands.

"Guards!" Leeha had shrieked gleefully. "Take him to the room next to mine, and lock him in."

A foul smell had filled the room as half a dozen of Leeha's morbid creations had lurched through a hidden doorway, hissing at Keira as they'd passed.

She'd recoiled from them, the night they'd stolen her from the carnival grounds, just a few days before, still fresh in her mind. Her wounds had still been healing.

Two of them had hauled Luukas off, and Leeha had ordered the remaining ones to "Take her down to one of the cells."

Keira had had no time to react before they'd had her by the arms and were dragging her away. As they'd reached the doorway of the tunnel leading down to the underground, she'd heard Leeha call out after them, "Remember our deal, witch!"

Current Day

She'd been down here ever since. She still wondered how Leeha had found out about her. Her family had gone above and beyond to keep her existence and her practicing a secret, to prevent something just like this from happening.

They'd brought Luukas down to the cell next to hers a few months after he'd arrived. How long ago was that now? Three years? Five? Keira had lost track.

She'd cringed under her blanket in the corner of her cell as they'd passed by, praying he wouldn't see her, and relieved beyond measure when he hadn't looked her way.

That relief was short-lived, however, for Leeha had soon grown tired of his continued resistance and had started calling Keira into his cell to participate in his "emotional rehabilitation".

Forcing her to use her magic, she'd pushed his limits to new heights, torturing him in ways that were so horrendous it made Keira gag, and gave her nightmares whenever she managed to sleep. Luckily, that wasn't very often.

If she started feeling rebellious and refused Leeha's wishes, all it took was a reminder of the threat to Emma to bring her back in line.

Keira hated herself for what she was doing to him, and that hatred grew more every day. For the gods were cruel - even crueler than Leeha - because somehow, over the years, in the midst of this nightmare, she had fallen for her vampire.

But she didn't see any way to get out of her part in all of this; at least not until she could get them out of there, and saw for herself that her sister was safe.

However, now that she was in the same cell, maybe there was something she could do to relieve his suffering, if only a little.

Pushing herself up off the floor, she walked over to the door and stood on her tiptoes until she could see out of the small window. A dirty-blonde head was on the other side, and Keira sent up a silent thanks. She knew this guard. He liked to leer at her through the door of her cell whenever she tried to wash herself with what little water they allowed her. Not that it helped much, without a change of clothes.

She'd been embarrassed at first, but eventually, she'd gotten over it. Let him look. Leeha wouldn't let anyone touch her. She needed Keira's magic to enable her to take out her sick frustrations on Luukas.

"Hey," she whispered. She knew he'd hear her. Vamps had excellent hearing.

He didn't turn around, but the slight tilt of his head told her that he was listening. Keeping her voice down, she made her play. "I have an offer for you, Blondie. Have they brought your dinner yet?" He turned his head slightly to the right and back to the left. "Ok. Good. I'll make you a deal. If you let me have your dinner, no questions asked, I'll provide you with a better one. Something from a real, live human, if you get what I mean." Lifting her arm, she waved her bare wrist back and forth in front of the small opening, smiling bitterly as his head whipped towards it and he inhaled deeply.

The guards were fed blood bags shortly after nightfall. Keira knew this because she'd heard them talking about it. She also knew that they detested bagged blood by the way they bitched about it. "Do we have a deal?"

She could practically hear him salivating as he gave a sharp nod.

She nodded back, even though he couldn't see her. Ok then. "Good."

As she headed back to her corner, she hoped like hell that this particular vampire had some semblance of self-control, and wouldn't get carried away with his meal. At least he seemed somewhat sane, unlike her new cellmate.

3

LEEHA

After leaving Luukas' cell, Leeha went straight to her private chambers. Closing the door, she locked it securely behind her. She needed a good soak in a nice hot bath. This business with Luukas was making her entirely too tense. He was just so stubborn. Most males would have broken years ago, but the fact that he hadn't only made her want him more. A lot of males looked good, but inner strength like that was so hard to find these days.

A delicious shiver ran down her spine as she envisioned that strength moving above her in her bed. She'd never had sex with the Master vampire, but she fantasized about it all the time when she was alone, and when she was fucking someone else. Imagining she was with Luukas was the only way she could get her pleasure.

Strolling over to her dressing table, she sat down to take off her ruby necklace. She rubbed her fingers over the stone lovingly. It was her favorite piece of jewelry. Her father had given it to her shortly before he was put to death for creating her.

It matched her eyes.

She missed him, her creator. He'd taken her from a life of neglect and starvation with the humans and adopted her into his family, protecting her and caring for her like she was his very own child.

In return, all he'd asked of her was a *tiny* little sip of her blood when he tucked her in at night.

A child's blood, he'd told her, was the best blood of all. It was fresh and innocent and pure, unlike an adult's blood, which had been muddied up with evil thoughts and deeds.

The first few nights after her arrival, she'd been frightened when he'd snuggled up behind her in her new bed, but he'd been so very gentle with her, just as a real father would. Pulling her hair back off of her neck, he'd inhale deeply, and tell her how very sweet she smelled.

She'd barely felt his fangs sliding into the tender skin of her neck, and when he'd start to drink, pulling on the vein, it had actually felt kind of ...good.

Over time, as she'd matured, he'd spent more and more time with her while "tucking her in". After he'd taken his nightly drink, he would pull her in close to him, whispering things in her ear; wicked things that made her skin burn and her body tense up with apprehension. He would pet her as he talked to her, running his hand down her arm and up her thigh, calming her.

He would tell her that she was beautiful, and that she was destined for greatness. He'd tell her that she was going to be queen someday, and lead beside their Master. He'd tell her he needed to prepare her for that day, so that by the time she was of age, Lukas wouldn't be able to resist her.

His petting had become more and more aggressive, his words more urgent until finally, one night, he'd taken her innocence and made her a woman.

She'd liked the idea of being queen.

When she was twenty-five in human years, her father had turned her into what he was, without Luukas' permission: Illegally, as it turned out. She had woken up as a vampire, half mad with thirst, and her father had been there with someone for her to drink.

They had shared the young girl's blood, and when she'd had her fill, Leeha had watched as her father had raped the human before draining her dry. He wasn't loving with the girl like he was with her. She was only a human, he'd explained. Not special like Leeha.

When he'd brought her a new meal the next night, she'd joined in on the rape.

A month later, her father had proclaimed her ready to approach Luukas. *He will not be able to resist you!* he'd announced.

But he'd been wrong.

Luukas had stared at her like she had grown two heads when she'd finally gained an audience with him, demanding to know where she had come from, and who had turned her.

Taking off her dress, she'd offered him her body, explaining to him how her father had prepared her to rule by his side, and to please him in bed. Swiftly getting over his shock, Luukas had ordered her to dress herself, and gently but sternly told her that her father was horribly misguided.

He'd apologized for her suffering, and told her he would have removed her from the household if he had known what had been happening there.

He'd called a female vampire who lived in his building, and had her take Leeha to her home to live until he'd dealt with her father.

A week later, he'd burned her father to death in the mountains outside of Seattle.

Grabbing her hairbrush, she brushed her hair up off of her neck with angry strokes, securing it with a clip. Admiring her reflection in the mirror, a small smile suddenly turned up the corners of her lips.

"If you're going to spy on me," she chided, "you may as well come over here and help me get out of this gown."

After a moment, Josiah, her young apprentice, crept out from where he'd been lurking in the bathroom. "I'm sorry, mistress. I was only in here checking that you have everything you need when you walked in. You surprised me is all, and it seemed like you wanted to be alone."

She followed his movements in the mirror as he came up behind her and unzipped her gown. If his skin hadn't been so dark, she would've sworn he was blushing.

"It's all right, Josiah. You can help me with my bath."

His eyes flew up to meet hers in the mirror, before he quickly dropped them again. But not before she'd seen his complete adoration for her.

"Anything you need."

Kicking off her heels, she stood and sashayed into the bath, the bare skin of her back tingling under his scorching gaze. Josiah was her greatest admirer, she knew, and he was often useful. However, he still had so much to learn.

Turning on the water, she added some lavender to her oversized tub, inhaling the calming scent before dealing with his actions earlier.

"What I need," she told him, as she came back into the room, "is someone who doesn't flee in fear from a hateful look."

Josiah hung his head in shame. "You're right, of course. I don't know why I let him get to me. It's not like he can hurt me."

She caressed his cheek with her cold fingers. "No, he can't. I wouldn't let him. You are too important to me."

Clenching his jaw, he lifted his head, a challenge in his brown eyes. "If I'm so important, what do you need him for? We should remove the witch's protection of fire and just leave him in the sun to burn. It's been seven *years*, Leeha. He's not going to change his mind. *I* can rule alongside you. No one will ever be more loyal or love you more than I do."

"We've discussed this, Josiah," she told him curtly. "I need him. He's over six hundred years old, and is the most powerful Master vampire of our time. Whatever example he leads, the rest of our kind will follow."

She looked him up and down, "Do you really think anyone would follow *you*? You're nothing as far as vampires go. You're barely ten years old. What good is that to me and my plans?"

Josiah looked away, the muscle in his jaw jumping in anger.

With a burdened sigh, she softened her tone. "Don't be cross with me. I'll let you burn him again tomorrow if it will make you feel better."

"Can I whip him too?" he asked petulantly.

She smiled, "Of course. He'll heal. A little more slowly these days, but he will." She left him then to go turn off the bath water. "Come, my love. I'll let you wash my back. And afterwards, we can discuss the building of our legion."

When he didn't follow right away, she put her hands on her hips, her head tilting jerkily to the side. "Don't pout, Josiah. It's not attractive."

Dropping his arms to his sides, he heaved a great sigh, unable to resist her. His tongue darted out to lick his lips as Leeha slid her gown off of her pale shoulders and let it drop carelessly to the floor. She wore absolutely nothing underneath.

"Come, Josiah." She entreated huskily, holding out her hand to him.

He ran his hungry eyes from the top of her red hair to her small toes. With a moan of defeat, he pulled off his shirt and followed her into the bathroom to wash her back and anything else she desired him to.

4

LUUKAS

Luukas fought his way up through the blackness, driven by an urgency he couldn't name. But as he faded in and out of consciousness, the throbbing agony that comprised his physical form tried to pull him back down into the sweet depths of nothingness.

He wanted to let it take him, so badly, but no...he needed to stay awake.

Bit by bit, he became aware of a soft slurping sound that seemed out of place in this, his own personal hell. Attempting to quiet his ragged breathing, he listened closer.

He heard the consistent *drip, drip, drip* of the water he could never taste, and he heard the light pitter-patter of the rats as they scurried down the hall outside his cell.

His stomach clenched. Ah, gods...were they eating him again?

It wouldn't be the first time he'd awoken to find them chewing on his wounds as he hung there, their soft squeaks clawing at his sanity...but no, that wasn't what he heard this time. This was more of a sucking sound.

His eyes cracked opened as another sound came to his ears, a voice: the angel's voice.

"Stop," she whispered. "You need to stop now."

Luukas squeezed his eyes shut again in disbelief. He had to be hallucinating.

The dark-haired angel was still in his cell, pressed up against the wall by the door, her ragged blanket falling from one shoulder.

She was in the arms of a man. He was hunched over her, and he was kissing her neck.

He heard her whimper and his eyes popped open again. They were still there. He wasn't hallucinating.

As he watched, his angel began to struggle in the blonde man's arms, and her voice got sharper and more frantic.

"Stop! You have to stop!"

The man didn't stop. A low growl reverberated from deep within Luukas' throat. His fangs slid down with aggression as he restlessly shifted his weight on his chains. But still, the man didn't stop kissing her.

No. Not kissing. Feeding.

That was no man, but a vampire—and he was feeding from his angel.

Rage surged through him. A rage such as he'd never felt before.

She started pounding on the vampire's head and shoulders with her small fists, trying to break his hold.

He ignored her like she was nothing more than an annoying gnat, tightening his hold on her as she struggled.

Luukas strained against his chains, the sounds erupting from deep within his chest becoming animalistic in nature as he fought to get to her.

All of the noise must have finally disturbed the feeding vampire. His head jerked up from her neck, leaving ragged gashes where he had bitten her. He released her from his hold and stepped back, not bothering to heal the torn flesh.

Luukas roared with fury at the sight, lurching towards the other vampire with bared fangs and mad, wild eyes. The chains clanged loudly as they pulled him up short, but the pain of his shoulders and body didn't even register past his overwhelming need to kill the other vampire.

MINE!

The bastard smiled at him as he casually wiped the blood from his mouth with the back of his hand, then sauntered out of the cell, pulling the door shut behind him and locking it again with a clank.

Yanking impatiently on his chains, Luukas lunged towards the door, his fangs aching painfully with the need to rip into the fucking bastard.

His roar of frustration echoed through the cell when the chains still wouldn't give. After a minute or so, he finally gave up and fell back against the rock wall, chest heaving with exhaustion, shoulders throbbing.

A small movement out of the corner of his eye caught his attention. He whipped his head around to the girl, who was trying to staunch the flow of blood from her neck with an edge of the threadbare blanket. She didn't look at him as she ripped off long strips of it, wadding one up to apply pressure and tying the other around her throat to hold it there.

His top lip pulled back off of his fangs in a snarl as the smell of her blood permeated the small room; the overwhelming need of his thirst so intense, he nearly passed out again.

She must have sensed the change in him, for her hazel eyes flashed up to his, widening slightly as she took him in. Quickly, she crouched down and picked something up off of the floor.

She eyed him warily for a moment, seeming to gather up her nerve, before cautiously coming toward him, staying just out of his reach.

Closing his eyes, he inhaled her scent, groaning aloud at the unbelievable smell of her. Ah. Gods. She was torturing him.

Then she spoke. "I have something for you, and I know it will be hard, but you have to try to keep it under control."

His eyes snapped open in confusion, to find her fiddling with a blood bag.

A fucking plastic blood bag.

He nearly laughed out loud. After all the shit he gave his brother, Nikulas, for drinking those things, and here he was, thinking nothing had ever looked better to him.

Except for the female tampering with the seal.

Finally managing to get it open, she glanced up at him with an apologetic look. "I'm sorry. I know these things taste like crap, or so I hear, but I couldn't take the risk of letting you drink from me with the condition you're in." She started to raise it to his mouth, pausing midair as she begged him once more, "Please. Control yourself, Luukas. Don't make me force you to. I promise I'll get you more blood as soon as I can." With that, she raised the bag the rest of the way up to his mouth.

Luukas' eyes rolled back in his head as the first drops hit his parched tongue. Sucking hard, he swallowed greedily as she poured the nasty stuff down his throat, and fought the urge to spit it back out.

Immediately, he felt the life giving fluid flooding his desiccated cells, the pain of his broken body flaring temporarily before it began to heal him.

But it wasn't enough...wasn't nearly enough. He needed more.

He desperately clamped his teeth down on the bag when she tried to pull it away.

"It's all gone," she told him firmly. "Let go."

But he couldn't let go.

She yanked it away from him, and he went into full survival mode, fighting for his meal, only to find himself thrown back against the wall and unable to move.

He smashed his head back into the wall with a loud roar of frustration, muscles pulled taut as he strained against her hold.

"Luukas! Stop it!" she ordered. "I won't let you hurt yourself more!"

Chest heaving with harsh breaths, he closed his eyes. He could still feel the blood working its way throughout his system. He tried to concentrate on that, and not on his lingering thirst, but it was impossible.

"More," he rasped out.

"I don't have any more, but I'll get you some at next meal," she promised. "Just hang in there, big guy."

Luukas could feel his body continuing to heal, not much, but just enough to close the worst of his wounds. It wouldn't last long, he knew. That sniveling little pet of Leeha's would be back soon to add some more. He never stayed away for long.

The angel was talking again. He focused on her words. She was insisting she'd bring more, that it wouldn't be long.

He calmed as he listened to her, opening his eyes to find her watching him guardedly.

"Why are they doing this to me?" He sounded pitiful even to himself, and he looked away from her, ashamed for the angel to see him like this.

She lowered her hand, and he felt the force that held him gradually ease up until he was free to move again.

Ah, yes. Not an angel. No, she was a fucking witch.

His eyes burned with hatred as he glared at her.

"Why are you *helping* them?" he gritted through his teeth before she could answer.

She turned away from him and his anger, taking the empty blood bag over to the corner she normally huddled in. Squatting down, she used her fingers to dig down into the dirt floor. When the hole was deep enough, she crumpled the bag and placed it inside, scooping the loose dirt back over the top, burying it. Once she was done, she stood and scuffed the top of it with her shoe, then walked over it a few times, until there was no sign that the earth had been disturbed there.

He watched her while she hid the evidence, his brows pulled down in puzzlement. He was so confused. Why was she helping him now?

"I don't understand. Please," he begged, "Please, talk to me."

When she finally turned back to him, her large eyes were brimming with tears.

"Listen to me," she implored him. "I don't want to do this! I don't want to help her hurt you! But I have no choice!" Her voice shook with emotion. "I can't stand what that bitch does to you, what she's been doing to you all these years, but there's nothing I can do about it. At least not yet."

"Years..." he repeated. "How long have I been here?" he asked.

She gave him a sad smile. "A long time."

He tried to gather his scattered wits together into coherent thoughts, tried to think of the questions he wanted to ask, but they stayed just out of his grasp. He felt as if he was losing his sanity, and it terrified him.

The angel/witch appeared in front of him. "Shhhh. It's alright, vampire. It will be all right. Sleep now."

She raised her hand, and he felt the weight of his body ease up, providing welcome relief to his mangled shoulders. He groaned aloud at the respite, his head falling forward with exhaustion as he let the blackness take him again.

5

SHEA

Shea screamed in agony as the hands wrapped around her wrists and ankles and tossed her into the back of a van, where more hands joined them to hold her down as the vehicle took off. She was thrown to and fro as the van veered around a corner, but the hands held her in place.

Their touch caused excruciating pain to shoot through every nerve in her body, blasting down her spine and out her limbs. Her arms and legs flopped around like a fish, in spite of the strength of the vampires restraining her. She had no control over her body anymore.

Mindlessly, she screamed with the pain.

A hand smacked down hard over her mouth to shut her up. Shea convulsed harder, her eyes rolling back into her head, her fangs slicing into the male's palm. She couldn't see. Couldn't breathe.

"What the fuck is with her?" A wheezy voice asked.

"Who the hell knows?" The answering voice was gruff. "Let's just get her to the boss lady. She can deal with her."

What felt like an eternity later, tires squealed, and the smell of burning rubber rose up from the pavement as the back doors of the van were flung open wide. Shea was lifted out of the van and hustled up a set of stairs.

At least the hand was off of her mouth now so she could scream again.

"Shut the door! Shut the door! Let's go!"

She was dropped onto a hard floor, and the hands were removed. Oh, sweet relief.

Shea sucked in air as she blinked open her eyes. Lights flickered above her head. The floor vibrated, and she felt wheels rolling underneath her again. They were moving.

A disembodied voice came over the speakers. "We're cleared for takeoff. Everybody sit down and buckle up."

Shea rolled her head to her right and then to her left, breathing hard, getting a feel for where she was. She was lying in the middle aisle of a small airplane.

"Should we buckle her up?" Wheezy asked.

"Nah, fuck 'er. Let 'er bounce around in the turbulence. Maybe it'll knock 'er the hell out, and she'll quit with all the caterwauling."

Wannabe gangster dude appeared to be the leader of her group of kidnappers.

She wondered if they also had Christian and Dante, Luukas' other two Hunters. She'd been looking for them when she'd been swiped right off of the street in front of their apartments, right before they were to leave to go meet Nikulas and Aiden.

She should've called Aiden, told him what was going on, before she just ran out looking for them.

Stupid, stupid! They'll have no idea what happened to the three Hunters who were supposed to meet them up north and help them get Luukas away from that bitch, Leeha.

A nervous voice from the front of the plane spoke up, "She's a Hunter, man. We should chain her up."

"Doesn't look like she's gonna be huntin' nothin' at the moment."

"But what if it's a trick?" the nervous one asked.

A swift kick landed in her ribcage, knocking the air out of her. Shea curled in on herself, moaning, pulling her knees up to protect her middle.

"It ain't a trick. Relax, idiot."

Conversation stopped as the plane hurtled down the runway. A few seconds later, Shea's stomach lurched as they became airborne.

"Where are you taking me?" she demanded weakly.

"She speaks, instead of screaming," Gangster wannabe-man announced. "Don't worry, honey. You'll find out soon enough."

Shea flopped over onto her back. Her body felt like it'd been through an electrocution. Maybe it had. She'd never been able to find out why the hell she'd started reacting this way whenever a male touched her, but it had started right after Luukas had disappeared.

If it would keep their hands off of her, she'd be more than happy to lay here and not cause any trouble. Besides, where would she go? Even if she somehow managed to subdue them all, she'd be stuck on this plane until it landed. She didn't know how to fly a plane, so she'd have to leave the pilot alive. That would be a sticky situation.

No, better to wait until they landed and she could regain her strength and find a weapon. Until then, she could play the weak, subdued female.

The flight was short, with relatively little turbulence, and they were landing again much sooner than Shea would've liked. She wished she'd had more time to recover, but she'd have to make do. She'd never had so many men touch her at once, or had a reaction this strong; it'd completely incapacitated her. And for a vampire, that was really saying something.

She pushed herself up into a sitting position as the four vampires who'd kidnapped her right off of the streets of Seattle unbuckled their seatbelts and prepared to disembark.

"Stay right where ya are, honey," Gangster-dude told her. "Skip, go get the chains from the front there."

The whiney one scurried to the front of the plane to do as he was told, returning with an armful of chains with cuffs on the ends. The big one grabbed her around the arm, and she let out a grunt of pain as he yanked her to her feet. As soon as she was steady, she tore her arm from his grasp.

"Don't. Touch. Me." she hissed at him.

He eyeballed her, a thoughtful expression on his bulbous features. "I'll tell ya what, girlie. You come along nice with us, and we won't touch you. But you try anything, and you'll be at the bottom of a man-pile again before you can blink, and I don't care how much ya scream. Got it?"

"Yeah, I got it." She held out her wrists like a good girl, and Gangster-dude clamped the cuffs on them, smirking when his fingers brushed her skin and she winced. He then took the other chain from Whiney and clamped those cuffs onto her ankles.

Dammit. They were silver. Not as lethal to vampires as the movies made it out to be, but not good either. Something about the metal weakened a vampire enough to where she actually began to worry about whether or not she'd be able to get herself out of this mess.

With Gangster-dude and Whincy leading the way, she shuffled off of the plane restrained by her chains, the other two big and silent types bringing up the rear.

They loaded her up into the bed of a pickup truck. Gangster dude and Whiney got in the front, while the other two big talkers hopped into the back with her. Sitting up on the sides of the bed, they watched her with exposed fangs, paying particular attention to the dangerous area of her boobs as they bounced along the rutted roads. She glared back at them, but they weren't to be deterred.

They obviously took their jobs of prisoner-watcher very seriously.

After a while, Shea gave up and let them stare as she watched the scenery go by through the misty rain, and tried to figure out where she was. If the snow-capped mountains were any indicator, they had flown north. They must be in Canada, and she was pretty sure she knew where they were taking her now.

They'd driven for about forty minutes when they pulled off of the main road onto a barely-there sidetrack. Bumping along on the dirt road, Shea gripped the side to keep herself from bouncing out of the truck bed.

Ten minutes later, they pulled up outside of an old barn that appeared to be on the verge of collapse. About half of the roof was lying on the floor towards the back, and as they entered the debilitated building, an owl flew gracefully down from the rafters, swooped out the hole in the roof, and into the night.

Gangster-dude shoved her down into a corner. "Sit. We're just gonna hang out here for a bit until we get the OK to bring you to Leeha."

"So you *are* Leeha's bitches." Shea sank to the rotted, wooden floor gratefully.

Gangster-dude squatted down in front of her. "That deal we made includes keeping that smart mouth shut. You wouldn't want me to have to keep a hand over it to shut ya up, now would ya?"

Shea gave him a stony stare, and wisely kept her mouth shut.

"Yeah, I didn't think so." With a snort, he stood and hitched up his jeans, then walked over to join the rest of his crew.

Shea settled back against the wall behind her with a sigh. Looking out the hole in the roof, she tried to determine how long they had until dawn. They'd all be huddled in the corner if they didn't hear from Leeha before the sun came up.

Three hours passed since Shea had been grabbed off the street and shuttled up to Canada, and they were still waiting it out in the barn. All four of her captors kept eyeing the sky with trepidation, worried about the oncoming dawn.

Really, couldn't they have found a nice cave or something to hang out in? Idiots.

She was beginning to wonder if they were ever going to get that call when Gangster-dude's phone went off.

"Mistress! Oh, Josiah. Yes, we have her. Yes." He was silent for a few minutes, his eyes growing wide as he listened and he looked at the others with alarm. "Yes. Right away. We're coming." Hanging up, he ordered the others to prepare to leave.

"Let's go, honey." Grabbing her arm, he pulled Shea to her feet, and gave her a push to get her moving.

"Let's go!" he yelled to the others. "We gotta go. We gotta go right now."

Hustling them all out the door, they loaded back up into the pickup and took off, back out to the main road.

"What's going on?" Whiney asked him from the passenger seat.

Shea scooted back in the truck bed until she was up against the back windshield, turning her head to listen through the glass.

"There's other vamps in the area. Leeha wants us to get back to the mountain pronto, and hide this one so they don't see her."

"What vamps?"

"Luukas' brother, and another Hunter. They've got a human girl with them too."

Nikulas! And Aiden! And they must've found Emma.

Shea smiled with glee at the two thugs occupying the back with her again. They didn't notice. Their eyes were trained on her cleavage, amply displayed by her low-cut cotton shirt. One of them kept running his tongue over the tip of his fang.

Perv.

Shea rolled her eyes. Honestly, not to brag or anything, but she was used to it. Men usually found her hard to resist for some reason, women too actually. She was always getting hit on with cheesy pick-up lines, usually something about her mossy-green eyes being hypnotizing, her pale skin flawless, her dark, wavy hair luxurious...blah, blah, blah.

One guy had even asked to paint her.

Right now, the only thing her "luxurious" hair was doing was blowing into her face so she couldn't see. Lifting her chained hands, she pushed it out of her face, ignoring the two idiots with the staring problems.

Let them look. It might be the last chance they'd ever get.

She watched the scenery pass by. It was dark, and there wasn't much of a moon to light the way, but she could see just fine. Before long, she started recognizing the mountain range they were approaching.

They were heading straight towards Leeha's fortress, which meant Nik and Aiden were most likely in their secret hideout, scoping things out. She could only pray that they were out watching and would see her.

They didn't pull up to the front, but circumvented the base of the snow-capped peak to head around to the hidden side entrance. The truck skidded to a stop amongst the pine trees, the vampires jumping out before the engine was turned off.

Shea stood up and leapt over the side also, not waiting for anyone to "assist" her.

Once inside, they took a sharp right, and walked single-file through a narrow tunnel.

One of her watchdogs hesitated, "We're not going to see the mistress?"

"No," Wannabe gangster-man told him. "I was ordered to take her straight to the altar room."

"We're going to the altar room?" Whiney sounded even whinier than usual.

"That's what I was told."

Wow. Even gangster-dude didn't sound like his usual macho self. What the hell was in this altar room?

"What's in the altar room? Besides an altar, I assume," Shea asked.

Whiney, who was directly in front of her, glanced back over his shoulder with worried eyes, but didn't deign to answer her.

This couldn't be good.

Other than the clanking of Shea's chains, they traversed the tunnels in relative silence, turning down so many different side passageways, Shea knew she'd never find her way back out of there. The place was like a creepy garden maze gone awry, and the air became colder and mustier as they descended further and further into the bowels of the mountain.

She was nearly convinced they were just going to keep walking straight down into the Christian's Hell when the tunnel they were in finally ended, opening into a spacious room lit with the flickering firelight of numerous torches hung at intervals along the walls. And right smack in the middle was, you guessed it, an altar.

It was large and made completely of stone, unadorned except for a brownish stain coloring the flat surface, with streaks of that same color running in rivulets down the sides.

She stopped just inside the doorway, not wanting to go any further inside. An evil presence suffused this room, floating through the air like an invisible fog. It was so heavy, she could practically taste it on the back of her tongue.

The altar caught her attention again, as it was the only thing in the room, and she looked closer, trying to decipher what it was used for. Then she realized what the stain was; it was blood. That slab of rock was a sacrificial altar.

Not good.

"What is this place?" she whispered urgently to Gangster-dude.

He smiled at her, some of his old macho charm showing, "It's Hell, girlie."

One of the others snickered nervously behind her.

Shea's heart began to pound rapidly as the adrenaline kicked in. She pulled on her chains, hard, testing their strength. Sweat beaded on her forehead when she realized there would be no escaping them, at least not easily.

They waited, the silence deafening in her ears, until she thought she would scream if something didn't happen. Long, tense minutes later, they heard sure and steady footsteps echoing from another tunnel entrance on the opposite side of the altar.

Shea held her breath, as did her escorts.

The footsteps grew louder. Whoever was coming was not making any effort to hide their presence.

Right before they got to the room, the footsteps stuttered and paused momentarily, and then picked up again, stronger than before.

Why the pause? Or had she only imagined it?

She didn't have any more time to think about it before their owner strode into the room.

Her first impression was of a large raven, perched on a man's broad, cloaked shoulder. It tilted its head, curious, taking them all in with one beaded eye. A black hood covered the man's head and half of his face; pulled down low so nothing was visible except his lean, clean-shaven jaw. His hands were tucked inside the wide sleeves, and the material fell all the way down to his feet, which were cased in black boots with treaded soles.

He came to an abrupt halt just inside the room, remaining on the opposite side of the altar from them.

"Who is this?" he demanded.

His voice was deep, and although soft-spoken, it had a strong timbre to it.

"She's the Hunter. Leeha ordered us to bring her straight here." Gangster-dude appeared to be the only one brave enough to speak.

"I won't use her, if that's what she's planning."

"I wouldn't know. She just told us to wait."

The cloaked man pulled one of his hands out of his sleeve, and held it up to the raven so it could hop onto his arm. He stroked its feathers with strong, sure strokes, and then set it down on top of the bloody altar as he paced around it to join them. The bird hopped across the surface, staying as close to him as it could.

He stopped directly in front of Shea, and she stiffened, staring up at him defiantly. Though only about a head taller than she was, or maybe even less, he exuded a dark power that gave her pause. But he wasn't a vampire, or a werewolf. A witch, maybe? But he felt different than the witches she'd known. The witches normally used the forces of the earth and nature to conduct their magic. It was a part of them. You could practically smell the natural elements in them.

But not this one: this one was different.

She searched the shadows under his hood, trying to make out his features, but he kept his head lowered, and his eyes downcast. Even so, he seemed to be studying her somehow.

"What's your name, vampire?"

"Shea." She felt compelled to answer him, whether she wanted to or not.

"You're a Hunter. Of Luukas'?"

"Yes." She saw no reason to try to lie to him. The rest of them already knew. Besides, lying wasn't her thing.

"Are you not afraid of me?"

"No. Should I be?"

He didn't answer, but his lips curved up at the corners. "Do not try to escape, vampire. It will do you no good."

"Yes, well, I'm a little chained up at the moment, so…" She shrugged.

Still directly in front of Shea, he dismissed the others. "You may go."

Her four captors didn't argue, but sped on out of there like the hounds from Hell were after them.

And maybe they were.

"So, what are you, exactly?" she asked with genuine curiosity.

He didn't answer her, but she hadn't really expected him to give up his secrets that easily. The raven flew back to his shoulder, and contemplated her with the same curiosity she did it.

"What's the bird's name?"

"Her name is Cruthú."

"She's your pet, huh?"

Reaching up, he stroked her feathers with long fingers. "She's my friend." There was a wistful quality to his words.

"She's beautiful." Shea meant it. The bird was beautiful. Her feathers were so black, they looked almost blue in the flickering light of the torches, and there was an eerie intelligence in her beady black eyes as they studied each other.

Suddenly, the bird hopped over to Shea, landing solidly on her shoulder. She watched, amused, as it made itself at home, pulling strands of her hair through its beak, and plucking at her diamond stud earring. Ducking its head, it rubbed against her cheek before it went back to the man. She chirped in his ear, then ruffled her feathers and settled in on his shoulder.

"It seems she would like to return the compliment," he professed.

"Uh, thank you, Cruthú."

Abruptly, he turned away and strode over to the other side of the altar. Shea was confused at first, but then she heard the footsteps. More people were coming.

How did he hear them before she did?

Leeha swept into the room, her sheer blue gown billowing around her. A young, dark-skinned vampire followed closely on her heels.

With hardly a glance at Shea, she stomped across the room, facing off with the cloaked male across the altar. "Why is she still standing there?"

He regarded her calmly. "I won't use her. Find another."

She pulled back, surprised. "But it must be her. The new ones are rotting away before they can be of any use to me. She is old enough, and she is one of Luukas', just like the others who survived." She turned to the dark-skinned male who'd come in with her. "Josiah, chain her to the altar."

The cloaked male was in front of Shea before Josiah could begin to carry out her order, protecting her. He had moved with the speed of a vampire or wolf, yet he wasn't either of those. How had he done that?

"I said. *No.*" The raven spread her wings, squawking loudly in agreement.

It seemed she had a champion, or actually two of them. Good. She had a feeling she was going to need them for whatever it was Leeha had planned for her.

However, she wondered if she was really all that much safer in the cloaked one's hands.

Leeha fumed with silent rage. "You *dare* to disobey me? Who exactly do you think you are, witch?"

"I'm not a witch, and you would do well to remember who it is that *you* are dealing with, vampire."

Shea shrunk back against the cold, stone wall behind him as the air became rife with malevolence. She would almost swear she could hear evil voices from another realm shrieking around the cloaked one, in unity with him, as he dared to stare down the horrors that swirled in Leeha's red eyes, unaffected.

No human could resist the pull of her eyes. They would drag them into their own worst nightmares, and have them on the floor, gouging their own eyeballs out, never to be sane again.

Leeha appeared to regroup, not backing down exactly, just trying a different tactic.

"You seem fond of this one. May I ask why?"

"No. You may not. But I'm not using her. Find another."

Leeha lost her patience, and spun away from him. "The others will be coming, if they survive, but I cannot wait until then! I need her for tonight!"

Calming the raven's ruffled feathers, he held his ground. "You will have to do without."

Leeha studied him with narrowed eyes, and then suddenly smiled sweetly. "I believe I can manage. I'll just have to think of some other welcome gift for my visitors."

She headed for the door. "Bring her along, Josiah."

"She stays with me."

She swung around to face him. "What for? No. She comes with me. Josiah!"

Josiah didn't move a muscle as the cloaked one turned his attention to him, daring him to try.

"Why don't we just leave her here, mistress? Maybe she'll annoy him enough that he'll change his mind."

Shea almost laughed at his pathetic attempt to avoid challenging the other male, but Leeha didn't find it quite as amusing.

Without a word, she gave the cloaked one a tight smile, then turned on her heel and slithered out of the room. Her young pet followed closely behind.

He waited until they were well and truly gone before he relaxed his stance and stepped from in front of Shea, dropping his head down again so she couldn't see him.

She stiffened her spine, wondering what he planned to do with her, and gave him a wary look. "So, what are you going to do with me?"

Ruffling the raven's feathers, he appeared to think about it.

"I don't know."

6

KEIRA

Keira's arm shook with the effort to hold Luukas elevated, until she was certain he wouldn't come out of it again for a while, and then she gently lowered him down again, easing his body weight back onto the chains.

Fucking Blondie. He'd taken too much blood. Her lightheadedness and growling stomach urging her on, she made her way back over to the door, hoping they hadn't switched guards for some reason. She sent up a silent thank you when she saw his straw colored hair. She needed to eat.

"Psst. Hey, bloodsucker. I need some food. And some water." She waited for a response, any response, but it didn't seem like there was going to be one forthcoming.

Glaring at the back of his head, she wished she could zap him, and force him to cook her a gourmet meal. But it wasn't good to stretch your magic around too much. It became less effective that way, and made a witch too vulnerable. And she was already spread thin keeping up the cloaking spell on everyone in the fortress, the incombustible spell allowing them to use fire on Luukas, and having the heavy burden of possessing his power.

Not to mention the recent blood loss.

Deciding her need for sustenance was more important than not angering a vampire, she stuck her hand through the small window opening and poked him hard in the back of the head.

"Hey!" she whispered loudly, "I'm talking to you."

Very slowly, the blonde vampire turned his head just enough for her to see his exposed fangs and the displeased look on his face.

Good, she'd finally gotten his attention.

"I need food, jerkoff. You took too much blood. And if *I* get too weak, so do my spells, and you'd better believe I'd throw you under the bus in a heartbeat when Leeha wonders why everyone suddenly knows we're here, and her prisoner goes up in flames. Besides," she added in a matter-of-fact voice, "If you feed me now, you'll be able to have some more nice, fresh blood tomorrow. Provided you leave me your bagged stuff again, of course."

He didn't respond for so long she began to worry she'd pressed her luck too far, but then, with a quiet hiss of displeasure in her direction that made her hair stand on end, he strode off to get her meal.

Keira breathed a sigh of relief when he'd gone, and leaned back against the wall to await his return. She hoped he'd bring enough water to allow her to clean the ugly wound he'd left. She could practically feel the germs crawling off of the filthy blanket to infect her, but it was better than slowly bleeding to death she supposed. At least with an infection, she'd have a fever, and with any luck would be completely out of her mind with delirium when she died.

Footsteps echoed down the corridor outside the cell and she pushed herself up off of the wall, not wanting him to see how vulnerable she actually was.

The bolt slid back and the door was cracked open. A bowl of mush was shoved at her through the opening, followed by two water bottles tossed onto the floor. The door slammed shut again, and she listened carefully for the bolt to be replaced back into the lock before she gathered up the bottles and took her meager meal over to the corner.

Sinking down onto the floor, she sat cross-legged and scarfed down the lukewarm contents before the taste – or lack thereof – could register. Once it was scraped as clean as she could get it and rubbed with dirt to prevent the local rats from seeking it out, she drank down half of a water bottle, saving the rest.

Belly full and thirst quenched, she stood up and crossed to the only semi-private recess in the room. Digging another hole, she relieved herself, using her blanket to hide her bare ass from anyone peeking in the window of the door. Finished, she yanked up her shorts, kicked dirt back into the hole, and went back to her corner.

Wrapped in her blanket, she curled up on her side and examined the vampire. He hung limply from the silver cuffs around his wrists, passed out cold. Thick chains led from the cuffs up to a wooden beam in the wall that could be swung out from one end, allowing him to be beaten on both sides, front or back. It disgusted her.

The blood she'd given him had healed the worst of his wounds that she could see, but he still looked like shit. That was good. She wanted to help him as much as she could, but she didn't want Leeha to suspect that she was doing so. If that happened, she'd get thrown right back into her own cell, and Keira had decided years ago that she liked having a roommate.

Plus, by being in here with him, she could do what she could to ease his pain a bit until she could think of a way to get them both out of there.

She must've dozed off, for she awoke to find the vampire's eyes on her, his expression unreadable.

Immediately alert, she sat up with a wince, and put her finger over her lips. Grabbing the half-full water bottle, she tiptoed over to him; quickly checking back over her shoulder to make sure Blondie wasn't paying attention. She didn't know if he'd really care what she was doing, as long as he got his fresh meals, but she figured it wouldn't hurt to be a little cautious.

As she unscrewed the top, she shot a quick glance up at Luukas, and her heart splintered inside of her chest at the utter desperation on his bruised face for that water. Hurriedly, she lifted it up to his lips.

He chugged it down in just a few swallows.

"More," he whispered urgently.

"I have more," she whispered back. "But let's allow that to settle first. If you drink too much, it might all come right back up."

His eyes silently pleaded with her, but she shook her head stubbornly. "Give it a little time, vampire."

With a huff, he turned his face away, and clenched his teeth together so hard she could see the muscles jumping in his jaw.

She scowled up at him. "Don't you go getting all surly with me. We have to be very careful. If the she-bitch suspects that I'm helping you, she'll throw me back into the cell next door, and I won't be able to get you anything from there."

Still not looking at her, he gritted out, "Don't feed vampire again."

"But, that's the only way to get you a blood bag..." she began.

"Don't care," he growled. "Don't do it again."

She shook her head. "I have to. I can't let you feed from me. You're so starved. You'd kill me." She lifted an eyebrow. "And the fact that you completely hate me wouldn't help things."

"I don't need it."

"Oh, really?" she scoffed. "Have you looked in a mirror lately?"

He shot her a dirty look from the corner of his eye: a semi-sane dirty look. Her lips twitched. Someone was obviously feeling a bit better.

A myriad of emotions crossed his face before it settled into just one: stubbornness. "No more feeding, witch."

"My name is Keira."

"No more. *Keira*."

"Why do you care anyway?" she wondered. "As hungry as you must be, I would think you'd take what you could get."

Confusion crossed his pained features. "I don't know," he admitted.

"Well, sorry, vampire, but I'll do what I need to do. There's no other way to get you more of that crap. I can't steal it. They never let me out of here."

Managing to get his feet under him, he braced his legs apart to hold himself up, standing spread-eagle against the stone wall behind him.

"Told you. Don't...need...it." Sweat trickled down his face as he struggled to hold himself up of his own violation.

Keira stepped forward to help him, but stopped as he ground out through clenched teeth, "Don't. Touch. Me."

That's appreciation for you, she thought, but allowed him to do it on his own, understanding his need to not appear weak in front of her.

Panting heavily through his open mouth, the extent of his efforts was obvious as his eyelids fluttered and he fought to stay conscious.

After a few moments, he looked at her from underneath his dark lashes. "Please," he rasped out. "Don't let him feed."

"We're still on this?"

He shot her another look.

"All right," she finally promised. "I won't."

Crossing her fingers behind her back, she told herself it wouldn't really be a lie if he didn't actually see it happening. Right? She'd just make sure he was knocked out again.

A look of such relief came his features, that Keira felt a surge of guilt for misleading him. But, dammit, it was for his own good.

"More water," he demanded.

Grateful for the change of subject, she spun around to get the other water bottle off of the floor, but she moved too fast. Throwing out her hands as a wave of dizziness hit, she barely managed to catch herself before her face smashed into the dirt floor.

She heard Luukas' indrawn breath along with the rattle of chains and sat back on her haunches. "I'm fine. I'm fine. Not getting an award for being graceful anytime soon," she jested sarcastically. "But I'm fine."

Grabbing up the water bottle, she carefully rose to her feet and shuffled back over to him. "Here you go."

He clenched his lips together into a flat line, staring at her with burning black eyes.

She gave him a look of disbelief. "What? You're not thirsty anymore?"

"Promise me. No more. Don't lie."

So he'd figured that out, huh? Guess she needed to work on her duplicity skills. She looked him directly in his fathomless black eyes. "I promise."

He must've believed her this time, for he gave her a sharp nod and opened his mouth for the water. After just a few swallows, he turned his head away. "The rest for you."

Screwing the top back on, she buried the bottle in her corner, hiding it from Leeha. Sinking down to the floor, she pulled her knees up and wrapped her arms around them, pulling the thin blanket close.

"I can help you, if you'd let me," she told Luukas as she watched him struggle to keep his weight off of the chains.

His eyes skittered over her way. "No! No magic."

"Ok," she relented. "No magic."

She hated just sitting there passively while he struggled, but she understood his fear of her. It was her fault that he was suffering. No one else's. Only hers. Leeha would have absolutely no power over him if it weren't for her and her magic. Not even with her army of rotting, demon hybrids.

Oh, yeah. Keira knew all about those things. Being locked up for years with nothing else to do tends to really sharpen your eavesdropping skills.

Multiple footsteps coming down the stairs outside the cell brought them both to sudden attention. The lock slid back and Leeha marched into the cell, followed by Blondie and that faithful dog, Josiah.

Keira quickly pushed herself up off of the floor, trying not to panic. She pulled the blanket up around her neck to hide her makeshift bandage.

What were they doing here so soon? They never came down twice in the same night. Gods, was it even the same night? She'd fallen asleep...but it had to be. Blondie hadn't come back to trade for more blood yet.

She watched as Leeha strode directly over to Luukas. Watched as Luukas lifted his lip in a snarl. Watched as Leeha realized he was standing on his own.

*Oh shit. No. No. No. No...*Panic overtook her as Keira watched her narrow her eyes at Luukas, looking him over with renewed interest.

She wasn't supposed to be back down here already! She NEVER came down twice in one night. Not in all the years they'd been here! Why now? Why tonight? She'll know! She'll know that she fed the vampire. Anyone with eyes could see the slight change in him, and vampire eyes were so much more perceptive. If Leeha had stuck to her schedule, had come down tomorrow, she wouldn't have been able to tell. The signs would've worn off enough by then.

Keira's eyes widened in alarm as Leeha leaned in towards Luukas, sniffing at him. She smiled bitterly, her head twitching to the side in that odd way. "You've had blood. I can smell it in you."

Luukas didn't confirm or deny her statement, just continued to snarl at her, a low rumble emanating from deep within his throat.

"But it's not the witch's blood," she guessed correctly.

She turned to the witch in question, red eyes seething with her displeasure. "How is this possible, witch?"

Keira swallowed hard, raising her chin. So, Blondie hadn't ratted her out after all. She dared not look at him, or at Luukas. "I don't know. I fell asleep. Maybe a rat got too close to his mouth."

Blood, death, despair...they roiled around within those blood-red irises, drawing Keira in until she felt the pull on her very soul. She forced herself to look away just in time.

Leeha studied her for a moment longer and then turned back to Luukas. "Is this true, my love?" Not waiting for an answer, she started pacing back and forth. "I believe there is more going on here, for it doesn't smell like the rodents who live here either. It *smells* like the bags of blood I give the guards when they're on duty. Now, *how*, I wonder, were you able to get a hold of one of those? Hmmm?"

Keira jumped as Leeha suddenly appeared directly in front of her. "Do you truly believe me to be a fool, witch?" she spat. "Do you truly believe I am that naïve?" Grabbing Keira's jaw with supernatural strength, she held her face still as she tried to catch her gaze. "Do you not remember our *deal*, witch?"

Keira's stomach clenched in fear. The female vampire could rip her head off with nothing more than a flick of her dainty wrist. But she dared not use her magic against her. Even if she managed to kill the bitch, and her minions, and released Luukas, how long would it take for Leeha's contingency plan to get to Emma? Days? Hours? Minutes?

Leeha was right; she'd never be able to get to her in time. She didn't even have access to a phone to call her and warn her.

"Leave her be!" Luukas's deep voice boomed through the small room.

Dropping her hand, Leeha spun towards Luukas, her sheer, forest green gown billowing out around her. "What did you say?"

Luukas's black eyes burrowed into hers without fear, and his voice dropped a few octaves as he repeated, clearly and dangerously. "I said, leave her be, you *fucking* cunt."

Keira would have laughed at the shocked expression on Leeha's face if the situation hadn't been so dire.

The shock was quickly replaced by a look of suspicion.

"So you like your witch now? After all she's done to you? Isn't this an interesting turn of events." Her voice dripped with sweetness, scaring Keira more than her anger. "Maybe you need a small reminder of what she's capable of?"

Keira was frantically shaking her head before she'd even finished speaking. "No! No. I won't."

"Oh, but I think you will." Leeha smiled at her. "Josiah, come here."

Josiah stepped forward eagerly, and Keira heard Luukas' low growl at the same time she noticed the whip in his hands.

Without thinking, she ran over and planted herself in front of Luukas. Though her head barely came to his shoulder, she tried to use her body to block his. "Don't touch him!"

This show of loyalty seemed to amuse Leeha to no end.

"And what are you going to do about it, witch?" she laughed out loud. "Are you going to stop me? Luukas needs to be taught a lesson. He isn't following the rules."

Keira sneered at the redheaded beauty. "Follow whose rules? Yours? You claim to care about him, yet you enjoy all of this!" She pointed at the whip Josiah was unraveling.

"But at least he will know that I'm not a hypocrite. I don't pretend to be something I am not. Now, step aside, before I decide that I don't need you after all."

Keira held her position. She couldn't do this anymore. She couldn't stand idly by and watch them torture the poor soul behind her. She sent up a quick prayer that Leeha would kill her quickly, and that somehow her sister would survive, if she were even still alive.

Without any signal between them that Keira could see, the guard, the same one who'd just fed from her a few hours ago, stepped up and lifted her bodily out of the way.

Leeha smiled her thanks at him. "You may begin, Josiah."

Keira struggled in the guard's arms, kicking and punching him as hard as she could.

"No! No! You leave him alone!"

Josiah cautiously approached the vampire who'd lost it again at the sight of her struggling in Blondie's arms. He didn't dare to get close enough to swing the wooden beam out. Instead, with a strong swing of his arm, he cracked the end of the whip across the front of Luukas' chest.

As Blondie took advantage of everyone's attention being on the vampire to grope her, Keira managed to get an arm free. Raising her hand towards Josiah, she was just about to send him crashing into the opposite wall when Luukas caught her eye and subtly shook his head.

With a sob, she lowered her arm.

7

LUUKAS

The whip whistled through the air and snapped across the front of Luukas' jean-clad thighs, leaving a trail of fire in its wake. Less than a second later, it tore across his cheek, slicing open a bloody streak of ragged skin.

Gritting his teeth, Luukas didn't utter a sound as the leather shredded his flesh. He knew if he did, the witch would try to protect him, and he wouldn't be able to do anything but watch as they killed her.

She had magic on her side, but the vampires had unnatural speed and physical power. She wouldn't be able to take all three of them out before they got to her. Even in his muddled state of mind, he knew this.

He wasn't sure how long the whipping went on. He lost track of the number of times he'd felt it tear into him. Lost track of the number of cries he heard from the witch every time Leeha urged Josiah on, her eyes glowing hot with blood lust.

After a while, he just got lost in the haze of the pain.

A few minutes, or hours, later (it was impossible to tell which), Leeha finally shrieked, "Stop!"

As Josiah lowered the whip with a frustrated snap, she stalked up closer to Luukas.

She was angry. Angrier than when she'd first come in.

Breathing heavily, Luukas blinked away the sweat and blood and lowered his eyes down to his stomach, where she was staring, and watched as the last wound healed itself within seconds.

Ah. That's what she was so pissed off about. He was healing nearly as fast as they were tearing him open. He gave her a bloody smile, and spit on the front of her gown.

Her face turned nearly as red as her eyes. This made him nearly laugh out loud, to finally be getting one up on her. But his smile fell as she whipped around towards his witch.

"Release her," she uttered calmly.

The blonde bastard who'd fed from Keira earlier abruptly opened his arms, and she fell onto her knees in the dirt at Leeha's feet.

Luukas bared his fangs and hissed at the guard, memorizing his face. For that, he would be the first one he killed, directly after Leeha and Josiah.

"Rise, witch," Leeha told her in that same placid tone.

He watched Keira push herself to her feet, yanking the blanket back up around her shoulders and neck, but she wasn't quick enough.

Without a word, Leeha reached out and yanked it away, exposing the makeshift bandage around her neck. For a moment, she looked confused, but then her eyes flashed over to the guard.

His guilt was written all over his face.

"You'd betray me to drink from *her*? So she could feed HIM?!" she snarled at him. "Look at me!" she screamed when he kept his head down.

He tried to apologize as he raised his eyes to hers, but all he managed to get out was, "I'm so s…" before his eyes widened in horror, and he slammed his hands onto either side of his head.

Luukas watched as the other vampire, his gaze locked to Leeha's, slowly lost his sanity, and his eternal life. Blood began to ooze from his eye sockets, nose and mouth, his jaw falling open in a silent scream.

Never taking her eyes from his, Leeha punched her hand through the guard's chest. When she yanked it back out, his still beating heart was in her small grasp. She began to squeeze it in her palm, gradually adding more and more pressure until, with a wet popping sound, it finally burst.

As the dead guard crashed to the floor, she dropped the remnants of his heart on top of him, and with a weary sigh, looked down at her blood-splattered dress. "Now look what you've both done. This was one of my favorite gowns."

Everyone in the room was frozen in place, afraid to make any sudden movements, as they watched her pluck at the delicate material.

Eventually, with a sigh of resignation, she lifted her head and looked around. "I apologize, I'm keeping everyone waiting, aren't I?"

Luukas watched her warily as her attention was drawn back to him. Wandering back over his way, she asked, "Now, what should I do with you, my love? I think you know you need to be punished, as does the witch. But...what?"

Clasping her bloody hands behind her back, she paced back and forth in front of him with her head down, deep in thought.

Barely able to hold his head up after his punishment, Luukas risked a glance at Keira, but she stood unmoving, in a state of shock from what she'd just witnessed. She just stared down at the dead guard, her blanket pooled around her ankles on the dirt floor, forgotten.

He looked over at Josiah the Dog, baring his fangs when he caught his eyes on him, finding a bit of enjoyment in the flash of fear it incited in his eyes.

Finally coming to a halt, Leeha smiled up at him sweetly, but directed her words towards Josiah. "Get a torch down off of the wall, will you please?"

Josiah narrowed his eyes at Luukas, the fear transforming into a gratified smile that lifted the corners of his full lips. He hurried to do her bidding.

So, it was going to be fire again. Luukas fought to keep his eyes open. The whipping had taken its toll on him, and he hung limply from the chains again. But he couldn't pass out. Only one thought kept ricocheting around his head: He had to protect Keira.

"Wait," Leeha ordered Josiah as he came back with the fire and waved it in front of Luukas' face. "We need to make sure he didn't manage to convince the witch to remove her spell. He has a death wish, but I don't want to actually kill him, after all."

He sneered at Josiah as the fucker sulked in disappointment.

"Keira! Come here."

As if in a daze, Keira lifted her head.

Anger flashed across Leeha's face again. "I said. COME HERE!"

He saw her jump at the shouted order, and she inched over towards them, leaving her blanket where it was.

Luukas let his eyes rove over her small form. Even in the state he was in, he couldn't deny that she was lovely. Her thick, dark hair tumbled over her shoulders and into her lovely face, nearly hiding her large hazel eyes. Petite as she was, she had full breasts and hips and shapely legs that tapered down to delicate ankles.

Was she thinner than before? He tried to remember. She always had that blanket pulled around her. Did they feed her down here?

He was jolted back into reality when he heard Leeha tell her, "Do not let him die."

Keira blinked in confusion. "What?"

Leeha spoke matter-of-factly. "We're going to burn him. Completely. I promised Josiah that he could."

Luukas swung his head over to Leeha, an animalistic growl coming from deep within his chest. He didn't need to see Josiah to know he'd be practically dancing with glee.

She smiled at him fanatically. "And I want him to feel everything, every tiny spark. I just don't want him actually damaged."

She placed a bloody hand on his chest. "We're going to cleanse you, Luukas. Cleanse your soul clean. Burn away all of this treachery. And then, I will be able to forgive you." Backing away, she gestured to Keira. "Go on, witch. You may begin."

"Are you completely out of your mind?" Keira gasped.

Leeha narrowed her eyes at the witch. "Do it, or he will burn to ash, and our deal will be null and void." She gestured for Josiah to step forward with the torch.

She won't do it, Luukas thought. There was no way she'd do it. Not this. She'd helped him. She'd sacrificed herself just to get him a little bit of blood. Got him some water. Eased his pain. She wouldn't do this. Not now.

Then why was he trembling?

Her eyes flew back and forth between him and Josiah, who was mere inches away from him now, a look of utter panic on her face. He watched in disbelief as her eyes began to overflow with tears, and she turned to him.

"Please, forgive me," she pleaded anxiously. "My first spell isn't strong enough for this much at once. And I can't let you die!"

A surge of adrenaline rushed through him as she lifted her graceful arms and began chanting, sending him one last desperate look before she closed her eyes, shutting him out.

He threw himself from side to side as Josiah advanced on him, bellowing with rage as he tried to break free. He knew somewhere deep in his psyche, that he wouldn't be able to come out of this with any sanity left. Not this, a vampire's worst fear. Not being burned alive. It would break him.

From what seemed like a great distance away, he heard Josiah cackle with glee, and he jerked his head around, a scream tearing from his throat as the first of the flames licked their way up his legs no matter how hard he tried to get away.

He could hear his skin crackling from the heat. He could feel it melting from the muscle. The smell of burnt hair and flesh filled his nose. His muscles began to cook like a thick steak on the barbeque, his blood began to boil, and through it all he heard her chanting in the background, her words background music to his screams.

The fire worked its way up his calves to his thighs, then upward toward his groin. His manhood retracted in a desperate attempt to avoid the ungodly heat...his balls shriveling up inside of him. But it was impossible. As the scorching heat licked between his thighs, Luukas forced himself to look down, made his eyes see that the fire wasn't actually harming him. Tried to get his brain to convince his senses that this wasn't really happening. But it didn't make any difference. He could *feel* it! Could feel every inch of his body being burned alive.

His throat was completely raw now; his screams nearly soundless, but he couldn't stop them.

Then, ever so slowly, the heat crawled up his stomach, the flames eating up the new flesh ravenously.

He thought he heard a girl crying, but he couldn't be sure. He couldn't focus on anything except the feeling of his flesh being incinerated from his bones.

The flames crept up his chest to lick at his face. He threw his head back, smashing it over and over against the wall. Trying to smash it open on the stone.

He couldn't scream anymore.

8

KEIRA

Keira was openly sobbing by the time Luukas finally lost consciousness.

"Get it away from him!" she cried, afraid to retract her spell too soon lest the flames actually ignite him. He'd be a pile of ash before anyone could react. "Get it away from him!!" she screamed louder.

Leeha shot her a look, but motioned for Josiah to remove the flames from his face.

"But I didn't even do his arms yet!" He whined.

A sound of disbelief burst from Keira, but she didn't take her eyes from Luukas.

"Well, there'd really be no sense in it now, would there?" Leeha turned away, disgust at Luukas' lack of endurance written all over her face. "He's lost consciousness."

"I guess not," he reluctantly agreed. With a sigh, Josiah pulled the torch away and took it back over to the holder on the wall where he'd found it.

Dropping the spell, Keira rushed over to Luukas' deathly still form. Running her hands along his face, his chest, his legs, even squatting down to his booted feet, she checked him for any physical damage. But he seemed ok. Even his clothes were intact.

Thank the gods! Her spell had held.

She glanced over her shoulder to find Leeha's eyes on her, a strange expression on her porcelain face.

Swiping at the tears running down her cheeks, she rose to her full height, and turned to face whatever her punishment would be for her part in all of this.

Leeha stared at her a moment longer.

"Wait outside, Josiah."

She waited for him to close the door behind him before speaking again. "I returned here tonight to see how you two were faring together, which I see now was much better than I had anticipated; A mistake on my part. I also came to let you know that I will be receiving guests this evening, and so will not be able to visit with my Luukas while I am entertaining. But don't worry; Josiah will be down to carry on here alone. No harm shall come to him while he is here by himself, witch, is that completely understood?"

She didn't wait for a confirmation. "Also, I will need you to drop that cloaking spell tonight."

Keira stared in disbelief. "You're not going to punish me?"

"Are you not the least bit curious who my guests are?" Leeha smirked.

Her head was still reeling with everything that had just happened, what the hell did she care who was coming? Unless they were coming to rescue her and Luukas, which she highly doubted.

But ok, she thought, not knowing what else to say, *I'll bite*. "By all means, tell me. Who in their right mind would be coming to visit you?"

Leeha's eyes lit up as she told her in a confiding tone. "A very handsome male. He reminds me a lot of my Luukas, only with blonde hair. And he's bringing a friend with him. A *lady* friend." Her brows lowered as she pouted. "I'm not sure what he sees in her, but my eyes in these mountains tell me he's extremely protective of the girl."

As Keira mulled that over, trying to figure out what the significance of these visitors could be, Leeha wandered towards the door to leave, adding as an afterthought, "Oh! Did I mention her name is Emma? And she looks quite a bit like...you."

"What?" Keira shook her head in disbelief. "What did you just say?" It couldn't be possible. It couldn't be her sister. What the hell would she be doing here?

"Not quite so defiant now, are we?" The door slammed shut behind Leeha and Keira heard her giggling with Josiah as the lock slammed into place.

They'd left her there, in the cell, with one dead vampire, and another one who no doubt wished he were.

Keira stared at the door in a daze. Emma was coming here? It couldn't be. How the hell would she have found this place? Thanks to her, they were cloaked, hidden from outsiders; A simple spell that most any witch could do. Anyone who happened to come upon it would see nothing but a snow-capped mountain like any other, without so much as a hint that anyone occupied it.

It was impossible that Emma could have found it.

Maybe the bitch was lying. Maybe this was her punishment! That had to be it. It was the only reasonable explanation. There was just no way in hell that her little sister could be anywhere near here. She was on the other side of the country in PA, and across the border. She didn't even have a passport!

And, Leeha had just shown her one of her sister's many posters not long ago, the ones with the headline "Please help me find my sister, Keira." She'd gloated over it. That couldn't have been more than two weeks ago. How would Emma have been able to find her between then and now?

Again, she shook her head. She couldn't have. There was just no way. This must be a trick; just another one of the head games that the bitch so enjoyed.

So why had she ordered her to remove the cloaking spell?

And who the hell was the male that was supposedly with her sister? She said he looked like Luukas...did she mean a vampire? Did a vampire find out where Luukas was and bring Emma with him? But why would he bring her along? A human?

Keira was at a loss. She didn't know what to think, what to believe.

One thing she did know, however, was that the dead body on the floor was the end of her trading blood for Luukas. The other guards weren't nearly as interested in her as this one was, and were much more afraid of Leeha.

And even if they hadn't been before, they would be now, once the word about Blondie's death got out.

Grabbing the body by the ankles, Keira attempted to drag it over closer to the door. She barely made it a foot before she fell on her ass with an "Oomph!" Three tries later, she'd managed to pull it a mere four feet or so, but at least it was farther away from Luukas and her stash corner.

She thought about trying to roll it onto her blanket and move it that way, but then what would she use for herself? She'd freeze to death down here, and she wouldn't want to use it if it had his blood all over it.

The body would have to stay where it was.

Picking up her blanket, she shook the dirt off of it as best she could. Mind still reeling with Leeha's departing words, she shuffled over to her corner and sank down with her back against the stone, pulling the thin wool around her body.

A howl shattered the stillness of the night, startling Keira awake, and she sat up with a start. Still half asleep and disoriented, she rubbed her eyes, and tried to get her bearings.

She must've been sleeping for a while. All of the torches except one had burned out, and lack of light caused shadows to leap along the walls like creepy puppets.

She'd felt so drained this morning. Literally. She'd barely remembered to undo the cloaking spell, before sinking back down into her corner to try and sleep. She must've slept through the entire day, dead body in the room and all.

Another howl sounded, closer this time, raising the hair on the back of her neck and goose bumps on her skin. She faintly heard a male voice shouting in answer from far within the labyrinth of cells.

There was someone else down here with them? She'd never heard anyone else in all the years they'd been here, and had always assumed they were the only "guests".

Hearing a ruckus on the stairs, she jumped to her feet and ran to the door.

Dammit, the window was too high! She couldn't see anything. Swinging around, her eyes landed on the dead vampire. He was beginning to disintegrate, but with the lack of sunshine down here, it was taking much longer than normal. She stomped on him a few times to see how solid he remained, and quickly decided he would do.

Adrenaline and fear flowing through her, she grabbed him by the ankles and dragged him close enough to the door so that she could step up onto his legs and see out the small window.

Just as she did, a body came hurtling through the air down the stairway, landing with a thud at the bottom. A gaping, bloody hole was all that remained of the guard's throat. She barely caught a blur of what appeared to be a huge furry creature lunge down the stairs after it, leap over the body, and disappear down the hall away from her cell.

What in the hell was that?

A loud crash came seconds later. The beast must've burst through another door. And then all was quiet again.

She held her breath, listening carefully, but heard nothing, until...there! More howling from deep within the mountain.

Silence reigned again for long moments. Hanging on to the door for balance, Keira leaned away and looked back over her shoulder.

Luukas was beginning to rouse again.

She studied him a moment, trying to assess his state of mind after what he'd been through the night before, but she couldn't really discern anything yet.

Turning back to the window, she let out a yelp as she found herself staring directly into a pair of glowing, green eyes.

Scrambling back away from the door, she stumbled over her own feet getting off of the dead vampire and landed hard on her backside in the dirt, those eyes at the door following her the entire time.

Once she was out of the way, the eerie green orbs zeroed in on Luukas. A low growl rumbled through the wooden door at the sight of him hanging there, and the eyes flew back to her, spearing her to the floor where she sat.

Keira shook her head frantically. "No! No! I didn't do this! It wasn't me! Well, it was, kind of...but I didn't want to! She threatened me! Threatened my sister, Emma! I didn't want to..." She was babbling, and had no idea if the thing outside the door could even understand what she was saying.

Her mouth snapped shut as the eyes suddenly dropped out of sight.

Sucking in a breath, Keira jumped to her feet. "Wait! Don't leave us here! Please!" She didn't know who, or what, was out there, but it couldn't possibly be any worse than their current hostess. Plus, if she could just get out of this cell, there would be a chance to escape.

She'd just taken a step towards the door to call after them again, when the entire wooden structure came crashing in, landing on top of Blondie. She threw up her arms to protect her face from the flying debris, and when she lowered them, an exceptionally large, brown, wolf-type thing stood on all fours on top of the door.

More muscular and less hairy than a normal wolf, it appeared to be some type of wolf hybrid. And when it swung its head her way, she saw an awareness in its eyes unlike any other animal she'd ever met.

Holy shit, she thought. A *werewolf*. She'd never actually seen one before.

"Duncan?" Luukas' voice was barely audible.

Tearing her eyes from the wolf, she glanced over at Luukas. His eyes were feverish in their sunken sockets as he stared at it in disbelief.

The wolf paced over to him on its huge paws, and as it did, another appeared in the doorway. It was also brown, though a lighter shade, a bit shaggier, and nearly as large, but had eyes so dark they looked black. Unlike its friend, this one stayed where it was, and kept looking out into the hallway, like it was afraid to come into the cell. It whined softly at its companion.

I know how you feel, Keira thought.

A cold nose nudging her shoulder made her jump. The first wolf was attempting to get her attention. Standing beside her, its huge head came up to her shoulder, and it was easily twice her size or more. She could ride the thing like a horse.

It nudged her again, harder this time, and looked up at Luukas' chains, then back at her. It repeated the movement until Keira finally caught on.

"Oh! Of course!" She paused, "What about Leeha?"

It shook its large head.

Did that mean what she thought it meant? Was Leeha not a concern anymore? What had happened to her? Keira could only hope that she had finally met her end, thanks to these wolves.

But, what would that mean for Emma? She'd never get to her in time if Leeha's contingency plan had gone into play. Not without help.

Deliberating, she looked back over at the vampire. If she were any kind of a good person at all, she would release him, and give him back his power. It's what she'd been planning to do all along.

She still had no clue as to his state of mind, however. What if she did all that and he was bat shit crazy, and killed them all in a psychotic frenzy?

Well, it would be no more than she deserved, after everything she'd put him through. And maybe he wouldn't be. Maybe, just maybe, he'd be so grateful that he would help her save her sister.

It was a long shot. More than a long shot. More like an impossible shot. But she had to try.

Closing her eyes, she began chanting the words that would undo the spell and give Luukas back his power. Her hair began to dance softly on her shoulders as she drew upon the earth's elemental energy, and the air stirred around her. She slowly lifted her arms, inviting it into her, becoming a part of it.

Distantly, she heard the wolves whining as the air currents picked up force, and her chanting got louder and stronger. Tilting her head back, she opened herself up from within, allowing the Master vampire's power to leave her and travel back to its rightful home.

9

LUUKAS

Luukas was confused as the girl began speaking in a strange tongue, saying words he didn't understand. Who was she?

He looked at the dogs (wolves?) that had broken through the door. He seemed to *know* them. Duncan, and...he couldn't recall the other one. They were inching slowly out of the room, their eyes never leaving the girl. Their hackles were raised on the back of their necks, and they whined softly as they crept backwards out the door.

Suddenly the air pressure in the room changed, came alive. His muscles tensed with the instinct to flee, feeling something wasn't right.

She raised her arms. Her voice rose in volume with each sentence, and she threw her head back. As the air grew dense with her sorcery, it lifted her body right off of the ground, until only her toes were dragging the dirt.

With a yelp, the wolves hightailed it out of there.

Weak, exhausted, and chained up as he was, Luukas could only hang there and watch as the girl...no, not the girl. The witch...yes! The fucking *witch*...cast her magic.

And he remembered.

He remembered her standing in front of him, looking much the same as she did now, as he was burned alive.

Remembered the sounds and smells of his skin melting and the meat roasting from his bones.

His mind recoiled violently from the memories. Hysteria rose within him, and he found it hard to breathe as he frantically looked down at himself. His heart pounded. How was this possible? How was he still whole? He had burned! He remembered! Remembered every excruciating second of it!

Am I in hell? The thought flitted briefly through his head, and was just as quickly gone.

His attention reverted back to the girl, the *witch*.

The word echoed through what was left of his mind. His lips peeled back from his fangs as they exploded down from his gums. He remembered others in the room when it was happening, their features hazy, but her...he remembered *her* very clearly.

He lunged forward on his chains, attempting to reach her with his razor sharp fangs. *Rip her open! Suck her dry! I'm so thirsty. Kill her! Burn her like she did to me!*

Suddenly her chest heaved upwards toward the ceiling and she opened her arms wide.

The witch fell to her knees on the dirt floor as Luukas was simultaneously thrown back against the wall, something slamming into him; a force so powerful, it knocked the breath from his lungs.

Gasping for air, his entire body went rigid, as the embodiment of hundreds of powerful life forces surged through him. Every vampire he'd ever created, every soul he shared, ripped through him like a tornado, embedding themselves as a whole back into his cells, before finally settling down within him like a sleeping beast.

In the sudden stillness, Luukas sucked in a deep breath, and then another. But he had no time to comprehend what had just happened, for just then, the witch lifted herself up off of the floor, her hazel eyes huge in her small face.

An evil smile spread slowly across his face, growing larger as she began backing away from him.

A howl sounded from somewhere high above them, a different voice, and the wolves answered from their hiding place in the hall, before running past the open doorway. But Luukas paid them no mind. His focus was on one thing, and one thing only.

The vile bitch in front of him.

Without even realizing what he was doing, he instinctively gathered his power within him, coiled it tightly, and then released it all at once with a blast of energy so strong, the entire mountain trembled. A tormented roar filled the room as his dislocated arms fell to his sides, the silver chains that had held him now nothing but clouds of dust that floated serenely to the floor.

Never taking his eyes from his prey, Luukas moved away from the wall for the first time in seven years.

The witch began to back cautiously out of the cell, like the wolves had before her. He could hear her rapid heartbeat. He could smell her fear.

And her sweet blood.

Steadily, relentlessly, he stalked her, pausing in the doorway only to slam his dislocated shoulders back into place against the wall.

She continued to back away slowly, her eyes never leaving his.

The backs of her heels hit the bottom of the stairway, and she started to fall, her arms pin wheeling as she tried to maintain her balance.

Before she could hit the stone, Luukas swooped in and grabbed her up into his arms, hauling them both up the stone steps with supernatural speed. Reaching the upper hallway, he swung his head from side to side, trying to decide which way to go. He recalled nothing from when he'd first been thrown down here.

The witch beat on him with her small fists. "Put me down!" she yelled in his face.

He threw her over his shoulder, wrapped one arm securely around her legs, and took off towards another stairway he'd spotted to his right.

Have to get out. Have to escape. Take the witch.

The stairway was a dead end. It literally led to nothing but a wall. How?

Luukas' anxiety grew, and he fought back the panic rising in his chest. Flying back down the stairs, the witch hanging on to his raw back for dear life, he ran back down the other way.

A door!

Releasing the force of his power before him, he blew the door apart by strength of will alone, and ran through. He found himself in a tunnel barely lit by torches, smaller than the previous hallway. Which way to go?

Have to get out! Have to escape! Take the witch!

He looked to his right, then his left, and back to the right again. Which way?

Up. Need to go up.

Bouncing his prize up to a more secure spot on his shoulder, he went right. He hadn't gone more than a few hundred feet when he saw another dead end ahead.

NO!

Sending out another burst of force, he shattered the stone and ran through.

The mountain quaked as Luukas burst through wall after wall, ascending ever higher through the maze of tunnels, until he felt the ground leveling out again. With a final, strong surge, he turned to the wall on his left and blew through it, dropping the witch to her feet but hanging on to her wrist.

She would not be getting away.

As the dust settled, Luukas found himself looking out into the cathedral-like space where it had all began, with *Leeha*.

He remembered.

"Keira!"

He felt the witch stiffen beside him. "Emma..." She breathed.

His head whipped around to see a small human female with bright hair running down the stairs in front of the throne-stage, calling for his witch. Pulling his lips back into a snarl, he hissed menacingly at her.

She paid no heed at all to the warning, and continued to run towards them.

Luukas growled low in his throat, his eyes never leaving her. His body tensed as he prepared to defend what was his.

A male vampire with blonde hair threw himself in front of her before she could reach the bottom of the stairway, plucking her right out of the air and holding her tight against the front of him. She struggled in his arms, demanding he let her go, but he held her fast, whispering to her, until she calmed a bit.

Still holding the human, he turned his head and looked Luukas up and down, a strange expression on his face.

Luukas bared his fangs at him too, and also at the wolves prowling back and forth at the far end of the room, just for good measure.

The blonde vampire set the human down, speaking to her sternly this time. Glancing back at the wolves, he turned to face Luukas, his expression relaxed.

"Luukas? Hey, big brother. It's just me, Nik."

Nik?

The vampire eased down another step. Luukas' heartbeat picked up again as he tried to keep an eye on both the vampire and the pacing wolves. Swinging his head back and forth between them, he finally settled on the vampire, as the beasts seemed to be keeping their distance.

Nik. He thought again. *Nikulas?*

He knew that name. Knew that face. From where? He tried to think back. Fractional pieces of his life before flashed through his mind.

My brother. Trust him?

He wasn't sure, but he sheathed his fangs a bit. Still, to be safe, he yanked the witch behind him.

"The witch is *mine*."

"Ok man, you can have her." The human female made a sound of protest, but the vampire – Nik - ignored her, easing down a few more steps.

"No one is going to take your witch. I just want to say hello to my brother."

Brother, yes. My brother. Nikulas.

He took a halting step into the room, scanning the area. Where was Leeha? He needed to kill her.

"Where is she?" he ground out.

"She's gone...She took Aiden with her."

Aiden?

"We came to get you out," Nik continued, "When she heard the wolves, she freaked out, and unleashed her monsters upon us." He indicated the room full of decaying carcasses around him. "We killed them all except for a group that took off with Aiden through that door." He pointed to the doorway where he and the human had been standing. "We can't get it open now. I don't know where she took him."

Luukas growled low in his throat as his lips twitched back off of his fangs. "I'm going to rip her apart. Slowly. *Painfully.*"

"Luukas!" Keira cried as, in his anger, his grip tightened on her. "You're hurting me!"

Hurting her? No! He couldn't hurt her! Luukas immediately loosened his hold, releasing her wrist, but his eyes pinned her to the spot.

"Leave us," he ordered the others in the room.

The wolves kept a wary eye as they took advantage of his distraction with the witch. They slunk past him through the hole in the wall to go find the rest of their pack, but he paid them no mind. He was incapable of tearing his eyes away from the female in front of him.

"Luuk, man. Let's just get out of here," his brother called from behind him.

A cold rage filled Luukas, so intense, it dropped the temperature in the room. The witch shivered before him, and wrapped her arms around herself.

She swallowed hard.

Rip her open! Suck her dry! Ah, I'm so thirsty. Kill her! Burn her!

"LEAVE! US!"

A silent moment passed as he and the witch stood with gazes locked: His intense with anger. Hers frightened, yet resigned.

Finally, he heard his brother urge the human female, "Come on. Let's go." Raising his voice, he called to Luukas, "We'll be at the hideout."

"What? No. Nik! NO!! Dammit, that's my SISTER over there!"

Luukas' upper lip twitched as the human argued with his brother.

"Nikulas! Stop! I'm not leaving without her!" A pause, "I will *not* leave without my sister."

The air began to vibrate, and at first, he thought it was his witch, but no. It wasn't her. This magic was similar, but different, and far weaker.

He didn't have long to wonder about it though. The *whoosh* of a large object soon came sailing through the air towards him. Without taking his gaze from his witch, he lifted his left hand and flicked the rock away from him with nothing but the will of his mind.

"Nikulas. You *really* need to remove her," he warned. "NOW. I'm not in the mood to play."

Keira gave him a hopeful look he didn't understand, before tearing her gaze away to plead with her sister, "Emma, it's ok. Luukas and I have some things we need to discuss."

"Sweetheart, that's enough. We're leaving." Nikulas' voice was firm.

"He's going to kill her, Nik!" she cried.

Yes. But first, feed. Then kill.

"No, he won't," Nikulas told her in a reassuring tone. "He's very angry right now, but he won't hurt her. You need to trust me here."

"You don't *know* that," the human insisted.

"Actually, I kinda do."

Luukas was swiftly losing his patience.

With an anxious glance at his face, Keira quickly interrupted them, "It's ok, honey. Go with Nik. I'll be out in a bit."

"Keira?" The human's voice trembled with disbelief and uncertainty.

With another quick glance at Luukas, Keira ordered, "Emma, just GO. I'll be fine."

"Come on," Nikulas insisted.

Her sister looked as if she was about to argue more, but then turned and stalked from the room in a huff.

Keira watched her go, relief and sorrow playing across her features. She turned back to Luukas, and drew herself up stiffly.

A cruel smile spread across his face.

"Luukas," she began haltingly, but he didn't give her any time to give him her excuses. There were no excuses he would accept for what she'd done to him.

He moved before he realized he'd meant to do so. One second he was standing in front of her and the next he had her slammed up against the wall behind her, her feet dangling a foot off the floor. One of his large hands was around her bandaged throat, and the other had a death grip on her wrists, holding her arms above her head.

He lowered his head until his icy visage was but an inch from her face. His glowing, green eyes burned into her with his rage. His lips were drawn back from his teeth in a snarl, exposing his massive fangs.

"I'm going to kill you. Slowly. And painfully."

Keira looked at him defiantly through her tears. Choking from his hold, she managed to rasp, "I...deserve...it. Just...don't...hurt...Emma."

Luuk tilted his head to the side as he stared at her with disbelief, his hatred of her sharpening his thoughts into something that sounded somewhat coherent.

"You *dare* to demand something of *me*? For years, you helped that bitch hold me here. Fucking *watched*," he yanked her towards him by the throat and slammed her back into the wall, feeling some satisfaction when she winced. "As I was tortured and starved, without a bone in your body feeling a bit of remorse, without one *ounce* of empathy for me."

"That's not...true...!" she gasped.

"SHUT UP! SHUT UP! You don't get to fucking ask for anything!" he roared into her face. "You don't get even a small feeling of pity from me. Nothing! YOU! BURNED! ME! ALIVE!"

Luukas was struggling hard to keep the madness in check, but he was losing the fight. He could feel the delicate bones of her throat under his hand, and imagined how good it would feel to crush them in his grip. He began to squeeze, smiling cruelly as her face turned a dark, mottled red.

Rip her open! Suck her dry! I'm so thirsty. Kill her! Burn her!

A single tear escaped and rolled down her cheek: just one tear. And the sight of that single fucking tear gave him pause...made his chest tighten painfully.

Hurting her? No! He couldn't hurt her!

Luukas squeezed his eyes shut.

Rip her open! Suck her dry! I'm so thirsty. Kill her! Burn her!

But that one brave tear undid him. "God *damn* you."

He loosened his grip on her throat and watched anxiously as she sucked in air, coughing, the color rushing from her face, the sudden paleness of her skin stark in contrast. Still effortlessly holding her up by the wrists, as he had been chained for so long, he placed his other hand on the side of her head and brushed the tear away gently with his thumb. Eyes wide with wonder, he cupped her cheek as he let his eyes rove over her exquisite face.

Gradually, he became aware of her lush body pressed against him. Her heart pounded and her blood rushed through her veins. Her delicious, unique scent hovered in the air around him, interlaced with...desire?

He instantly ached to bury his fangs deep in her neck. Gods, he was so thirsty.

Her full breasts pressed into his chest, and his cock throbbed painfully. It was strange, feeling his cock hardening again, feeling the almost painful pleasure of it.

He wanted to kill her and fuck her at the same time. Maybe he'd fuck her first, and then kill her. Why not? She deserved nothing less.

And she wanted him. He could smell her desire, stronger than her fear. How could that be possible?

No, feed first.

He snarled at her again as he thought about the past...what? Years? She owed him for what he'd been through. What *she'd* put him through. Moving faster than she could track, his mouth slammed down hard onto hers at the same time he ripped the bandage from her throat.

She gasped at the assault, and he used the opportunity to invade her mouth with his tongue. He wasn't gentle. He kissed her ferociously, thrusting his tongue in and out of her mouth, sucking, feasting; the taste of her easing the madness, centering all of his awareness on nothing but her.

His fangs scraped her lips and a drop of her blood touched his tongue. He growled deep within his chest, holding her head firmly to his.

It wasn't enough. He wanted more. *Needed* more.

Tearing his mouth from hers, he grabbed her by the hair, roughly pulling her head to the side to expose her neck to his hungry view. Her breathing was ragged in his ear, and the sharp scent of her fear grew thicker around him.

Her plump veins pulsed rapidly just under her translucent skin. He put his nose to her neck, inhaling deeply, reveling in her scent for just a moment.

Rearing back, he struck like a snake, sinking his fangs deep into her succulent flesh. She stiffened in his arms as he felt her vein pop and her warm blood began to gush down his throat. He swallowed greedily, his eyes rolling back in his head as an instant feeling of euphoria spreading throughout his emaciated body.

MINE.

With a groan, he let go of her wrists. Her hands immediately went to his shoulders, but rather than push him away, they clung to him. Putting his arm around her waist, he pulled her hips into his throbbing erection as he sucked hard at her neck.

Her blood was like nothing he'd ever tasted before. It ran down his throat and burned sweetly through his body like a fine liqueur. Luukas' body responded eagerly, her blood healing him, renewing him.

He pulled her impossibly closer as he dropped to his knees and sat back on his heels, pulling her down with him and holding her on his lap, her knees to either side of his hips. Her hands gripped his strong shoulders and she moaned as he rocked his hips up, trying to push himself into her core through their ragged clothes. His cock felt like it was about to burst, but he couldn't bring himself to let go of her long enough to remove their clothes.

He rubbed himself against her, seeking relief, moving faster and faster. Lifting his head from her neck, he moved his mouth to her ear and ordered, "Come for me, Keira. Come for me...NOW."

Her body responded instantly to his words, and with an incoherent cry, she convulsed in his arms. He struck her neck again, groaning deep in his throat, and pulled her down onto him as he ground up into her, hard. With her sweet, sweet blood running down his throat and her cries in his ears, he yelled out against her neck as his cock swelled impossibly larger, before violently releasing as he came.

She went limp in his arms as he continued to rock against her, more gently now. Taking one last tiny pull, he removed his fangs from her throat, and ran his tongue over the wounds to help heal them.

He growled dangerously as he felt the previous wounds there from the other vampire who'd fed from her. Who'd fed from what was his.

Pulling her limp body close to him, he rose to his feet, adjusting her in his arms.

I'll fucking kill him.

But wait, he was already dead. Wasn't he? Luukas tried to remember. Yes, Leeha took his heart. He remembered now. He wouldn't get to kill the vampire who'd fed from his female.

And that pissed him off. He bared his fangs at the empty tunnel, but no one was there to take out his anger on.

He turned in a circle. Which way? He stepped back out of the tunnel into the main room. It was empty also. Everyone had gone. But where? What had Nik said?

The hideout. Yes.

He glanced down at his witch. She hadn't opened her eyes.

Can't hurt her!

He frowned, lifting her up closer. He could hear her heartbeat. It was still strong.

Spotting the narrow tunnel Nik and the human had taken, Luukas headed that way, holding Keira close against his chest so as not to bang her limp form against the stone.

He followed the human's scent until he came to a larger opening. A creek ran by, flowing through the mountain. He followed it upstream until he came out of the mountain.

It would be daylight soon. He would have to hurry.

10

AIDEN

Three sets of steel doors, each one four feet thick, slid down from the ceiling behind them as Leeha led them down the passageway.

Aiden glanced back at the slabs of metal in amusement. "If you wanted me to stay for tea, luv, all you had to do was ask."

He received a shove in the middle of his back from a yellow-clawed hand, as her monsters hissed at him to move faster.

"Alright, alright. You don't have to push." Wrinkling his nose at their ripe odor, he caught up to Leeha.

"So, where are we going?"

"Shut up, Aiden!"

He grinned at her.

"Whatever happened to 'I'm so happy to see you, Aiden. Let's go wallow in other earthly pleasures, Aiden?' It's not my fault you're frightened of wolves. I want to go wallow."

"SHUT UP!" Leeha screamed at him. She flinched as a howl came from the direction they'd just come from.

He supposed he'd just have to be patient.

"Just give me a hint," he told her five seconds later.

Patience was obviously not his strong suit.

Leeha spun around so fast he nearly collided into her small form. Smiling down into her lovely, furious visage, he kissed the tip of her finger when she stuck it in his face.

Taking a deep breath, she lowered her hand, curling it into a fist as she visibly attempted to calm herself. "Much as I would love to go 'wallow' also, there are other things I need to take care of right now. You can stay out of my way, or not. But if you don't, my love, I will be forced to remove you, Aiden."

She reached up and touched his cheek softly, her eyes hurt. "You've already betrayed me by bringing those Scottish hairballs to my door, ruining *everything*. Don't push your luck."

"Actually, they sort of invited themselves along. Like I said earlier, luv, if you would just stop stealing people..."

She narrowed her eyes at him, the blood-red irises gleaming dangerously.

He held up both hands in a placating gesture. All right, he'd play along.

For now.

"I'm sorry, poppet. You're right. I shouldn't be distracting you when you are so obviously distraught. Tell me what I can do to help."

She smiled at him, sweet as sugar. "Stop talking."

He grinned back at her roguishly. "Done."

Gently, she wiped the blood from his mouth where she'd backhanded him on the stairs, turned, and continued on.

Which reminded him. That backhand had been unusually powerful, even for a vampire. There was something more going on here, and Aiden was bound and determined to discover what it was.

11

LUUKAS

Luukas rushed through the cool night with the witch in his arms. He didn't look back. Sword ferns whipped against his legs with their wet leaves, but luckily, it wasn't raining at the moment. The tall pine trees hid him and his precious cargo from any watchful eyes, his footsteps silent upon their fallen needles that covered the ground.

He took a deep breath of the fresh night air. The first fresh air he'd breathed in years.

The witch's blood circulated through his deteriorated muscles, giving him a strength and energy that he hadn't felt in a long time, if ever.

Yet, he barely noticed. His focus was on one thing, and one thing only. He had to find the hideout...needed to get out of the open before the sun rose. After finally escaping from his hellish prison, he wasn't about to let something as insignificant as sunshine finish him off.

He ran with a desperation born from the need to escape the horrors of this place, not really aware of where he was, or how he knew which way to go. He just ran, following the mountain range.

It didn't take him long to reach the hidden entrance of the hideout. He eyed the brush at the foot of the snow-capped mountain. How to get in? Pacing back and forth, his pulse raced as he studied the foliage.

There!

Shifting Keira to one arm, he pulled back the branches and stepped into the long passageway, pausing a moment to let his eyes adjust. It was pitch black, but he didn't need a light. His vampire vision allowed him to see just fine.

He traversed the tunnel cautiously, and came to the open cavern he and his council had been using for years to keep an eye on Leeha and her brethren.

No one was there.

Carrying the witch over to the fire pit in the center, he gently laid her down in the shelter of the large stones surrounding it, and sat down near her to wait out the day.

He knew he should be plotting, planning, but was unable to think ahead past the next few hours.

He closed his eyes, quelling the panic that was trying to rise in him.

Just get through the day. Worry about the rest later.

They hadn't been there long when he heard someone coming. Placing himself between the witch and the tunnel entrance, he held himself perfectly still and listened.

Footsteps came down the tunnel, closer and closer.

Luukas took up a defensive stance, fangs bared, hands fisted at his sides. As the steps neared the cavern, he hissed in warning.

The footsteps slowed, then stopped completely.

"Luukas?"

That voice. It was familiar.

"Luuk? I know it's you. I can feel you from here. It's just me, bro. Nikulas."

The footsteps started up again, slower this time, easing cautiously towards him until Luuk could make out the blonde vampire from earlier.

Nikulas. My brother.

Relief flooded through him. His brother was here. He would help him. He wasn't alone.

Nik raised his hands in a peaceful gesture. "It's ok, man. It's only me."

Luukas rose up from his crouched position to his full height, retracting his fangs slightly.

"The witch is *mine*." He growled at his brother.

Nikulas smiled sadly. "I know she is, man. It's ok."

He came closer, not making any sudden moves.

"You look better," Nikulas observed.

"I fed."

Nik nodded. Heading over to the wall, he took one of the torches off of the wall, dipped it in a barrel of some kind of liquid, and lit it.

Luukas' heart took off, pounding in his chest as he growled, and skittered away from the dancing flames.

"She won't be able to see when she wakes up." Nikulas said in way of explanation, placing it slowly back into its holder with a frown.

Still moving slowly and deliberately, he walked over and sat down on one of the rocks, leaned forward, and put his elbows on his knees. He didn't say anything else, just stared at the cold fire pit.

Keeping a close eye on the lit torch, Luukas eventually copied him, sitting down by his witch. "The human?"

Nik's expression didn't alter as he told him, "She's gone."

"Why?"

"We sort of got into a fight." Nik smiled wryly. "Of course, if she'd known you two were in here, she wouldn't have left. But it's a good thing she didn't," he commented, eyeing Luukas uneasily. "You must've passed us somehow on the way here. I was so intent on following her, I didn't even notice."

Luukas frowned. "I don't understand."

"Keira is her sister. She's worried about her."

"Then why did she go?"

"I guess she didn't feel that she had a choice. Keira told her to, and I wouldn't help get her away from you."

Luukas bared his fangs again. "The witch is MINE."

"I know, man. It's cool. I'm not going to try to take her away. She's yours." Nik's voice remained calm, non-threatening.

He looked over at the female in question. Cocking his head to the side, he frowned. "Dude, she's too cold. Her lips are blue. Is she alright?"

"Her heart is strong."

"You need to cover her."

"With what?"

"Good question. We should probably start a fire, and then we can all get some rest."

"No! No fire!" Luukas scooped Keira up off of the floor, reappearing over at the tunnel entrance with her before Nik had the chance to stand up.

Nik paused halfway up, and sat back down, a strange look on his face as he took in Luukas' reaction. "No fire?"

"No!"

"OK. All right. No fire, then."

When he deemed it was safe, Luukas came back and rejoined him, carefully laying the witch back down where she was.

Should've brought her blanket. He hadn't thought about that. He put his head in his hands, squeezing it between his palms in frustration. Stupid, stupid. Why hadn't he thought of that?

"Hey man, it's ok. Don't stress yourself out about it. You can lay by her and keep her warm."

"I just...can't...*think*." He felt a hand on his shoulder, and he flinched.

Nik pulled his hand back, a sad smile on his face. "Sorry. I just...never mind. Let's try to get some sleep."

With a nod, Luuk eased himself down next to the witch and pulled her in tight against him, wrapping himself protectively around her small form.

"We'll leave right at sundown," Nik said quietly. "We'll have to walk until we can get to some kind of civilization again. From there, I can order a car or something to get us back to Seattle."

Luukas nodded again. "All right."

"We'll need to get home as quick as we can." Nik continued. "Your female needs food and water, and you both need a few hundred showers and some clean clothes."

Nik looked at him questioningly for a second, and then with a small shrug, he made himself comfortable on the other side of the cold fire pit.

He felt the connection with his brother, and it comforted him somewhat, but he also sensed something wrong.

"What's wrong with you?"

Nik looked over at him in surprise. "I'm all right. And, Luuk?"

"What?"

"I'm very glad to have you back, brother."

Luukas couldn't answer him, unable to get his thoughts past anything but getting the hell away from there.

12

NIKULAS

Nikulas woke with a start and immediately searched for his brother. He found him sitting up against one of the rocks with the witch in his lap, wide awake, his eyes jumping nervously around the room, fangs half exposed.

It fucking killed him to see his brother like this; the Master of their colony, the strongest vampire of his time, reduced to a fearful shell of a being.

And it was his fault.

Luukas hadn't noticed that he was awake yet, and that worried him, but he took advantage of the opportunity to get a better look at the two of them.

Luukas was wearing the same clothes he'd worn the night he'd left, and he imagined Keira was also. They were both filthy, but apparently that hadn't bothered them overmuch, for he smelled the distinct smell of sex on the two of them.

He also smelled her blood. It flowed within his brother, which would explain all of the "mine" stuff.

He never would've dreamed in a million years that Luukas would find his fated mate in the witch who'd been helping Leeha hold him captive all these years. But, apparently, he had. There was no denying it once he'd had her blood.

On the up side, he didn't have to worry about him killing her for revenge now, and he was very glad he wouldn't have to fight his own brother to save her. He may make her life miserable for a while, but he wouldn't hurt her. Nik knew this for a fact.

On the down side, he would never let her go. She'd never be able to go home to be with her sister. This he also knew for a fact. He needed her blood for his very survival now, or he would die the true death. Once mated, a vampire would slowly wither away without the blood of his or her mate.

A story Nik used to think of as a fairy tale, until it had happened to him.

The witch was still out for the count, and Nik frowned with concern. Although he knew his brother would never be capable of purposely hurting her, he wasn't so sure that his current state of mind would allow him to properly care for her. And he couldn't let anything happen to that female. It would completely destroy not only his brother, but also his Emma. Keira was the only family she had left.

But he also knew he'd be lucky to be able to get anywhere near her, and he understood why. He had the same crazy possessiveness with Emma. She was his, and his alone, given to him by fate - that bitch. He'd known it the first time he'd tasted her blood.

Actually, whom was he kidding? He'd known it the first time he'd seen her through her kitchen window. But the blood... yeah, the blood had confirmed it in a major way.

Seeing Emma anywhere in the vicinity of another male drove him nearly as insane as his brother appeared to be, so yes, he understood.

He'd had to let her go though. It was good that they'd gotten into that fight outside Leeha's lair. It was good that she hated him now for not helping her take her sister away from Luukas. She'd never asked for this strange vampire mating, and he refused to ask her to give up everything for him, just to be his feedbag. Because that's basically what she would be. He needed her blood now to survive, and her blood alone. Without it, he was going to die the true death. Drinking his normal diet of bagged blood should slow it down a bit...maybe...but it was still going to happen.

And he was ok with that, because he didn't want to live without her.

He just needed to hang on long enough to help his brother get back home and make sure he was going to be ok, and help him find their missing Hunters.

Luukas' eyes locked onto him the moment he moved. He kept his movements casual, not moving too quickly, so as not to alarm him. Yawning, he sat up and stretched his arms over his head. "Did you get any sleep?"

Luukas shook his head.

"How is Keira doing?" He pointed at the girl with his chin.

With a confused look on his face, Luuk looked down at the female in his arms like he'd just realized she was there. "I don't know. Her heart beats."

"Good, that's good." Nik slowly scooted over closer to them and leaned over to get a closer look at her. His brother pulled her in closer to his chest.

"I'm not going to try to take her away. I would never do that, man. I just want to make sure she's ok."

After a pause, he got a quick nod.

"Cool. I'm just going to check her pulse, ok? Just gonna touch her wrist for a few seconds." His brother kept a close eye on him as he carefully reached out and put two fingers on the pulse in her wrist. It could've been stronger, but it was nice and steady. Nik breathed a sigh of relief.

"Ok. Let's get you guys home."

"She's ok?"

"She will be if we get her back to Seattle tonight."

Luukas was up and heading out the tunnel entrance before Nik finished the sentence. Chuckling, he put out the torch, leaving it upside down as a sign for Aiden that they went home should he make it back here, and followed them out.

Luukas was eerily quiet the entire trip home, speaking only when absolutely necessary, and in as few words as possible.

They made good time hiking through the wilderness. Luuk still held Keira, so they were able to move at vamp speed.

The night air was cold, but that was probably a good thing. He assumed his brother had probably taken quite a bit of blood. Honestly, he was surprised he'd managed to stop at all, starved as he'd looked when he'd first seen him. He only looked slightly better now.

Once out on the main road, he flagged down a passing car and "persuaded" the driver to let them drop him off at the nearest gas station, and to give them his vehicle, as a gift. They also had no trouble getting back across the border into Washington with no passports and an unconscious girl. The perks of being a vampire were pretty cool sometimes.

A few hours later, they were back in Seattle.

Nik parked the car in the garage under their downtown apartment building. He'd get rid of it later. Right now, he just wanted to get his brother upstairs and get them both clean and warm. He would worry about everything else after they were settled.

The private elevator whisked them up to the top floor, and Nik was glad to see his brother stride confidently to the door of his apartment. At least he remembered where he lived.

"I have a key." Pulling it out of his pocket, Nikulas unlocked the door and ushered them inside.

"Do you want to put her down on the couch? Your arms must be feeling it by now, even for a vampire."

Luukas was standing very still just inside the door, taking in the wall of windows, the modern kitchen and furniture, the limestone floor and high ceiling. "No."

"Ok. How about we get you cleaned up then? Maybe it'll wake her up, and we can get some food and water in her. If not, we may have to take her to the hospital."

Nik strode off to the bedroom on the right. He stood in his brother's bathroom a moment, thinking. Shower or bath? Bath, he decided, and turned on the water to fill the tub. She couldn't very well stand if she was unconscious. Besides, they could use a good soak. He assumed the nudity thing wouldn't be an issue.

In the bedroom, he found some clean clothes for the two of them, and laid them on the bed. That done, he went out to get Luuk, who was exactly where he'd left him.

"I'm running a bath. Come on. Let's get you guys cleaned up." Once Luuk was following him, he went in and turned off the water. Not sure what his brother would be able to manage on his own, he hesitated to leave.

"Luukas? Do you need help in here?"

When he didn't answer him, Nik hurried to reassure him. "It's alright if you do. I know you've been through a lot."

In the first show of real emotion since he'd found them at the hideout, his brother turned burning eyes on him. "You *don't* know. Now leave."

Guilt bore down on him, so heavy he was surprised he was able to remain upright. So he just nodded and closed the door behind him.

He'd just go scrounge up some food.

13

LUUKAS

Luukas laid the witch down carefully on the rug in front of the tub. A bath. Yes. She needed to be cleaned. Hunkering down beside her, he took a handful of her shirt in each hand and ripped it right up the middle, then down both arms. Moving to her shorts, he yanked them open, sending the button flying, and pulled them down her legs, sliding off her slip-on shoes along with them, and throwing it all in the corner.

Sitting back on his heels, he let his eyes wander down her curvy body, clad in only what used to be a white bra and little cotton underwear with purple stripes. Reaching out, he cupped one of her full breasts, then ran his hand down her soft belly, over her hip, and down the outside of her shapely thigh.

Feelings he didn't understand made him scowl down at her, and he pulled his hand back, leaving her in her bra and underwear.

Can't hurt her.

He ripped his own shirt off, throwing it into the corner on top of hers. The tub was big. They would both fit. Rising up off of the floor, he took off his boots and peeled off his bloody, sticky jeans. They joined the "to be trashed" pile in the corner. He wasn't wearing anything else.

No emotion was reflected as he caught sight of himself in the mirror. He looked nothing like the vampire he remembered anymore. He was thinner, and the recent gashes from what they'd done to him covered his torso and legs. Twisting around, he looked at his back, crisscrossed with lash marks and still half raw. He idly wondered how long it would take them to heal, and why there were no burns?

But what surprised him most were his eyes. They were no longer grey.

They were black.

He spun away from his reflection, unable to stomach the sight of those stranger's eyes.

Sliding his arms under the witch, he lifted her limp form and lowered them both into the deliciously warm water, propping her up between his legs with her back against his front. She moaned softly as he settled them in the warm water, her eyelids fluttering.

His cock stirred at the feel of her lush ass against him, and he ground his teeth together, fighting the urge to roll his hips and increase the contact.

No. Can't hurt her.

With his cupped hands, he scooped water over her front and onto her hair, letting it run down her face, washing away the dirt. He found the shampoo bottle and dumped some on her head. Using both hands, he gathered up her long hair, massaging the shampoo through it.

She moaned again as he rubbed her scalp, one small hand lifting out of the water to touch his bare knee.

"Luukas?"

He stilled at the sound of her voice.

Rip her open! Suck her dry! Kill her! Burn her!

Can't hurt her!

The two instincts battled fiercely within him, making his head pound.

His hands tightened on either side of her head. *How easy it would be to crush her skull*, the darkness told him, until her eyes popped out and her brain matter oozed between his fingers.

"Luukas? You're hurting me!"

Can't hurt her!

He released her head instantly, dropping his hands into the water on either side of her, breathing hard.

"I *want* to hurt you." His voice was raw with the battle raging inside him.

"Luukas, I need you to *help* me," she whispered.

Help her. Yes. He would help her.

She pushed her soapy hair back out of her eyes and struggled to sit up. He pushed against the backs of her shoulders to help her. She flinched at his touch, relaxing again when he only steadied her.

"Where are we?" she asked weakly.

"Home."

"Your home?"

"Yes."

"Where is my sister? Where's Emma? And the other vampire?"

"Nikulas...my brother...is in the other room. Emma left."

"Left to go where?"

"I don't know."

She peeked back at him over her shoulder, started to say something, but then turned back around without speaking, but not before he noticed a slight blush creeping over her skin.

She seemed to be thinking about something. "Luukas? Would you help me shower? Please? So we can rinse off?"

"Yes."

Bending his knees, he sat up and reached down by her feet to lift the plug, then stood up and yanked the curtain closed. He turned the water on, and then pulled the knob up. As he straightened up, he grabbed her under the arms and brought her to her feet, holding her steady.

"Thank you," she told him shakily. "I'm sorry, I would do this on my own if I could."

He kept a grip on her arm as she stepped into the spray to rinse out her hair. "Gods, this feels so good."

Turning around carefully, she kept her eyes closed and hung on to his forearms as she tilted her head back, letting the warm water wash away the years of grime. She lifted her head back up, blinking away the water, and her eyes flew open wide as she caught sight of his naked form. Quickly, she averted them to the side.

"Would you hand me that bottle please?" she asked him huskily, pointing to the body wash.

He stiffened, clenching his jaw. "What's wrong? You don't like to look at me? At my wounds? The wounds *you* helped them inflict? Am I ugly to you?"

She shook her head. "No! No, you're not ugly to me. Not at all." She stared him right in the eye, not looking away, but not looking anywhere else.

Not sure why it even bothered him, he got the bottle, and squeezed some soap onto a cloth, lifting it up out of her reach when she went to take it from him. "I'll help you."

She steadied herself against the shower wall as he ran the soapy cloth over every trembling inch of her, enjoying her sharp intake of breath when he ran it slowly over her breasts and between her thighs.

When she was as clean as he could get her, he helped her rinse off. Grabbing a white towel off of the rack, he slid one arm around her waist and lifted her out of the shower, then wrapped it around her.

"Sit and wait." He pointed at the closed toilet.

Hugging the towel around herself, she sank down gratefully onto the toilet seat.

Luukas washed himself quickly and efficiently. Twice. The soap and water burned his raw skin, but he didn't care. She was right. It felt good to be really clean.

Turning off the water, he grabbed the matching towel and dried himself off before wrapping it around his narrow waist and stepping out.

He noticed her bra and underwear had made their way into the pile as he washed, and her towel was firmly wrapped around her.

She shivered, her eyes tired as they glanced at him apprehensively.

Clothes. He'd seen clean clothes somewhere.

Leaving her where she was, he walked out into the bedroom and saw two sets of clothing on the bed. Both contained a pair of his drawstring lounge pants and a T-shirt.

He picked a set and strode back into the bathroom.

"Lift your arms."

She did, and he slid a shirt over her head and torso. Squatting down in front of her, he helped her place her small feet into each pant leg, and then lifted her to a standing position with his hands around her waist. She steadied herself by hanging onto his bare shoulders, and he pulled the pants up her legs, tugging the towel off of her when it got in his way.

He sucked in a quick breath when she was revealed to him for a split second before the T-shirt fell and covered her.

Recovering quickly, he pulled the pants the rest of the way up and tied the drawstring so they'd stay. His clothes were big on her, but at least she was clean and dry.

Picking the towel up, he squeezed as much water from her long hair as he could. He found a brush, and patiently removed all of the snarls as she sat complacently.

Not asking her permission, he picked her up and carried her out to the living area, setting her down on the couch.

"Do we have anything for her to eat?" he asked Nik.

"Yeah. I grabbed some stuff from my place real quick while you guys were in there. I'll get it ready while you go get dressed."

Nik headed into the kitchen.

Luukas hesitated a second, then nodded once. Leaving them to it, he went in to dress himself.

14

KEIRA

Keira watched the hot, blonde vampire who'd been with her sister as he rummaged around in the kitchen.

He glanced up with bright, blue eyes and gave her a crooked smile when he caught her staring.

"Hi. I'm Nikulas. Luukas' brother."

"I'm..."

"Keira. I know," he interrupted. "Emma's sister."

"Where is she?" she asked him quietly.

He paused, knife in hand, midway through the apple he was slicing.

"She's on her way back to Pennsylvania, I would imagine."

Making short work of the rest of the apple, he set it aside.

"Why did she leave?"

"It's a long story."

"Please, tell me. I haven't seen her in years."

The microwave beeped, and Nik pulled out some oatmeal, stirring it. He brought that, the sliced apple, and some bottled water over to Keira, setting it on the coffee table.

"Do you need help?" he asked her.

She shook her head, and carefully swung her legs off of the couch to sit up and eat.

"Tell me, Nikulas," Keira insisted.

Falling into the chair opposite her, Nikulas gave her the short and sweet version, "She was angry at me for not trying to 'rescue' you from my brother. We fought. She hates me now. I followed her when she ran off and made sure she made it back to the Hummer safely, and then she drove off. I found you two in the hideout right after."

Keira chewed a slice of apple. It was a Fugi, Emma's favorite.

Tears filled her eyes. "You did the right thing. Luukas...he needs time to adjust."

Nik nodded, and a look of understanding passed between them.

"Are you not angry with me?" she asked. "You *do* know it was me keeping your brother there, right?"

"Yeah, I know," he told her solemnly.

"Then why are you being so nice to me?"

He held her eyes as he told her, "Because your sister swears that you would never be so evil on your own. She thinks you were there against your will, and I believe her."

"Leeha threatened Emma's life. Swore to me that she'd kill her if I tried anything or didn't do as she asked." She sniffed and looked away, and then back at Nikulas. "I detested every single moment of it," she confessed adamantly. "I *hated* doing what I did. But I had to choose - Luukas or my sister. I chose my sister, and I would do so again."

They were silent for a while, Keira's crunching on the apple the only noise in the room.

Nik cleared his throat. "I didn't hurt her."

"I know."

"Did he hurt you?"

Keira didn't need to ask who "he" was. "No, not really."

"What happened to your neck? That wasn't him?"

"No. That was another. One of Leeha's guards."

"That bite doesn't look very good. Make sure you keep it clean."

Keira nodded. "I will."

"He won't, you know. He won't hurt you."

Keira was confused for a moment before she realized that he was talking about Luukas again. "You sure about that?"

"I am. You're his."

Keira stopped chewing, swallowing the piece of apple whole.

"His?" she repeated.

"Yes. You know what that means?"

She avoided answering his question. "How do you know?" she challenged instead.

"I know because he told me. Not in so many words. Actually," he scoffed, "in just one word. *Mine*."

Keira took another bite of apple, her mind racing. She knew exactly what that meant. Her parents had taught her all about vampires and their ways when she was young.

"She misses you," he told her, changing the subject again. "She's never given up looking for you, just so you know."

"How did you find her?" She took a bite of oatmeal. "*Why* did you find her?"

"We received word recently that you went missing around the same time Luukas had, and we connected the dots. But, we didn't know if you were taken against your will also, like Luukas, or not. I found your sister and brought her along for leverage in case you proved to be difficult."

"We?" she asked him.

"Aiden, Shea, Christian, Dante, and myself. They are Luukas' Hunters, part of the vampire Council here."

She was well aware of who they were.

"Are they here?"

Nik shook his head. "No. Leeha took Aiden during our rescue attempt, when the wolves showed themselves." He smiled roguishly. "She *hates* wolves. The others…I don't know where they are," he admitted. "They were supposed to meet us up there when Aiden and I arrived with Emma. We received a call from them right before we left PA, and haven't seen them or heard from them since. Running into the wolves was pure luck. I have no idea what happened, but I need to find out before..." He cut himself off. "They've all been acting weird ever since Luuk went missing. Who knows what could've happened?"

Keira glanced up sharply. "Weird, you say?"

Nik narrowed his eyes at her. "Yeah, very weird. Why?"

Keira glanced towards the closed door of the bedroom before whispering to him softly. "I may know something about the others who are missing."

"What?" He demanded.

Keira told him the truth. "I don't know where they are. But...I'm sure you know, Leeha is insanely obsessed with having Luukas for herself."

Nik nodded. "Yeah, that's been going on for a long time. That's why Luuk went to meet her that day, hoping he'd finally be able to talk some sense into her."

"I don't think she's capable of 'sense', Nikulas. Trust me on that one." Keira put the empty oatmeal bowl on the coffee table. "I don't know where they are. However, I know why they've been acting strange. She made me put a curse on all of you."

"She made you *what?*" His mouth dropped open in disbelief.

"Curse you. All of you. Except Luukas. I guess torturing him to within an inch of his life was satisfying enough for her," she said bitterly. "She wanted to throw you off his trail. She wanted you all to be as miserable as she is, wanted me to make it impossible for any of you to find someone to care about and be happy: partly because she'd be jealous, and partly because she's just a psycho bitch. She knows all of your weak points, and made me expound upon them."

"What was the curse?"

"She wanted you to believe you were a killer, knowing the guilt would eat you alive. Christian I made into a complete whore. He is physically unable to *not* have sex, and never with the same person twice. He needs to find multiple people a night to do it with; when all he really longs for is to find one girl he can be with in a faithful relationship. Shea cannot be physically touched by a male, it causes her excruciating pain."

"That explains a lot," Nik interrupted. "She used to be so affectionate, until the day Luukas disappeared and she hugged me. As soon as she touched me, she stiffened up and jumped away. I was too distraught to think much about it, and she just played it off. But now that you say that…I can't even remember the last time she so much as sat within arms distance of any of us."

Now that her belly was full, Keira felt her eyelids getting heavy. "Dante will always be in darkness, when all he wants is light." She yawned. "The curses cannot be broken. But I tricked her. I added a little something to each curse, a way out."

Keira fought to keep her eyes open, but it was a losing battle.

"What way out? Keira? What way out?"

She wanted to answer him, but all she could manage was one word before she floated into sleep.

"Witches."

15

CHRISTIAN

Christian groaned, slowly blinking his eyes open.

What the fuck happened?

He remembered leaving the apartment building and taking a shortcut through the alley. He'd been on his way to see that cute little stripper he'd been eyeballing, to work off some stress before they left on the rescue mission to get Luukas. But, it appeared he'd gotten intercepted.

So, where the hell was he now?

He rubbed the back of his neck, trying to chase away the headache pounding in his skull as he looked around. He was in an empty box within a larger, windowless room. Granted, it was a large box, more like a small room, but it was a box nonetheless. The box had three walls made of what looked like reinforced steel, and one wall made of glass. The floor and ceiling were made of the same material as the walls.

Glass? Really? Christian smirked as he stopped rubbing his neck. Whoever it was that had put him here was stupid enough to put a vampire behind glass? Thinking that would hold him?

He cracked his knuckles as he walked up to the front wall. The only bad thing about this was that he was about to cut the fuck out of his fist. But there didn't seem to be any help for it. He sure as hell wasn't staying in here and waiting around for his kidnappers to reappear.

He looked through the glass, searching the corners of the outer room as far as he could see, but it was just an empty room. There wasn't even anywhere someone could hide, as there was no furniture other than a tall, leather-covered bench on the one side angled toward him, and a floor-to-ceiling pole in the center of the room. He didn't see any hidden cameras either.

Good deal. Fisting up his right hand, he pulled back and slammed it into the glass. It bowed out with the force of his punch, but didn't shatter as he'd expected it too, returning to its original shape.

Christian frowned. He'd hit that sucker pretty good. It should've broken easily. Taking a deep breath, he pulled back his fist again, letting it fly as hard as he could.

Again, the glass bowed out with his punch and then returned to the way it was.

What. The. Fuck.

This was obviously no ordinary glass. For the first time since he'd woken up, Christian began to get nervous. His fangs punched down in frustration as he tested each of the other walls in turn, punching, kicking, and body-slamming them until he had to stop or risk injuring himself in a way that would take too long to heal. He didn't want to be incapacitated in any way when he met his hosts. His nervousness blossomed into full-blown anxiety.

He wasn't getting out of here that easily.

Out of breath, he sank down into the corner, and tried to calm himself. Tried to think.

He didn't remember anything after he entered the alley. Was he even still in Seattle? Who would do this to him?

He racked his brain for answers. Had he upset somebody's boyfriend or husband? It was entirely possible. Christian didn't ask many questions of the human females he fucked. He didn't really care if they were taken or not, or where they were from, or what their name was. He'd never see them again in any case. He was only ever with a female once, and once he'd had her, any and all desire he'd felt for her was gone. And then he was on to the next one, and the next, until the rising sun chased him home.

The next night, he would do it all over again. The only time he didn't follow this routine was when he was fighting or sleeping.

Such was his life since their Master had disappeared, and he had no idea where it had come from, or how to stop it. All he knew was that if he tried to resist his urges to have sex...well, let's just say it wasn't good.

He'd only attempted to refrain one time, and he'd managed to go two nights without being with anyone. The next night, when he'd gone to Shea's apartment to get with her and Dante about how they were going to handle a group of rogue vamps in the area, he'd felt like a strung out heroin addict. He'd taken one look at the female Hunter, and had completely lost it. Dante had had to physically remove him from the premises, before he'd forced himself upon her and raped her, or worse. And that would've been bad. Really, really bad. Thank the gods Dante had arrived before him.

So, yeah, there was a very good chance that he'd played with the wrong female, and she'd cried to her male about how she'd been drugged and seduced, through no fault of her own, into cheating on him.

But how would a human male know to put him in something like this box cell? It wasn't common knowledge among the humans that vampires lived among them. As a matter of fact, vampires went out of their way to avoid them finding out. If they did somehow, they were treated to a good old-fashioned memory wipe and were sent on their merry way, safe again in their ignorance.

Christian jumped to his feet as a hidden panel in the back of the room slid open. His eyes narrowed in on the empty doorway, waiting for his host to reveal himself. But no man ever came into the room. Instead, an ethereal creature glided towards him. A creature dressed in nothing but a gauzy, white camisole, matching short skirt, and slinky heels. Her skin was so pale it was nearly translucent. Her lips were a pink cupid's bow. Her hair such a bright, peachy color, it reminded him of the rays of the sun streaming through the clouds at sunset. As she moved closer, he saw strands of blonde interspersed throughout the peach, only adding to the sunset effect. It was pulled back from her face, with only a few strands left loose to frame her features.

He wanted to pull the pins out of her hair and watch it ripple down around her face like fire.

He walked towards her as she neared him, stopping only when he came into contact with the glass wall. She hadn't looked at him or spoken to him, yet she completely entranced him. His heart pounded as he watched her come closer and closer still. Her eyes were downcast, and he wished she would lift them so he could see their color.

She stopped at the pole, and he groaned aloud, placing his palms on the glass. She was still too far away from him. He wanted her closer.

Music bled into the room. A smoky, seductive beat that pulsed through his body, and she started to dance.

He watched, mesmerized, as she strutted around the pole, and then gripped it with one hand while she let her body go into a free fall around it, keeping her eyes down the entire time. Finding her footing again, she dropped down into a squat; the pole between her legs, gripping it with both hands. Ass first, she rose up to her full height, only to turn around and slide up and down the pole, her hands above her head as the pole separated her perfectly rounded ass cheeks. Her skirt rode up as she writhed on the cold metal, giving him teasing glances of something white and sparkly and barely there, scarcely covering the mound between her soft thighs.

Christian pressed his forehead to the glass as she started undoing the hooks on the back of her shirt, helpless to look away.

Facing away from him, she let it float down the front of her body. Crossing her arms in front of herself, she covered her breasts with her hands, and then teasingly dropped one hand to swing around the pole again.

Through it all, she kept her eyes down and her expression never changed.

His cock pounded in his pants. His fangs ached to sink into her pale skin.

He was truly in hell.

16

NIKULAS

"Keira? Keira?" Nikulas sighed heavily and flopped back in the chair. Dammit. She'd passed out again. Well, at least he'd gotten some food into her.

He wondered what was taking his brother so long. Pulling the blanket off of the back of the couch, he lifted Keira's legs back up onto the cushions and covered her up before wandering over to the bedroom door.

Knocking softly, he announced himself before going in. "Luuk? It's me."

Cracking the door open, he peered inside. His brother stood with his back to the door, dressed in the clothes he'd laid out for him. His arms were crossed over his chest, and he was staring out the wall of windows at the lights of the city.

Walking into the room, he joined him there.

They stood in companionable silence, staring at the beautiful city of Seattle, until Luukas broke the spell.

"How long have I been gone?" His voice was rough.

Nik dropped his eyes to the floor, ashamed to say it out loud. "Seven years."

Luuk's sharp intake of breath was the only sign of emotion he showed. After a long moment, he said, "Seven years should be nothing to a vampire as old as I am. But it felt like so much longer than that. What they did to me..." he dwindled off, unable to finish the sentence.

"I didn't know where you were." Nik felt the need to defend himself, but the excuse sounded flimsy even as he spoke it. "As soon as we realized something was wrong, I got everyone together and we went to Leeha's lair to get you, but you were gone."

"I wasn't gone."

Nik's eyes snapped over to his brother. "What?"

Not taking his eyes from the view, Luukas said in that same chilling tone, "I wasn't gone. I was there. She had me chained in the catacombs."

"That's impossible!" Nik clenched his fists at his sides. It couldn't be!

"We were there! We searched the place! No one was there! And there weren't any 'catacombs'...we looked...all of us..." he stuttered to a halt.

Please tell me it isn't true. Tell me I did not leave my brother there, right under my nose, all of these years.

"Luukas, how is that possible? We were there. We searched every inch of that place."

Luukas shrugged. "I was there. She never moved me."

Nik searched his brother's profile, but it didn't seem like any more information was forthcoming.

He risked another question. "How did she manage to keep you there?"

"The witch."

Nik nodded. "Yeah, I know it was the witch, but how did she do it?"

"She took my power."

"Keira can do that?"

"Yes. When the wolves came, she was chanting, and then we escaped. I have it back now."

"Holy shit. I didn't know there any witches left who could still do that."

"Why now?" Luukas wondered aloud. "Why come for me now?"

"We recently found out Keira had gone missing right before you did by sheer luck. Put two and two together." He rubbed the back of his neck. "Soon as we found out Leeha was back in town, well...when we *thought* she'd just come back to town, I went to Pennsylvania to get her sister for leverage, and then we went to get you."

"Where are the other Hunters?"

"I don't know. They were supposed to meet us at the hideout. They never showed." He decided to keep the news that they'd all been cursed on the down low for now.

"Luckily, the wolves did. They just happened to be there of their own accord. What are the chances? Leeha had Marc for some infraction or another. Cedric wouldn't say much about it." Nik frowned as he thought about the bit of fun the wolves had thought they'd have with him. A 'bit of fun' that had ended with Emma being attacked by those fucking grey monsters of Leeha's after they'd kidnapped her from right outside the hideout in broad daylight, when Nikulas couldn't follow them. Thank the gods he'd made it to her in time.

"And now she has Aiden, correct?" Luukas interrupted his thoughts.

"Yes. He was standing too close to her, as usual, and was overpowered. She ran off when the wolves showed up, and took him with her."

A slight smirk turned up the corner of Luukas' mouth. "Are you sure he was overpowered?"

Smiling, Nik shrugged. "Who knows with Aiden? It wouldn't surprise me if he came waltzing in the door a few days from now, full of tales of how he took out the entire place all by himself." His smile was gone as quickly as it'd appeared. "But I'd like to go look for him anyway, once you get settled again."

His brother stiffened beside him. "I don't know that I could help…that I could go back…"

Nik laid a hand on his shoulder, "You don't have to, Luuk. I can do it. Besides, the wolves owe me, and," he smacked him gently on the arm, "I need you here to keep an eye on that witch out there."

Luukas visibly relaxed as he turned away from the window to look at Nik for the first time since he'd entered the room. "How is she?"

Searching his brother's strange, black eyes for some remnant of the over-confident male he'd been before, he saw nothing but pain and uncertainty in the soulless depths. "She's sleeping again, but she ate before she passed out."

Luuk nodded. "I'll need you to fill me in on everything that's happened while I've been gone before you leave Seattle."

"Do you want to do that now?"

"No. Not tonight. Soon."

"Alright. Just let me know when you're ready. Will you be ok here by yourself?"

Luukas gave a nod, and turned back to the window.

Nik did the same. He was happy to stand there for a bit and just enjoy the fact that his brother was standing next to him again. He'd never admitted this out loud to anyone but Aiden, but he had been seriously scared that he'd lost him forever.

After a while, he heaved a sigh and turned to leave. Much as he'd like to hang around for the remainder of the night, he had a car to get rid of before dawn.

"I need to go down to my place, make some calls, see what I can find out about our missing Hunters, and get rid of our ride."

"I'll be fine."

Nik almost smiled. Even after everything he'd been through, his brother was still a stoic son of a bitch.

"I'll come back tonight. Check in on you guys, ok?"

Luuk nodded.

Not knowing what else to say, Nik headed for the door. "Alright then. I'll see you later." Leaving the bedroom door open, he checked on Keira and then headed down to his place.

Once inside his own domain, he leaned against the door and took a deep breath. Too many emotions were going on inside of him.

He missed Emma.

He missed Aiden.

He was worried about his brother and his witch.

Leaving Luukas here alone while he went to find the others was dangerous. If anyone found out he was here on his own, he'd be an easy target for someone to challenge his position. Especially in the condition he was in now. But luckily, as far as Nik knew, they had managed to keep his brother's disappearance and rescue on the down low. As long as he stayed in the apartment building, he should be ok.

Wandering into the kitchen, he found some bagged blood in the fridge and threw it in the microwave. He nearly gagged trying to drink the stuff, but he forced himself to finish it. How the hell had he ever lived on that shit before he'd met Emma? Or rather, before he'd tasted Emma. But she wasn't here, and he needed to keep up his strength as much as he could until he found the others. Once they were all home, he could let nature take its course.

He wondered what death would be like.

It couldn't be any worse than what he was feeling now.

Tossing the now empty bag in the recycle can, he picked up the phone. He had a lot of calls to make.

At least Luukas appeared to be somewhat in his right mind, and getting better all the time. Nik had been really worried about him for a while there.

17

AIDEN

Aiden enjoyed the sultry swing of Leeha's hips as he followed her deeper into the interior of the mountain. She walked like that just to rile him up, he knew, and like the hot-blooded male he was, it worked brilliantly. He'd follow that plump derriere into the depths of hell itself.

And it appeared that that might be exactly where they were going.

Distracted as he'd been by the female's voluptuous assets, he hadn't been paying much attention to their surroundings. He really needed to work on his attention span.

"Are you quite certain we shouldn't chain him, mistress?"

Apparently, he also hadn't noticed that somewhere along the way, a young, dark-skinned vampire had joined them. He marched along beside Leeha, the stiffness of his spine indicating that the stick stuck up his arse was quite large.

Leeha gave him such a look that he immediately lowered his eyes and dropped back into step beside Aiden.

He glared at him out of the corner of his eyes. "I don't like you."

Aiden put his hand on his chest, his feelings hurt. "You don't *like* me?"

"No."

"But, you've only just met me. How can you not like me?"

"You need to leave."

"Ah. But your mistress would be very upset if I were to do that, especially without saying goodbye. Besides, she promised that we would 'wallow' in our earthly pleasures before the wolves showed up. She owes me a wallowing and I'm not leaving until I get it."

The young vampire clenched his teeth so hard, Aiden could practically hear the enamel cracking from the stress.

"If you believe for one minute that I would let you lay a finger on her, you're sadly mistaken." He lowered his voice. "Leeha is mine."

Aiden barked out a laugh, "Ha! Leeha is no one's but her own. And if you think you're male enough to change that, you're in for one hell of a bloody awakening."

Leeha's voice rang out angrily, "If you two are quite finished?"

Aiden gave him a look. *See what you've done?*

He glared back at him, but said no more.

They'd been walking for quite a long time. How deep did this bloody mountain go?

He'd just began to consider having a go at persuading Leeha into ditching her reeking guards and her boy toy, and finding a dark corner where they could be somewhat alone, when she took a sharp right and then a left.

Glancing up from the enticing female in front of him, he saw they were entering a small altar room.

"Aiden!"

Aiden's head swung around, Leeha's ass forgotten. "Shea?"

He frowned at his hostess. She appeared none too pleased, although not surprised, to see his friend standing next to the altar in the center of the room, chained to the heavy rock.

"What's she doing here, Leeha?"

Never taking her blood-red eyes from the female in question, Leeha tilted her head jerkily to the side. "I do keep asking myself the same question. She was to be...taken care of by this time. However, it seems that plan has been changed."

"Are the other Hunters here also? Christian? Dante?"

"I'm sure I don't know what you mean. Why ever would *I* have them?" She gave him a dazzling smile.

He eyed that smile with a good dose of distrust. It was never good when she was this bloody happy, especially after what had just gone down aboveground.

"What do you mean by 'she was to be taken care of'?" he asked her warily, although he wasn't certain he really wanted to know.

Her boy toy cleared his throat and stepped between them to gain her attention, ignoring Aiden completely.

"Mistress. What are we going to do with *him*?" he asked, tilting his head towards Aiden. "We can't just let him have free rein in here."

Aiden took offense at his tone. "*Him*?" he mimicked. "Is that some secret code word for 'rival for my true love's attentions'? I am standing right here, you realize."

The vampire stiffened, and Aiden knew he'd hit a nerve. He grinned at the back of his head.

"There are no rivals for my mistress's attention. Especially not from a swarthy, grey-eyed Brit like you," the vampire gritted out between clenched teeth.

Aiden's smile widened.

"Well, aren't you a cheeky one?"

He was definitely jealous. This could work to his advantage.

But back to the question at hand: "Poppet, you haven't answered me. Why is my mate here chained to this slab of stone, deep within the underground of your home? And why does this place in particular give me the heebie-jeebies?"

Leeha ignored both males, directing her question to Shea. "Where is he?"

Shea cocked an eyebrow. "He who, exactly?"

"Don't get impertinent with me, vampire. You know whom I'm speaking of."

Shea looked as if she was about to deny it, but then shrugged nonchalantly. "I don't know. He and his bird went off that way somewhere after he secured me here." She pointed over her shoulder with her chin.

"Josiah, go find him," Leeha ordered.

"Mistress, I don't know if it's a good idea to leave you here alone..."

"Go find him! NOW!"

His hands balled into fists, but he grudgingly left to carry out her order, throwing a warning look at Aiden on his way out.

"I can trust you not to do anything stupid, my love, yes?" Leeha purred as she ran her hand down Aiden's large bicep.

"Yes," he answered, curious as to what she would do or say next.

Shea sounded like she was choking on something.

"Good. Because I want to show you something."

She grabbed his hand and gave him a tug to follow her, and Aiden took the opportunity to give Shea a wink of reassurance.

She pulled him over to the altar, excitement lighting up her features. "Do you have any idea what this is?"

Linking his hands behind his back, he strolled casually around the piece, unobtrusively checking Shea for injuries when he got to her. He didn't see anything obvious.

Good.

"Hmmm. Well, I would gather from the blood stains so artfully seeped into it that it's an old, sacrificial altar of some sort." He paused at the one end, his forehead wrinkling as an unpleasant thought occurred to him. "I do hope that's not the reason Shea is chained to it."

Leeha avoided his eyes, her smile faltering.

"Now poppet, you understand that I cannot allow that," he told her sternly, like he would to a child.

With a pout, she ran her hand lovingly over the rough surface of the stone. "Don't be cross with me. It seems that's not going to be possible now, in any case."

Aiden crossed his arms. "I am *quite* angry with you right now, Leeha. But I would be more so if something had actually come of your plan. Is that what you wanted to show me?"

Her smile reappeared, blinding him with its brilliance.

Her Evilness was bad news, he knew, and pursuing her would only lead to heartbreak on his part, but for some reason, he couldn't seem to resist her.

He smiled back, his anger forgotten.

"No. That is not what I wanted to show you, I didn't realize she would still be here, but no matter." She continued to lovingly caress the surface of the altar. "This is no ordinary altar, Aiden, but a link between the dark realm and our own. The "heebie-jeebies" you feel in this room are not just your imagination."

Aiden and Shea both glanced around uneasily.

Leeha continued, her voice filled with reverence. "This altar is my greatest secret weapon, found quite by mistake shortly after I arrived here. It will enable me to become everything I've always aspired to."

"Which is what, exactly?" Shea asked.

Leeha shot her an angry glance for daring to interrupt, but answered the question. "Why, to become the Master vampire of this entire region, of course, to start with."

Aiden scoffed. "Luukas is the Master vampire here. And being that he's recently escaped your evil clutches…"

Shea gasped, "He did?"

Aiden continued, "And isn't likely to allow you to one-up him again, how exactly do you think you'll be getting away with this plan?"

"It's quite simple, Aiden. This altar allows me to create my own army. An army that will be invincible once I work out a few…kinks." Arms flung wide, she spun in a slow circle, flinging her head back with joy.

The hair on the back of Aiden's neck stood on end, and from the way Shea's eyes were shifting around nervously, she felt it too. The room suddenly felt…alive.

"This *room*, this room and this altar are doorways. Doorways that let the darkness through." She came to a stop, her eyes maniacal, blood and shadows swirling within their depths. "There are demons here, tied to this altar by an ancient curse. The demons speak to me. They want to be of this world, but of course, they cannot, as they're not corporeal. But I found a way to help them with that, quite by accident, when one of my vampires displeased me while in here. They whispered to me, told me what to do with him. I found a way to make them physical beings again, with the ability to leave this room, and in return, they give me their complete and utter loyalty."

Aiden tapped his pursed lips with his index finger, brow furrowed as he thought on what she'd just told him. "So, what you're jibber-jabbering about, basically, is that you're giving evil demons bodies to possess, and in return they're going to help you take over the world. Did I miss anything?"

Clasping her hands in front of her, Leeha nodded excitedly.

"And the stinking pack lined up in the tunnel out there, I take it they're the results of the 'kinks' you need to work out."

"Yes. But I believe I know how to keep that from happening now."

He looked at her with new eyes, impressed. "That's *quite* the diabolical plan. Even for you, sunshine."

She preened beneath his gaze. "Thank you."

Aiden allowed her her moment, and then clapped his hands together loudly. "So this has all been fun, but I really need to go now. And I'll be taking Shea with me. Much as I hate to do it, we'll have to postpone our 'wallowing' for another time. If you would be so kind as to show us the way out, luv?"

She had the decency to look sincerely apologetic. "Ah, my Aiden. You know I cannot do that. You will need to stay here with me now. If I allowed you to leave, you would try to foil my plans, and I cannot let you do that. Don't try to deny it," she scolded when he opened his mouth to speak, "you know you would."

"You're quite correct, I would," he acquiesced. "So, now what?"

She only smiled wistfully at him.

Bloody hell. *That* smile was even more worrisome than the happy one.

18

LUUKAS

Once Nikulas left, Luukas went out to the other room to check on the witch. She was curled up on the couch, her dark hair spread out around her head like a halo.

She was his angel, but looks could be deceiving.

Rip her open! Suck her dry! Kill her! Burn her!

NO! Can't hurt her!

Luukas pressed his palms to either side of his head and pressed, trying to contain the two sides warring within him. His emotions were riding a razor's edge.

Part of him wanted nothing more than to destroy the fallen angel on his couch. It wanted to rip into her, slake his never-ending thirst, and throw what was left of her, piece by piece, off of the balcony to the street below to be set upon by the crows.

But the other part of him, ah...the other part, wanted to do nothing but hold her and make her his, wanted to love her and protect her from anything and anyone that may hurt a single hair on her lovely head.

Even if that someone was him.

Can't hurt her.

Luukas lowered his arms as that side of him won, for now. Taking a deep breath, he closed his eyes for a moment, opening them again only to look around the room with wide, wary eyes.

His past life, before his imprisonment, felt almost like a dream. It was surreal to be back - surreal and a little bit frightening, if he was going to be honest. He was glad Nikulas was the only one here. Glad the others weren't here to see him like this.

That was wrong, wasn't it? To be glad something had happened to them?

He frowned in confusion. Not glad something had happened to them; just glad they weren't here to witness his weakness. Hopefully, by the time they were found, he would be back to normal; or as back to normal as he would ever be again.

How could he ever go back to what he was?

But he had to; he was their Master, their maker. Not just to the council, the Hunters, but to all of the vampires in the area.

Did they even know what had happened to him? The civilians? He'd have to remember to ask Nik about that.

They must. He didn't see how his brother would've been able to hide it for so many years. How would they have explained his absence when his colony came to him to settle a dispute or ask for advice, as they so often did?

His heart sped up and sweat beaded on his brow as he thought of all of the responsibilities he would have again. As a Master vampire, he was responsible for hundreds of lives. Lives he'd created. Some of which had traveled with him overseas to start a new life here. They would all be looking to him to guide them, to protect them, to lead them.

Had they felt his pain, his hunger, his fear, while he was gone? Could they feel his panic now? He was a part of them as they were a part of him. Had they all suffered along with him?

He gulped in air as he fought his growing panic, his emotions flicking out from him like shots of electricity to rattle the lamps and the paintings on the walls. His eyes flew wildly around the room as memories, and the feelings they evoked, flooded his mind: memories of his past, memories of his torture, and the uncertainty of his future colliding inside of him, twisting around in his mind.

Slamming his trembling palms to either side of his head again as his heart pounded, he spun towards the windows, then back around, not knowing where to go to escape his own mind, until his eyes landed back on the small female asleep on his couch.

The witch.

The angel.

A calmness overtook him as he watched her sleep, focusing on her deep, even breaths. He matched his breathing to hers, everything else leaving his mind, as he unconsciously pulled his power back within himself.

He focused on nothing but her until the dawn beckoned him to join her in sleep. Lifting her up off of the couch, he carried her, blanket and all, into his room and laid her gently on the bed. Lying down beside her on top of the comforter, he covered them both with her blanket and pulled her in tight against him, her back to his chest. Wrapping his arms around her, he breathed deeply, inhaling her scent, closed his eyes, and fell into a natural sleep for the first time in seven years.

19

KEIRA

Keira slowly became aware of birds singing happily, and smiled slightly as she listened to them calling back and forth.

Gods, it was hot.

Wait. Hot? How could it be hot? It was always freezing cold in the bowels of the damn mountain. And where had the birds come from?

She cracked open her eyes. The shadows on the wall in front of her told her that the sun was just setting, and she was in a bed. A real bed! Turning her face, she breathed in the fresh, cool scent of the soft pillow her head was resting on.

As she attempted to roll over to shove her entire face into it, she became aware of a heavy arm wrapped around her middle, and warm breaths hitting the back of her neck.

Memories of the night before rapidly returned: She was in Luukas' apartment, and this was his muscular arm wrapped around her middle.

She chewed her bottom lip, and tried to decide how to feel about that.

Other memories popped into her head. Luukas enraged with her, his hand wrapped around her neck while she struggled to breathe. Luukas drinking greedily at her throat, the sounds of his pleasure and the memory of him pulling at her vein making her muscles clench deep inside her core. Luukas pulling her down onto his lap, surging against her, pure lust heating her blood as he'd ordered her to come.

And, wow, had she ever. Of course, it'd been years since she had sex. No wonder it'd felt so good.

She reminded herself to breathe while she attempted to calm her fluttering heart. It wouldn't do for him to wake and find her in such a state. There was no hiding these things from a vampire's heightened senses.

She focused on the shadows moving across the wall and thought about absolutely nothing until her heartbeat returned to normal.

Wait a minute. The sun was just going down. How come he wasn't a pile of cinders?

This *was* a vampire's home; she guessed it would make sense to have it sun-proofed somehow.

In any case, much as she'd love to stay all snug and warm and sleep some more, nature was calling.

Inch by careful inch, she eased her way out from underneath his arm, managing to make it out of the bed without disturbing him.

Tiptoeing across the room, she opened the door that she assumed led to the bathroom. Instead she found rows and rows of clothing in a huge, walk-in closet; suits, shirts...even ties.

She imagined Luukas healthy and dressed in a designer suit. He would command the room, but he did that no matter what he was wearing. Still, the image brought an interested lift to her eyebrow, until her bladder urged her to quit fantasizing about a hot vampire, and find the damn bathroom already.

Closing the door again quietly, she found the bathroom and gratefully locked the door behind her.

Like the rest of the apartment, the bathroom was clean and modern. All pale blue and white, with dark walnut cabinets, a walnut and cream marbled counter with two sinks, and a tiled floor. It was similar to most apartment bathrooms, except for the tub and shower combo. The tub was oversized and deep, and every woman's bubble bath dream.

Her blood heated up again as she remembered being in that bathtub.

Finishing her business, she gazed over at it with longing. Though she planned to take full advantage of that tub again someday, right now she could really go for another shower; a shower with scalding hot water and a Brillo pad to wash with. Even then, she didn't know if she'd ever feel really clean again after all of the years she'd spent in Leeha's "guest quarters". But she sure as hell planned on trying.

Mind made up, she turned the water on and stripped out of her oversized clothes. She pulled open the drawers, wondering if there were any...yes! A razor! She'd had just about all she could take of the hippie-chick look. Not that there was anything wrong with that. To each their own. The natural look just wasn't normally her thing.

Stepping into the tub, she sighed with pleasure as the steaming spray hit her, and for long moments, did nothing but enjoy the hot water pounding on her shoulders.

She wondered how long she was going to have to stay here. Even after her day's sleep, she still felt run down. Maybe in another day or so, she could start thinking about heading home.

That is, if Luukas would let her leave. If what she'd guessed, and Nikulas had confirmed, was true, there'd be no leaving for her. Once a vampire had found their mate, only their blood would keep the vampire alive. Without their mate, they would die.

She sighed as she grabbed the shampoo bottle.

He was angry with her, more than angry with her, and with good reason. Honestly, she was shocked that she was still amongst the living. Of course, if he was capable of realizing the full implication of what she was to him, he had to keep her alive and well.

She didn't deserve to be, and she wouldn't hold it against him if and when he finally snapped and took his revenge, even though her reasons for doing what she did were sound.

Weren't they?

Yes! Yes, of course they were. What was she supposed to have done when Leeha told her what she was meaning to do, and the consequences if she didn't go along with it? Just let that stupid bitch kill her little sister? Her only family? Emma was innocent in all of this. As a matter of fact, she had no idea about any of it. She didn't even know she was a witch!

Well, actually, she did now it seemed, thanks to Nikulas. But she had no idea about the history of their family, and why her parents had kept it hidden from her. She had no idea that her older sister has been practicing her entire life in secret, strengthening her magic. She had no idea her parents had been part of a powerful coven, or why her family had left the protection of that coven.

Their parents had kept Emma in the dark about it all to protect her, and Keira had agreed to keep the secret. Her little sister was everything in the world to her. She would die to protect her, and almost had a few times.

But now that she was out of that hellhole, she planned on making her way home to Emma, come hell or high water, if for no other reason than to talk her into moving out here so they could be together again. However, she had a feeling it wasn't going to be easy.

Chewing her lip, she tried to come up with a plan while she scrubbed herself clean and shaved. Maybe she'd be able to talk to

Luukas, tell him about her sister and what Leeha had threatened to do to her. Maybe he'd understand, like his brother. Leeha's threats foremost in her mind, she was worried about what Emma would find upon arriving home. Surely Luukas would let her go.

She flashed back to his growled declaration once they'd been free of the tunnels: *"The witch is MINE."*

Or, maybe not.

OK, on to plan B. She'd have to make her escape during the day, when Luukas wouldn't be able to follow her. She'd need money for a plane ticket, and a way to get to the airport. That was her biggest obstacle right now, as far as she could see. Getting away would be relatively easy, as long as she could make it outside of the building and into the sunshine.

Piece of cake.

Turning off the water, she stepped out of the shower and dried off, putting Luukas' clothes back on. Hunting around in the drawers again, she found a toothbrush and some toothpaste and brushed her teeth. Twice.

She almost felt human again.

Pulling her long, brown hair back, she braided the wet mass down her back and tied it with a rubber band she'd found. She really needed a haircut. The stuff had grown nearly halfway down her back while she'd been gone, and she hadn't been allotted haircuts like Luukas. Apparently, Leeha hadn't wanted him to get too uncivilized in appearance, so she'd sent in Josiah to trim him up occasionally and shave him every other day or so. He did so, grudgingly, and carelessly, and when the risk of Luukas waking up while it was happening was little to none.

Rolling her eyes at the absurdity of it, Keira turned off the light and eased the door open.

Luukas was still exactly where she had left him. Tiptoeing past the bed, she made her way out to the main room, closing the door behind her. She needed to eat, and find a phone to call her sister. She had to be worried sick. Even if Emma hadn't made it home yet, she could leave a message on their home voicemail to warn her about Leeha, and let her know that she was okay and that she'd join her as soon as she was able.

She was glad Emma had actually listened to her and had left when she did. If she hadn't, there was no telling what Luukas may have done to her. He'd been starved and tortured for years. He hadn't been in his right mind.

She bit her lip as she wondered if his mind would ever be "right" again.

Turning on a few lamps to fend off the encroaching darkness, she made her way into the kitchen and found another apple in the fridge. Biting into it, she savored the juicy sweetness for a few seconds, and then began raiding the cupboards for more food. All she found were a couple of protein bars.

Grabbing two, she got some water and took her bounty over to one of the stools on the other side of the counter. While she ate, she planned, and by the time she'd finished, she knew what she was going to do.

Although she had a pretty good feeling that she would get no help from Luukas, his brother was a different story. She would ask Nikulas for the money for a plane ticket. A loan. She'd pay him back as soon as she got home, and could get to the bank. He would do it, if not for her, then for Emma. She'd seen the way he protected her. And she knew he had the money. They all did. Any vampire worth his salt that'd been alive as long as he had would have a small fortune stashed away by now. She'd just have to get him alone the next time he stopped by, as she was sure he would. It shouldn't be too hard to maneuver a way to speak to him privately for a few seconds. That's all she would need.

Finished with her meal, she threw away her trash and washed her hands. There was no phone in the kitchen, so she decided it was time to explore the place.

Heading in the opposite direction of the sleeping vampire, she gave herself a tour.

Peeking in the half-opened door on the other side of the apartment from the master bedroom, she found a guest bedroom. A quick perusal from the doorway didn't reveal any telephones, so she didn't go in to explore further. However, nestled in the corner of the living room was a glass walled office, if the desk and file cabinets were any indication. And if any room would have a phone, that one would, and...bingo! There it was: a cordless phone sitting right on top of the desk.

With a satisfied smile, she yanked it off of its holder and listened for a dial tone. Punching in the numbers she'd known by heart her entire life, she wandered over to the office window to watch the last rays of the sun disappear over the Sound while she waited for it to ring.

Halfway through the first ring, the phone was ripped from her hand.

"What the hell?" Spinning around she came face to face with a very large, very intimidating, very *awake* vampire.

"No phone." He gritted out between clenched teeth.

Turning, he slammed the phone down on the edge of the desk, shattering it. Then, for good measure, he destroyed the cradle for it also, ripping its cord out of the wall and smashing that on the desk too.

Without another word, he turned on his heel and flew through the apartment at vamp speed, destroying the phones in both of the bedrooms.

Dammit. She should've looked in that spare room first. Maybe he wouldn't have found her until after she'd gotten through.

Keira stood at the window where he'd left her, her eyes narrowed as she tried to track his movement throughout the apartment. Catching a blur of color going past the office doorway, she stomped after him. "I can't even call my sister?"

He stopped abruptly, spinning towards her so fast she collided with his wide chest. "No."

"No-o?" she countered.

"NO."

They stood at an impasse, black eyes glaring into hazel, until Keira finally took a step back, lifted her chin and crossed her arms defiantly.

"So, I'm not allowed to use the phone. Am I allowed to leave?"

His eyes widened fearfully and his breathing became shallow. "No."

Keira observed his reaction with interest. This didn't bode well.

"You can't just keep me locked up here forever," she told him.

He narrowed his eyes at her. "I think I can."

"No, you can't. You can't watch me every single second, Luukas."

The stubborn expression on his face told her he believed otherwise.

She sighed and dropped her hands to her sides. "Look. I am so, so sorry for everything you've gone through. Really, I am. And if there were any way at all that I could go back in time and figure out a way for what happened to *not* have happened, I would! But, I can't."

His upper lip lifted in a sneer as he leaned down into her face. "*You* are the reason it happened. *You* are the one who did those things to me. *You*, are not going anywhere until I decide what to do with you."

His dark eyes smoldered into hers.

She could swear she felt them burning right through to her very soul.

"How could you do those things to me?" he asked, his voice husky with betrayal.

Tears filled Keira's eyes and rolled down her face. She didn't bother wiping them away. "She said she would kill my little sister if I didn't do as she said." Lifting her arms out to the sides, palms up, she tried to make him understand. "I had no choice..."

He barked out a harsh laugh. "Oh, you had a choice. You're a powerful witch. You could have destroyed her easily, but you didn't. Why not? If you're so innocent?" He didn't give her a chance to answer. "I think you're not so innocent. I think you were in on it with her the entire time. I think you still are."

"No! That's not true!" How could he believe that of her? He had to have seen how much she was repulsed by her own magic every time she was made to assist that evil bitch! How could he not have seen that?

"Luukas, you can't really believe that I would do something like that of my own violation," she implored him.

"Why not? I was *there*, witch. I was the one you tortured, the one you starved, the one you fucking BURNED ALIVE!" he roared.

Spinning away, as if he couldn't stand the sight of her anymore, he gripped his head with his hands, a harsh sound escaping him.

Keira stood silent and still, afraid to say anything, afraid to move, afraid to so much as breathe.

He visibly trembled before her, fighting for control. So she stood as still as a statue, not making a sound, while he battled his demons, and prayed he would get a grip on them before he remembered she was there.

After a few very long, very tense moments, he lowered his arms and straightened up. Without looking at her, he ground out, "I want to shower. You're going to come with me." Reaching behind him, he grabbed her wrist and tugged her into the bedroom with him.

"But I've already showered!" She tried to escape his grasp, but his grip was too strong. She had no choice but to allow him to pull her along.

Once in the bedroom, he didn't hesitate, but yanked her into the bathroom with him, shutting and locking the door.

Dropping her wrist, he proceeded to ignore her and walked over to start the shower.

She watched, unable to look away, as with his back to her, he yanked his T-shirt over his head, then untied his pants and let them fall to the floor.

Not yet back to his full health, he was nonetheless a sight to behold. His back was broad, sculpted, and muscular; his beautiful skin marred only by some still-healing lash marks. Her eyes followed those muscles down to his tight ass and long, muscular legs. Slowly raising her eyes back up to his strong arms and shoulders, her belly clenched deep within her, and she squeezed her thighs together, swallowing hard.

"If you're done staring at me, I'll get in the shower now. Do not leave the room. I would catch you before you made it to the bedroom door." Yanking the curtain back, he stepped into the tub, quickly pulling it closed again behind him.

He'd sounded almost...disgusted. Disgusted that she was looking at him?

She scowled at the shower curtain. And how had he known she was staring?

In spite of his warning, it crossed her mind to try to run for it, but in the end she just leaned back against the door and waiting for him to finish. Because, as much as she wanted to leave, he hadn't been lying. She knew she wouldn't get very far, not unless she used her magic on him.

And *that*, she absolutely refused to do.

She would never use it on him again. Ever. No matter what. Not even if he did snap and try to kill her. She didn't think she could bring herself to do it even if she wanted to.

The water shut off, and Keira spun to face the door just as he yanked the curtain open. She wasn't about to get busted staring again.

Neither spoke as he dried off. It wasn't until she heard him opening drawers that she turned back towards him, assuming it was safe.

He had the towel wrapped around his narrow hips, the muscles in his arms and shoulders rippling under his skin as he searched for something. She tried not to stare, but it was impossible not to. Her eyes kept traveling back to him of their own accord.

She watched him brush his hair and his teeth before she noticed that he was avoiding his reflection. Like, seriously avoiding it. Her heart ached in her chest at the realization. Was he really so different now? She didn't think so. He'd already started to fill out again, and his wounds were healing with her blood.

The only things that hadn't changed back were his eyes. They were still a deep ebony, dark and haunted, rather than the bright grey they'd been when she'd first met him.

So maybe it wasn't just his physical appearance that he shied away from, maybe it was what he saw in those stranger's eyes.

He'd been correct earlier, of course. She was the reason that this male standing in front of her, though still beautiful in her eyes, was nothing like the strong, confident male she had met seven years ago.

She looked down at her hands twisting in front of her, guilt eating away at her insides, unable to watch him avoiding himself any longer.

Lost in her thoughts, she didn't notice he was standing in front of her until he lifted her face up with a finger under her chin. Turning her face to the left and then to the right, he let his eyes rove over her features and down her throat.

His jaw clenched and his nostrils flared as he stared at her neck.

Keira was confused at his reaction until she touched the bite. It was sore. She supposed it didn't look any better than it felt.

Releasing her jaw, he scowled at her slicked back hair.

"Come," he told her, indicating that she should open the door.

Obediently, she turned and opened the door, walking out into the bedroom. Stopping in the middle of the room, she stayed where she was and averted her eyes as he found some jeans and a T-shirt and got dressed.

Barefoot, he wandered over to the floor to ceiling windows to stare thoughtfully out at the lights of the city.

She cleared her throat. "So, um, what exactly are you planning to do with me?" For her answer, she got a whole lot of silence, so she tried again. "Luukas? What are you planning to do with me? Because if you're going to kill me, I really wish you would just do it and get it over with."

"I don't know," he finally admitted gruffly. "I want to kill you, witch. I want to hurt you as you've hurt me. But, I… can't."

Tentatively, she joined him at the window.

"You can't?" Why she was arguing the point, she had no idea. She should be happy that he couldn't kill her, not trying to talk him into it!

He was silent again for so long she didn't think he was going to answer her, but then, in a voice filled with wonder and disbelief, he whispered, "Because you're mine."

So he did understand.

He turned to face her, and she inhaled sharply at the hunger in his eyes. Instinctively, she took a step back, but he grabbed her upper arm.

"And I'm thirsty."

Keira's heart began to pound, her blood rushing to the surface of her skin as he slowly pulled her towards him.

His eyes lit up, and she knew he could hear it.

"Um. Luukas, I don't know if this is a good idea." Placing her palms flat on his firm chest, she tried to hold him off. "Luukas...no. Please."

But he just smiled at her lazily, exposing his fangs, and wrapped her braid around his other hand. Pulling her head to the side, he exposed her pulsing artery to his hungry gaze.

Without warning, he reared his head back and struck, sinking his fangs deep within her.

Keira's cry of alarm gradually turned into a helpless whimper as he began to drink, each pull sending a jolt of electricity straight to her groin. Her hands fisted in his soft T-shirt, pulling him closer.

He moaned softly, erotically, as he fed, and her legs went weak at the sound. Wrapping his arm around her waist as she sagged against him, he pulled her tight up against his hard torso. She could feel the thick length of him rapidly growing against her belly, and her body responded with a rush of wetness between her thighs.

Just when she thought she was going to pass out from the myriad of feelings rushing through her, he lifted his head from her throat, kissing and licking the wound to heal it. Trailing soft kisses up her neck and over her jaw, he released her braid, and gripped the back of her head with his large hand. She couldn't escape as he claimed her lips, kissing her softly at first, and then deepening the kiss. Thrusting his tongue into her mouth, he growled low in his throat as he tasted her.

Breaking off the kiss, he leaned his forehead against hers; breathing hard, and then suddenly bent down and scooped her up into his arms.

Keira threw her arms around his neck as he carried her over to the bed and gently laid her upon the mattress. Claiming her lips again as he followed her down, he eased his weight down on top of her, nudging her legs apart with his knee. He settled between them, holding himself up on his elbows on either side of her head.

Keira moaned as he devoured her mouth, lifting her body to meet him as he rolled his hips into her, the zipper of his jeans rubbing against her through the thin cotton of her pants. She resented the two layers of clothing separating them from each other, longing to feel his skin on hers.

He stopped moving, breaking off the kiss and holding himself off of her. She felt him trembling.

"What's wrong? Why are you stopping?" she whispered.

He tucked his head into the curve of her shoulder, breathing heavily, not answering her. Nuzzling her neck, he groaned aloud.

"Luukas? Please. Don't stop." Turning her face towards him, she tried to catch his eyes with hers as she tightened her arms around his waist and lifted her hips, needing to feel him. "Please..." She didn't stop to question what she was doing;

she just knew that she wanted him. And right now, she felt like she would explode if he stopped.

She continued to arch up against him until finally, with a defeated sound, he lowered himself back down to her. Shoving a hand underneath her ass, he held her still as he ground into her, hitting her clit through their clothes.

Keira cried out with longing. She needed more.

Grabbing the bottom of his T-shirt, she lifted it up as far as she could, tugging until he finally slid his knees up to either side of her hips and sat up to yank it off. Taking a piece of her shirt in each hand, he tore it clear in half, exposing her to his view.

She shivered as the cool air hit her bare skin, her nipples puckering under his heated stare. She tried to pull him back down, but he grabbed her hands and held them still while he ran his eyes over every inch of her exposed skin.

Letting go of one of her hands, he skimmed her nipple with his palm, tilting his head as it tightened even more. She gasped when he pinched it hard, before taking the weight of her full breast in his palm. It filled his large hand, swelling into his palm as he kneaded her. Releasing her other hand, he took her other breast, feeling its weight, before pinching her nipples again.

Keira gripped the comforter as she arched towards him, her legs moving restlessly, wanting still more. She was wet and throbbing, and they still had their pants on.

"Luukas! Please," she begged.

"Please what, witch?" he taunted her, his black eyes wide and intense.

So, he wanted her to beg, was that it? Fine. She would beg.

"Please, be with me. I want you so much," her voice was breathless with desire.

His lips parted on a hiss at her bold words, then closed as his eyes narrowed and he lowered himself back down onto the bed.

Kissing her hard and quick, he wasted no more time, and began to work his way down her body. His mouth was hot and wet as he kissed his way down to her breast and lapped at her nipple, sucking it into his mouth before nipping at it with his teeth.

Keira cried out, her hands in his soft hair, urging him on.

Moving to the other side, he followed a similar path, working it into a hard bud as she strained against him.

Shifting his weight to the side, he ran a hand down her soft curves, his eyes following its path hungrily. He untied her pants, and slid his hand under the waistband.

Her legs fell open of their own accord as he palmed her, and then slid his long fingers between her slick folds. He growled again as he felt her, hot and wet for him.

Taking her nipple with his mouth, he rolled it between his teeth as he slid a long finger inside of her.

Keira's eyes rolled back at the sensation. It'd been so long since she'd been with anyone like this, other than what had happened back in Leeha's cavern. The fact that she couldn't remember being this turned on by anyone else, she conveniently pushed to the back of her mind.

He pulled his finger out, only to have another one join it, and began to thrust them in and out of her, all the while playing with her sensitive nipple with his teeth and tongue. Removing his fingers, he moved them up to her swollen clit, rubbing it in slow circles.

Keira's body moved with him, building toward orgasm.

He sped up his fingers, at the same time sinking his fangs into her areola, and Keira cried out as she crashed over the edge, hard and fast.

20

LUUKAS

Luukas lifted his head to watch his witch as she came undone beneath him. Her skin was flushed and damp, one hand gripping the comforter and the other tugging at his hair as she arched into his hand without shame.

He wished her eyes were open.

Easing her down from her orgasm, he ran his fingers lightly through her pussy. She was so fucking wet.

His cock throbbed in his jeans, and he could wait no more. With one more lick at the blood seeping from her nipple where he'd bitten her, he stood up and shoved his pants down, stepping out of them and then pulling hers off too.

Crawling back over her, he nudged her legs apart and poised himself at her entrance, enjoying the feeling of her arms wrapping around his neck and shoulders.

"Open your eyes, Keira," he ordered, his voice raw with need. "Look at me."

She did, and he watched her beautiful hazel eyes widen as he thrust into her tight sheath, burying himself up to the hilt. She cried out as he filled her so suddenly, throwing her head back.

"No! Open your eyes. Look at me!"

He wanted to see her, and he wanted her to know who was fucking her—who was possessing her.

She locked her gaze to his and he began to move, sliding himself all the way out and then quickly slamming back in. Gods, the *feel* of her. Her full breasts pressed against his chest, her soft thighs wrapped around his hips, and her hot channel squeezed him as he thrust in and out, savoring these feelings that he hadn't felt in so long.

Lowering his head, he kissed her fiercely, groaning at the sweet taste of her. He couldn't remember ever having a woman that made him feel like this.

MINE.

The word reverberated through his head as he broke off the kiss. Rearing up, he quickened his pace, slamming into her as she gripped his biceps, holding her eyes with his. His balls tightened as he felt his impending orgasm. He wanted to make it last longer, wanted to work her up again, but found he couldn't stop.

"Touch yourself," he ordered.

She didn't hesitate to do as he told her. He watched as she found her clit and started rubbing herself, her other hand going to her breast to play with her nipple. The sight nearly unmanned him.

He pounded into her, his eyes going from her face, to her breast, to her small hand touching herself. "Ah! I'm going to come. Come with me, Keira!"

"Yes!" she cried out. "Luukas!"

At the sound of his name on her lips, he threw his head back with a roar as he came, hearing her cry out loudly as she joined him. He continued to thrust in and out as he pulsed inside of her, her contractions forcing every last drop from him.

Falling on top of her, he rolled to the side, bringing her with him, not wanting to crush her.

Holy fuck.

He lay still and silent for a few minutes, catching his breath, enjoying the calmness of his mind; a calm he hadn't felt in seven long years.

Reaching up, he pulled the tie out of her hair and ran his fingers through the damp strands, spreading it out to dry. He liked her hair down.

"Luukas?" Her angel's voice broke into his thoughts.

"Hmm?"

"How old are you?" she asked.

"Over six hundred years."

"Where did you come from? When you crossed the ocean?"

"I'm from Estonia."

"Luukas?"

"What?"

He felt her take a shuddering breath against his chest. "I truly am so sorry for everything I've done to you. If I'd felt I had any other choice..."

Why did she insist on trying to apologize to him? Nothing she said or did would ever make him forgive her.

Nothing.

Extracting himself from her arms, he got up off of the bed, found his jeans and yanked them on. "Get up. Get dressed. You need to eat."

She searched his face for a moment, and then, with a sigh, sat up and found her pants. Standing up, she carried them over to the dresser as she pulled off her ruined shirt and searched his dresser drawers for a new one. Finding one she liked, she sashayed naked into the bathroom, closing the door. The lock clicked behind her.

He felt himself growing hard again at the sight of that luscious, bare ass.

Clenching his jaw, he reminded himself who she was...of what she had done to him. He would NOT fall prey to her charms. He would NOT forget. He would use her delectable body, for blood and for sex, and then he would kill her when he grew tired of her.

He would find another female that tasted just as good, and who made him just as hard.

Stalking out of the bedroom, he went to check the supplies in the kitchen. He never kept food here, there wasn't ever any need, and he didn't know how much Nik had brought up from his place.

Thinking of his brother, he wondered for the first time what was going on with him and Keira's sister. The thought left him again as his witch came out of the bedroom, immediately diverting his attention.

"What kind of food do you like? There isn't much here. We could order something."

He watched her make herself at home at the kitchen counter as she thought about it, her eyes lighting up as she told him, "I could totally go for a huge, greasy pizza. Thin crust. With mushrooms. And iced tea!"

He gave a nod. "Done."

"Just one question," she stopped him before he could walk away. "How are you going to order a pizza when you've destroyed all of the phones? Surely you're not planning on leaving me here alone to go get it? As I'm not allowed to leave?"

He narrowed his eyes at her smirking face. How indeed? Walking over to the front door, he opened it just enough to stick his head out.

"NIKULAS!"

Closing the door, he walked calmly back to the kitchen.

A second later, his brother burst through the door, "Luukas! What's wrong? What can I do?"

He smiled as the smirk fell from her face. "The witch would like a large, greasy pizza. Thin crust, with mushrooms, and an ice tea."

Nik put his hands on his narrow hips, eyeing his brother with confusion. "You know you can just pick up the phone and order it from that place down the street, right? They deliver."

"I destroyed the phones."

Nikulas lifted an eyebrow. "You destroyed the phones? Why?"

"Because he doesn't want me calling Emma," the witch informed him.

"Because I don't want her calling anyone," Luukas clarified.

Nik scratched his head. "Uh, ok. I'll order the pizza." He looked questioningly at Keira, and she gave him a reassuring smile.

"Don't forget the mushrooms, please."

He nodded, and with a strange look thrown his brother's way, left to go order the food.

Luukas watched her toying with a pen that had been lying on the counter. She looked up, her eyes dancing with mischief.

"Nikulas is kind of hot."

He clenched his jaw, refusing to rise to her bait.

"He's really nice too."

Luukas lifted an eyebrow.

"And he does that same exact thing with his eyebrow."

Rolling his eyes, he got some water out of the fridge.

"So," she put her elbows on the counter and rested her chin in her hands. "What do you want to talk about?"

"Why do we need to talk about anything?"

"Well, what else are we going to do? Stare at each other all night? You don't seem like the 'Charades' type."

"No."

"Tell me about your life growing up in Estonia."

She smiled encouragingly at him, and his breath caught at the sight. He couldn't remember ever seeing her smile like that, so relaxed. Of course, there hadn't been much reason to do so in the time they'd known each other.

He cleared his throat. "What would you like to know?"

"What was your family like? Where in Estonia did you grow up? What was it like there back then? Is Nikulas your only sibling?"

He frowned at her barrage of questions.

"My parents were peasants. We had a farm in Estonia. It was cold. Except in the summer, when it was warmer, but the sun never set. Or at least it seemed like it didn't. And yes, Nik is my only sibling. We had a sister, but she died as a child."

"I'm sorry." Her eyes softened, and he frowned. He didn't need her pity.

He shrugged. "It was long ago. I don't really remember her."

"How old were you when you were turned?"

"I was thirty years of age."

"How did it happen?"

He heaved a sigh, but she just raised her eyebrows at him expectantly.

Setting his water bottle on the counter, he leaned on his elbows across from her, linking his fingers together. "I went out to check on my wife before getting ready for bed, to see why she was taking so long checking the cattle, and I found her in the arms of a vampire. He was feeding from her. I...froze, unable to process what I was seeing, until he dropped her dead body to the cold ground."

"You were married?" she asked softly.

"Yes."

"Did you have any children?"

"No. Not yet."

"Then what happened?" Her hazel eyes were filled with horror for him.

"I attacked him, planning to either kill him or be killed. I thought I had a chance, even though I had no weapon. I'd never seen a creature such as that before, and he was smaller than I, and would be weaker, or so I believed. He played with me for a bit, like a cat with a mouse, until I'd worn myself out. Finally, as I stood weaving before him, bleeding from the many wounds he'd inflicted, I gave up and demanded that he kill me. I didn't want to live without her."

She sat back in her stool, and regarded him seriously. "You loved her that much." It wasn't a question.

He nodded. "Yes."

"Do you still miss her?"

He straightened up and shrugged. "I don't really remember the feelings I had for her anymore. And my life is different now. She wouldn't fit into it anymore."

She urged him to continue. "You still haven't told me how you became a vampire."

Luukas looked down at his hands gripping the edge of the counter. "The vampire that killed her…I guess he was impressed by my tenacity. He laughed at my demand, and had me on the ground, drinking from me, before I could protest. Next thing I knew, I woke up in his home. And I was…different. The hunger was indescribable, and all consuming. I panicked, believing myself to be a monster, and tried to run off. But he stopped me, calmed me down. We went out and fed together, and he taught me everything he knew. We were together for a long time. He was lonely and was glad for the companionship."

"Where is he now?"

"He's dead."

She sat up straight, a hand over her mouth. "Oh no! What happened?"

He looked her right in the eyes. "I killed him."

Her eyes widened, and when she finally spoke, her voice was disbelieving. "You killed your Master?"

He nodded once.

"Holy shit. I didn't even know that was possible. I was always taught that you guys had some type of weird bond with the one who created you."

"We do."

"Then how, why did you...?"

"He was an ass. He was reckless, irresponsible, and uncaring. He put us in danger needlessly, playing games with the humans. We always had to move around so the lynch mobs wouldn't find us; we could never stay in one home for any amount of time. He killed without remorse when he fed. I grew tired of it. And, I needed revenge for the killing of my wife."

"So you'd planned to kill him all along."

"Yes."

"Are you still planning on killing me?"

His expression became strained, and he clenched his jaw, but his eyes were direct and his voice didn't falter. "Yes."

She took a deep breath and exhaled slowly. She didn't look surprised, or even afraid. She looked resigned. She gave him a sad smile.

A knock at the door broke the tension, and Nik walked in with a large pizza box in one hand and a large to-go cup in the other. "One X-tra large, greasy pizza with mushrooms, and a large iced tea." He set it on the counter near Keira, and went to grab her some paper towels.

"Thank you, brother," Luukas told him sincerely.

"Sure. No problem." He smiled at the witch. "If you make me a list, I'll go down to that 24-hr market in a little bit and pick up some more stuff for you."

She nodded her agreement, her mouth full of pizza, and gave him a thumb's up.

Luukas watched as she closed her eyes, a blissful expression on her face as she chewed. A small smile played around the corners of his mouth at her obvious enjoyment. He found he...liked...seeing her happy.

Clearing his throat, Nikulas asked, "So, how're things going here? You're looking better."

Was he? He wouldn't know. He refused to look at himself in the mirror. Actually, he was considering smashing them all. "I'm fine."

Nik looked like he was about to say more, but then closed his mouth and gave him a nod. "Good. Ok. Well, if you don't need anything else, I'm going to head back downstairs. I got a hold of our security guys here and they're bringing me the video footage from the garage. See if we can see any of our missing Hunters leaving the building. I don't know that it will give us any clues, but it won't hurt to look."

Luukas nodded in agreement. "Let me know if you find anything."

He assured him that he would. Then, with a smile and a wave at Keira, he was gone.

It seemed her line of questioning had been deterred by the arrival of the pizza, so Luukas left her to eat, wandering over to the windows. He loved looking out at the lights of the city. *His* city. Once.

He rubbed the back of his neck as he remembered that he'd meant to ask Nikulas about his vampires, and what, if anything, they knew about him being gone. He would have to remember to do that.

Shoving his hands in his pockets, he again fought down the ever-present feeling of panic that'd been welling up within him since coming home.

Would they notice that he was different? He had to be different. Although he was feeling slightly more...sane, he was having a hard time recalling the vampire he used to be before he was taken.

He only knew what he was now, and that he was a far cry from what he used to be.

21

KEIRA

Keira had never tasted anything better in her life than this greasy, cheesy pizza. Her eyes practically rolled back in her head as she tore off another huge bite, burning the top of her mouth, but she didn't care. She didn't even care if she couldn't keep it down. It was the first real junk food she'd had in years.

She kept an eye on Luukas as she ate, concern creasing her brow. He looked so lost, standing at the windows as he was. He nearly always looked that way, except when he was interacting with her.

And that had been some serious "interacting" that had gone on just a bit ago. No wonder she was so hungry.

Most girls would probably be all kinds of freaking out right about now. Finding out that a traumatized vampire wanted to either kill you or keep you "to have and to feed from" forever could do that to a girl. But Keira knew what the deal was. A vampire claiming his mate was not something to be taken lightly. And she could try fighting it, or she could accept the fact that she belonged with Luukas, and enjoy the hot vampire sex.

It wasn't like she didn't know him. They'd spent the last seven years going through hell and back together. Hell that she was largely responsible for. If he could get over the urge to kill her, she might even get the chance to make it up to him.

Besides, would she ever meet another male that she was this attracted to? From the moment he'd stepped from his vehicle that early summer night, she'd been drawn to him, and she still was, more so now than ever.

Unable to squeeze any more food into her belly, she regretfully closed the box and put it in the fridge for later. Her vampire was still deep in thought by the window, so she went in and brushed her teeth again. Twice.

Returning to the main room, she found he hadn't moved.

"What're you thinking about?"

He glanced at her over his shoulder, his vacant eyes running over her face and body, and then went back to contemplating the city lights.

Well, obviously he wasn't going to be very talkative tonight, so she wandered over to the office. She thought she remembered seeing some books lined up on one of the shelves. Grabbing one without even looking at the title, she took it over to the couch and curled up to read. Flipping it over, she saw the title, "The Complete Tales and Poems of Edgar Allen Poe." Good choice.

She read throughout the night, one eye on Poe and one on Luukas, taking occasional breaks to refill her teacup and make the grocery list.

She didn't know how he could stay so perfectly still for such a long time. It unnerved her. But every time she tried to engage him in a conversation, he would just give her that vacant look, if he bothered to acknowledge her at all.

Until finally, as the first rays of the dawn were peeking over the horizon, he left the window and without a word, set her book aside, lifted her off the couch, and carried her into his room with him. Once there, he placed her gently on the bed and crawled in beside her. Pulling her towards him, he tucked her against the front of him and wrapped himself protectively around her.

She didn't complain, knowing it would get her nowhere, but snuggled down into the soft bed, and drifted off to ravens knocking on chamber doors.

Keira groaned. It was so cold. She should get up and move around, but she was so tired. She just wanted to sleep. It was always so cold down here in the bowels of Leeha's mountain.

"Keira!"

Her teeth rattled as someone shook her, hard.

"Keira! Wake up!"

Luukas? He was free from the chains? Oh, thank the gods! But how did he get free?

"Fuck! What do I do? What do I do?"

His voice came to her from everywhere at once. She wished he would hold still. It was making her head pound.

She tried to ask him to get a blanket for her, but nothing came out but another pathetic sounding moan. What was wrong with her? Why was she so tired?

It was that idiot guard. He'd taken too much blood.

She heard a door open, then another, and then heard Luukas screaming for Nikulas again. She didn't want another pizza; she still had some leftover in the fridge. She needed to tell him.

And why was he calling Nikulas? Had Leeha captured him too?

"Luuk..." she rasped.

Her throat hurt. No wonder she couldn't talk. She must be getting a sore throat. Not surprising considering the quality of the air down here.

She tried again, "Luukas."

"Shhhh. Don't talk. Nik is on his way, he'll know what to do."

The door burst open and she heard the heavy tread of boots coming across the floor.

"Oh, shit. What happened?"

"I don't know!" Luukas' voice was strained. "I woke up and she was like this. I don't know what's wrong with her. She wouldn't wake up. I don't know what to do."

She felt a cool hand on her forehead, and heard a low growl as it rested there.

"Don't growl at me, dude. She has a fever."

"From what?" Luukas gritted out.

"From this." The cool hand on her forehead gently turned her head to the side. "This bite is infected. Look at it."

She winced as someone gently probed at the wound on her neck. Stupid thing, why wouldn't it heal?

Damn vampire.

"What do I do?" Luukas asked.

Why were they talking about her like she wasn't even there? She struggled to open her eyes to tell them she was awake, only to find two handsome faces peering down at her anxiously.

"Keira?" Nikulas leaned closer. "Can you hear me?"

What kind of question was that? Of course she could hear him. She wasn't deaf, just tired.

"I'm cold," she managed to say.

Luukas immediately flew from the room, returning with an armful of blankets that he then proceeded to pile on top of her.

Nikulas glanced sideways at him. "Luuk, we need to get this fever down, man. She's burning up. I don't know that more blankets are a good idea."

"She's cold," he stated in a tone that brooked no argument.

"I know, but we need to get the fever down. Hey, come here a second." Grabbing his brother's arm, he dragged him over to the doorway, and asked in a low voice, "You've fed from her, right?"

Luukas gave him a sharp nod.

"You haven't offered your blood to her? Completed the bond?"

The bond? Keira frowned as she huddled under her mound of blankets, shivering as she watched them from under heavy eyelids.

Luukas tore his eyes from her to look askance at his brother. "The bond. The mating bond? That isn't real."

Nikulas chewed the inside of his cheek, heaving a sigh. "Yeah, I didn't think so." Clapping his brother on the shoulder to get his attention again, he looked him directly in the eyes. "It *is* real, man. And you need to complete it, or I don't know if she's gonna make it, and then neither will you."

Luukas straightened to his full height. "No."

"No?" The shocked expression on Nikulas' face was almost funny. Surely he'd faced his brother's stubbornness before in all of their years together?

"NO."

"But," Nikulas glanced sideways at her, lowering his voice. "That bite is really infected. I could try to get her some antibiotics, but I don't know that they'll help much. She's undernourished, and with you feeding from her, I don't know that she'll pull through without your blood."

Luukas said nothing.

"Luukas!" Nikulas shouted, all caution that she would hear him aside. "She might *die*, man. Do you get that?"

Luukas turned cold, black eyes to where she lay on the bed. "Then let her die." He left the room then, leaving Nikulas staring after him, dumbfounded.

Shaking his head with disbelief, he came back over to the bed, and adjusted the blankets over her. "I don't get him. One minute he's freaking out because you're cold, and the next he's sentencing you to death."

"Not his fault," she told him, her voice raw. "He wants to kill me, but I'm too irresistible."

Nik chuckled. "I'm going to go get you some antibiotics. I'll be right back. Hang in there, ok?"

She gave him a weak nod and attempted to smile.

Luukas didn't return after Nikulas left. Although she'd hoped their time together last night would've helped matters, it seemed he hadn't overcome the urge to have her dead. And, actually, going this way would be ideal for his revenge plan. She would be dead and he wouldn't have the guilty conscious of being responsible for it.

Although, how much guilt would a vampire who'd killed his own Master actually have?

This really wouldn't be such a bad way to go, she mused again. Definitely better than Luukas snapping her neck and draining her dry. Well, the draining wouldn't be so bad, she kind of liked that part, but the neck snapping wouldn't be pleasant at all.

She would really appreciate a drink before she went though. And she needed to talk to Nikulas about Emma, ask him to look out for her. She had no one else.

Her last thought before she drifted off again was of her sister, running through the field in her short, billowy, summer skirt, laughing as Keira chased her.

22

DANTE

"Would you drive faster? We don't know how long he's going to stay out. And this is one mother fucker I do NOT want to tangle with."

"Relax, he's chained. Even if he wakes up, he can't do anything. Besides, the sun is coming up. He'll be dead till sunset."

Dante kept his eyes closed and his breathing steady, taking stock of his body for injuries while he listened to the conversation going on in front of him. Other than the awkwardness of being chained with his arms behind him and his knees bent so his heels were touching his ass, he appeared to be uninjured. Good.

He remained prone, listening, waiting for the right moment to let them know that he was awake, keeping the element of surprise on his side.

And it was definitely "them", plural, he was dealing with. He remembered a driver and two male passengers. They had jumped out of a black SUV to "check on him" after the driver had barely missed sideswiping him, right in the parking garage of the apartments he lived under.

One had attempted to sneak up on him, and when he'd confronted him, he'd made the mistake of turning his back on the other one, who had jabbed a needle in his neck. Whatever the fuck was in there had knocked him out cold.

"Are you sure about that?" The third one confirmed his presence. Three males. Not that it mattered. Dante had no issue with killing a female.

"Both of you shut up. We're almost to the plane."

Dante quietly tested the chains. They were silver. He could tell by the drain on his muscles, which meant these fuckers knew what he was.

However, they hadn't done enough homework on the vampire they were dealing with if they believed silver chains would be enough to restrain *him*. Or sunlight, for that matter. As disciplined as he was, he could stay awake all day if necessary.

Slitting his eyes open just enough to be able to see, Dante confirmed that no one else had joined the group while he'd been napping. He saw only the driver, an older man with a bald head, and two more sitting behind him, both of them younger and inexperienced looking. Dante himself was trussed up on the floor of the vehicle just behind the two passengers where the third row of seats should have been.

As inconspicuously as he could, he took a deep breath, scenting them.

Humans? Whoever had ordered this had sent *humans* to capture a vampire?

A sinister smile spread across his face.

With a quick, hard yank, he broke the chain attached to his cuffed wrists.

"Fuck! Fuck! He's awake!"

"He broke his chains! Stop the fucking car!"

The vehicle swerved as the driver peered over his shoulder to see what they were panicking about. Dante took the temporary distraction to reach down and break the chain between his cuffed ankles while the humans braced themselves for a crash that never came.

Moving faster than any of them could track, he rose up to one knee, and broke the first one's neck. Wrenching it to the side, he sank his fangs into the still-pulsing artery, sucking down great mouthfuls of blood. Throwing the body aside, his eyes shot over to the other male, giving him a bloody grin when he screamed.

Suddenly, a ray of morning sun hit him directly on the face, as the driver opened the wide sunroof before he had the chance to snap the other's neck.

Hissing in pain, Dante retreated quickly to the shadows at the back of the vehicle. He kept his eyes trained on his prey as he crouched there, blood dripping from his mouth, his smoking skin already healing.

Like a cornered animal, he waited.

"Shut up!" The driver screamed at his hysterical companion. He glanced back at the dead one. "Fuck. Fuck!"

The passenger finally got it under control and took off his seat belt and slid off the seat, placing his back against the middle console. Wide eyes zeroed in on Dante's exposed fangs and stayed there. "What the hell do we do now?" he asked the driver in a high voice.

"I dunno. Let me fuckin' think a minute. We're ok as long as the sunroof is open. He can't get past it without becoming a shish kabob."

"You also said the chains would fucking hold him!"

"I was told that they would," the driver spat.

"But how are we going to get him into the plane? He'll kill us as soon as we're out of the sun."

"I don't know! I said let me think!"

They drove on in silence, the human in the back never taking his eyes from Dante.

He distantly wondered why? Did he prefer to see death coming for him? If he were the human, he would rather not know. He'd rather die instantly and unaware like his friend had.

Fifteen minutes later, they pulled up in front of a large airplane hanger in the middle of nowhere, but didn't drive in.

By this time, the passenger watching him was nothing but a statue of silent fear. Dante could smell it oozing from his pores.

"Stay here," the driver told him. "I'll be right back."

"Are you fucking crazy? You can't leave me here with him!"

"You'll be fine as long as you stay where you are. I've got guns in my car, brought 'em along just in case. I won't be long."

The driver got out, slamming the door behind him.

Dante cocked his head as the passenger slid farther away from his dead friend and closer to the door, putting his hand on the handle.

Dante leaned forward, placing his hands on the floor. "You don't really think you could escape before I got to you, do you?"

The human's eyes bulged from their sockets as the stench of urine filled the small space. Dante sneered, inhaling the sour smell of the human's terror.

Just then, the driver returned and yanked the door open, calling an end to his fun with the passenger.

"Jesus Christ! Did you piss yourself? Really? Get the fuck out of the car!" He grabbed the passenger by the back of the shirt and yanked him out into the sunshine, handing him something.

"Take this, and get into the drivers seat. We'll drive in with him and I'll get him onto the plane."

Walking around to the rear of the vehicle, he opened the back door while the other one got into the driver's side. Dante shrunk back away from the sun, now caught in the middle between its rays.

"See this, asshole?" The first driver pointed a semi-automatic pistol directly at Dante, and pulled back the hammer. "I'd behave if I were you." Stepping up onto the hitch with the door open, he hung onto the roof with the other hand and told the driver to go.

Dante barked out a laugh as the vehicle pulled slowly forward. "A gun won't stop me, *asshole*."

"This one will. It's made with special bullets. Exploding bullets. It'll blow a hole in you so big it'll cut you clean in half."

Narrowing his eyes at him, Dante studied his features, looking for any telltale signs that he was lying.

He saw none.

"My buddy up front there has another one of these, so even if you managed to get to me, he'd shoot you before you could get us both. Hell, he may shoot you anyway, out of sheer fright. So, I wouldn't make any sudden moves if I were you. We'll be rid of each other soon enough."

The SUV stopped just inside the hanger, and Dante weighed his chances of overpowering the two of them in spite of the driver's warning before either had the chance to fire at him. He wouldn't even hesitate if it weren't for the fact that he could still feel the effects of the silver. It would slow him down. Not much, but enough to make him not want to risk it.

The older human stepped down from the hitch as the nervous one came around to back him up. They stepped back, giving him plenty of room to get out, guns raised at the ready.

Dante crept forward on his hands and feet, and lowered himself slowly out of the vehicle, combat boots landing with a loud thud on the concrete.

Indicating the plane with the barrel of his gun, the driver indicated for him to lead the way.

He stayed where he was just long enough to make them nervous, wiping his hands on his jeans, and then he smirked and headed towards the plane as they followed behind him.

The pilot waited by the bottom of the steps as they approached, and he was also packing.

Dante ignored the three gun barrels aimed at him and looked up, intrigued. This was no ordinary plane. This was a V-22 Osprey, a military aircraft that could fly long distances like a jet, yet could take off, hover, and land like a helicopter. How the hell had three homeless looking humans gotten a hold of one of these?

"Get in, asshole."

Cold metal jabbed him in the back until he started up the stairs.

Once inside, Dante halted, awaiting further instructions. The interior was lined with troop seats.

Another jab in the back with the barrel of a gun. "Back of the plane, find a seat."

Though it irked him to play along, Dante did as he was told. They may or may not be bluffing about the guns, but he wasn't going to take the chance. He had no desire to die today.

He found a seat and sat down, while the humans strapped themselves in towards the front.

Guns trained on him, they taxied out of the hanger and took flight.

23

NIKULAS

Nikulas rushed back to the apartments as fast as he could go, without raising suspicion from the hoard of humans on the crowded Seattle streets.

As he dodged tech nerds and tourists, he shook his head, again, at his brother's words. He couldn't believe that Luukas would really let that female die, not on purpose, not like this. The urge for revenge must be overwhelming for him, but if the witch was truly "his" like he kept shouting to everyone, it wasn't possible for him to let her die. Not if Luukas felt for her anything near what he felt for Emma.

The constant ache in his chest expanded into a gaping, jagged hole at the thought of his female's lovely face. His head pounded, his throat ached, and his gums burned from the memory of her sweet blood. Her large, hazel eyes followed him everywhere he went. He couldn't escape the memory of her, and he didn't want to.

More and more every day, he felt the physical effects of being without her, and he just couldn't be sure how, when, and where it would get worse. It seemed to be coming in spurts. He'd feel a bit better right after he choked down some bagged blood, but it only lasted a few hours, and then his energy level would fall and his body would begin to ache. He imagined it was similar to what human's felt when they had the modern flu. He had to feed a lot more now just to try to stay somewhat level, and to enable him to get through a night while resembling any type of normalcy. When dawn came, he fell into his bed like the corpse he soon would be.

And it had only been a few days since she'd left.

Pushing the thought of her eyes, so like Keira's, out of his head, he concentrated on the task at hand. He couldn't let the witch die, if not for Luukas' sake, then for Emma's. He'd do whatever he had to do to keep that from happening.

Ducking through the front entry of their apartment building, he hit the stairs, beating the elevator up to the top floor, even in his weakened state. With a quick rap on the front door, he let himself into Luuk's apartment.

"Luuk? I'm back. I brought the antibiotics, and some more food."

The apartment was quiet. Setting the food on the counter, he glanced around, but didn't see his brother anywhere, so he headed for his bedroom.

He knocked again, softer this time, and cracked the door open. Still no Luukas. Walking over to the bed, he saw that Keira had fallen back to sleep.

He shook her gently by the shoulder. "Keira? Keira? I need you to wake up now. I've got the antibiotics for you."

Her eyelids fluttered, and he set down the pharmacy bag on the nightstand while he went into the bathroom to get a glass of water. Dumping a couple of pills into his hand, he slid an arm behind her to help her sit up a bit. Her skin felt way too hot, even through her clothing, and he frowned.

"Here you go. Open your mouth. That's it." Lifting the glass to her mouth, he pushed the pills between her lips and helped her to take a drink, then gently lowered her back down to the bed.

"I'll be back before dawn to make sure you take another dose," he promised.

"Thank you, Nikulas," she murmured. Burrowing into the blankets, she was asleep again before he managed to get the top back on the pill bottle. He left it, and the glass of water, on the table beside her.

Closing the door quietly behind him, he set out to find his brother. He found him in the spare bedroom, sitting on the edge of the bed with his head in his hands.

Nikulas cleared his throat. "I gave her some antibiotics. She'll need to take some more before you crash at dawn. I can come back, so you don't forget."

Luukas lifted his head and stared at him coldly with those foreign, dark eyes. "You shouldn't have bothered. She deserves whatever happens to her."

"How can you say that, man? She's not a bad person..."

"Do you know what she did to me in there, little brother?" Luukas interrupted him. "Do you *know* what she put me through?"

"She had no choice, Luuk, you know that."

"No choice?" Luukas scoffed with disgust. "She had a fucking choice. She chose to help Leeha with her sick plan to, I don't know, break me down or whatever the hell it was she was trying to accomplish. She *chose* to help her by taking my power. She *chose* to help her by keeping me weak. She *chose* to hold me immobile with her magic while they beat me, whipped me, salted my wounds...she *chose* to help them while they fucking burned me alive."

Nikulas' couldn't have heard that correctly. "Burned you?" he breathed. "That's not possible."

His brother stood up, and began to pace back and forth. "Oh, it's completely possible when you have a witch chanting a spell during the process. A spell that allows you to feel every single inch of your skin and muscle sizzling away in the flames, allows you to feel your own blood boiling, while not allowing any actual harm to come to you at all."

Nik's mouth fell open, and he quickly closed it again.

What the hell was he supposed to say to that?

Crossing his arms over his chest determinedly, he stepped in front of his brother, halting his incessant pacing. "She also gave your power back to you, and correct me if I'm wrong, but she hasn't lifted one finger to harm you since you both left that place. She's stayed here with you..."

"Because I won't let her leave."

"Of her own choice. She's an extremely powerful witch. You know as well as I that she can leave here whenever the hell she wants."

He pushed his hair back off of his face. "She hated doing that to you, Luukas."

"And you would know this, *how*?"

"Because she told me, and I believe her. Leeha threatened to kill her sister if she didn't do as she was ordered. Her *sister*, Emma. The only family she has left. She had to choose. And she didn't even know you at the time. I would've done the same."

Luukas lifted his chin defiantly, a bit of that old cockiness showing, and remained stubbornly silent.

Nikulas sighed dramatically. "Well, if you hate her so much, maybe I'll just take her down to my place, and take care of her there."

Spinning on his heel, he only made it one step before he had a face full of angry vampire. The temperature dropped and the air stirred around them with Luukas' fury, rattling the lamps and lifting the bed quilt.

His brother bared his fangs at him, "The witch in MINE," he hissed. "You won't be taking her anywhere. *Brother*."

Nik leaned forward, his own fangs bared in challenge. "Then *help her*, you stubborn bastard. Give her your blood. It will heal her."

Luukas hissed at him again as they faced off, his rising anger pulsing in the air, whipping out at his brother.

Nikulas' muscles began to ache from holding himself against the invisible force of the Master vampire's wrath, but dammit, he refused to give in on this.

Suddenly, the pressure eased.

"No." Sheathing his fangs, Luukas backed off first. Drawing his anger back completely, he turned and left the room without another word.

Nikulas sucked in deep breaths of air, not quite sure how he'd gotten out of that one unscathed. If his brother had been back to his normal self, he never would've put up with such an act of disobedience, not even from his own brother.

Following him out into the other room, Nik refused to give up. "Just think about it, Luuk. If she *is* your mate, and you let her die, you won't be far behind her."

Before he left, he tossed out one last parting shot, "You'd have escaped Leeha's torment, made it back home alive, only to let her win anyway."

He thought he saw Luukas stiffen, but didn't hang around to be sure.

Exiting the stairwell on his own floor, he found he had visitors in the form of four very large, very exhausted werewolves, in human form, sprawled in the hallway outside of his door. They jumped to their feet as soon as they saw him.

"Nikulas!" Cedric, the leader of the pack, greeted him with his heavy Scottish brogue, his startling, blue-white eyes shining happily in his tan face. "We thought we'd stop by tae chat and see how things were goin' with Luukas."

Nik ushered them all inside, closing the door firmly behind them before answering. "Did you guys find anything after we left?"

"No, we dinna. I'm sorry, my friend. We searched th' entire place, every passageway we could find. It's like they disappeared with Aiden into thin air."

Lucian spoke up, his gravelly voice and cynical demeanor reminding him of Dante, but that's where the resemblance ended. Dante looked like a tatted-up biker who'd been through hell and back a few times, whereas Lucian looked more like he should be on the cover of a magazine with his dark auburn hair, high cheekbones, and stormy blue eyes.

"After we found each other again, we went as deep as th' tunnels would take us. All we found were some more cells, all empty, and all looking like they'd never been used. Seems she only had Marc," he nodded towards his friend, "the witch, and Luukas down there."

"I never heard anyone else there but th' three of us," Marc confirmed, his dark brown eyes somber.

Cedric picked up the conversation again. "We found Leeha's private quarters. All empty, yet all of the lass's things were still there. If they did take off, they didn't bother tae pack first, which is why I think they're still in that mountain somewhere. Leeha would never go anywhere without all of 'er fancy frocks."

"But you said you searched the entire place. How could she still be there? There's nowhere she could hide from those big noses of yours." Nik ducked to the side as Duncan, the self-proclaimed ladies man of the group, chucked a glass bowl at him from the table in the foyer. Catching it before it smashed into the front door, Nik scowled at him.

"Dude, I like that bowl. I put my keys in it."

Duncan grinned good-naturedly. "Ye'd best be watchin' yerself then, or ye'll be finding yerself a new bowl."

"You guys wanna go sit down?" Nik offered, placing the bowl carefully back on the table. "You're making me feel crowded in here."

He shooed them into the apartment, feeling like he could breathe again with the extra space. Nik wasn't exaggerating about them not fitting in his foyer. They were all at least 6'2", with Cedric topping them off at 6'7", and not one of them weighed less than 220 lbs. They made him feel downright scrawny in comparison. Especially considering that werewolves were the only other supernatural species who were any threat to a vampire. They were the only ones who could actually beat them in a fight. And if one of their pack was in danger, they were a force to reckoned with.

A force Nikulas hoped he'd never have to experience.

Luckily, they were on the same side, and had been for hundreds of years.

"So, Marc, what unforgivable offense did you commit to land yourself in the dregs of hell with my brother?"

"It wasna me, 'twas Lucian." He took a seat at the bar, the others hovering near him. "She just took me because I was the one who was in the wrong place at the wrong time. Besides, you know all of us wolves look alike," he smirked. "She didna even care that she had the wrong one. Just plucked me away, claiming she needed a new pet."

Four sets of eyes looked at Lucian expectantly. He looked back like "Whaa?"

"Lucian," Cedric ordered, "Tell Nikulas here what you did tae cause all of this. He deserves to know."

Lucian's lips lifted into something resembling a smile. It didn't quite make it. "I killed Thomas."

"Who's Thomas?"

"You dinna know who Thomas is?" Cedric questioned.

"Not our Thomas?" Nik retorted. "Thomas? Our friend who's been with this colony since the beginning? I thought he'd just gotten a wild hair and was off scaling a mountain or something. He does that sometimes."

"No. Thomas has been with the she-bitch all of this time." Duncan clarified.

Nik's mouth dropped open for the second time that day. "No fucking way."

"Aye, way. He was 'er right-hand." Cedric flopped down onto Nik's oversized armchair, causing it to groan in protest. "We were attempting tae have peace talks with 'er, ye know, make a deal like we have with ye. She's been encroaching on our territory up north, and when we confronted 'er about it, she laughed, and said she would keep 'er vamps wherever she liked. So I arranged for us tae meet in private. She refused tae show up 'erself, but said she would send Thomas. I agreed, and sent Lucian, as he was the only one available." Cedric shot said spokesman a look, and he lowered his head, refusing to meet his leader's eyes.

"I take it he didn't agree to the terms?" Nikulas guessed.

"No. He didna," Lucian confirmed. "And what's more, he refused tae negotiate at all. He'd only shown up tae pass on Leeha's message that she will do whatever the hell she pleases, and if we got in 'er way, she would wipe out our pack. So," he shrugged carelessly. "I wolfed out, and ripped his jugular from his throat."

Cedric shook his head, regarding his pack-mate as if he were an errant child.

Duncan knocked him upside the head. "And ye got our brother taken for yer impulsiveness."

"I can see where that would piss her off," Nik agreed.

Lucian lifted his chin defiantly. "We got him back."

"Lucky for ye," Marc growled.

"Alright, alright." Cedric glanced around. "Where's yer lassie, Nik? I'd like tae see th' wee kitten. S'long as she promises to no' make things move around on their own and such." He shivered at the thought.

Nik sat down on the couch near Cedric.

"She's not here."

"Well, where is she? I'd be careful letting that one out o' your sight. She tends tae get 'erself into trouble."

Nik shot him a dirty look. "Only when there are mischievous werewolves around."

Cedric leaned forward, one hand over his heart, his long, black ponytail falling over his shoulder as he declared earnestly, "I swear to ye, my brother, if I'd had any idea those things were out there, I never would have sent 'er off on 'er own like that tae be captured. I thought a few normal vamps would jump out, and then we'd know how many we needed tae kill tae get inside. We coulda' surprised 'em that way." His blue-white eyes stared directly into Nik's, his sincerity easy to see.

Nikulas smacked him on the knee. "I know, man. I'm not gonna say it's all right, because it's not. That was fucked up, what you did."

"Truly. We were just havin' a bit o' fun. We never thought any harm would come tae ye're lassie. I will make it up tae ya, I swear."

Leaning forward, Nik caught his eyes with his own. "I'm holding you to that."

Cedric reached out a hand, which Nikulas took and shook firmly.

"I could actually use some help now," Nik told him. "Finding our Hunters."

"Done. Ye dinna even need to ask."

Duncan waited until the deal was concluded before asking, "So, how is our Luukas? He seemed a bit…and I mean no offense, but…*off* when we saw him last."

Nikulas leaned back wearily, the constant worry he felt inside written all over his face. "I don't know. He has Keira up there…"

"Th' witch that helped tae torture him?" Cedric exclaimed.

The other three wolves recoiled from Nik's words, crossing themselves superstitiously.

"Yeah, the witch," Nik said in his best Wizard of Oz voice, wiggling his fingers at them.

"Dinna make fun, man," Lucian growled. "Witches are no' something to be taken lightly."

Laughing, Nik agreed. "No, you're right. Except this witch in particular is seriously ill in Luukas' bed at the moment. I don't think you have anything to worry about."

"Ill? How do you ken she's no' just faking it?" Cedric asked suspiciously.

"Because she's got an infected vampire bite and is running a fever so high, she could almost pass for one of you."

"Luukas did that to her?" Duncan asked in disbelief.

"No. Luukas would no' do that. It was probably one of the guards. Am I right?" Marc asked.

"That's what she said," Nikulas agreed.

"Aye, I thought I heard one complaining about 'the witch and her deals' as he brought us some food. 'N how he should've just kept the 'bagged shite' for himself."

"Bagged shit? Bagged blood?"

"Aye." Marc confirmed. "Leah fed the guards bagged blood when they were on duty."

"What did Keira need bagged blood for?" Nik's voice trailed off as he said more to himself than anyone else, "Unless she needed it to feed Luuk. Would she have risked herself on purpose like that?"

"What're ya whisperin' to yerself over there?" Cedric asked.

Nik just shook his head, saying dismissively, "Just wondering if she did it for Luukas."

"But, why would she 'ave done something so daft?" Duncan asked Marc.

"Because she is Luukas'," Nikulas answered. "His mate."

"Like you 'n Emma?"

"Yes."

"No shite," Cedric breathed.

"No shit."

The wolves crossed themselves again.

24

LUUKAS

Two nights had gone by since his brother had brought the pills for Keira. Whenever Nikulas came to check on her, Luukas stopped him at the front door. He told him that he'd had a change of heart, that he was making sure she took the drugs, and that she was getting better. His brother was skeptical, but given no other choice, he'd go back to his search for the Hunters.

In truth, he was doing no such thing, and she wasn't getting better. She was getting drastically worse with every hour.

The dark side of him, the one that craved her death, the one that craved vengeance, laughed gleefully as it watched the witch suffer. It rejoiced in every jagged, red line it saw creeping out from the wound in her neck, until there were so many they resembled a spider's web covering her upper torso. It clapped its hands with delight at her feverish mumblings. It got a hard-on as it watched her fumble weakly on the nightstand for the medication.

She'd knocked it off of the nightstand the first time she'd tried to get it. He'd left it on the floor.

He was going to have to finish her off soon. His brother was getting more and more suspicious. He'd argued with him and had tried to force his way in to see her the last time he was here.

Luukas had ripped the locks from the door after he'd left, so he couldn't sneak back and use his key. He'd barricaded it shut for good measure.

Rip her open! Suck her dry! Kill her! Burn her!

Luukas stood at the foot of the bed, watching her as she struggled to breathe. He smiled an evil smile as she thrashed under the covers, her eyes rolling back in her head. It appeased him somewhat to see her in such painful agony.

But it still wasn't enough, wasn't anywhere near enough. It wasn't anywhere close to the pain *he'd* gone through because of *her*.

The wound on her neck was a raging red, the spider web of infection bright against her pale skin. Puss oozed from the bite. He would need to get new sheets when this was done.

Can't hurt her!

Shut up!

Squeezing his eyes shut, he attempted to suppress the other part of him, the one that wanted to keep her as his own. Forever.

She does not deserve to be mine. She deserves to suffer.

His brother's words came back to him, *"If she is your mate as you say, and you let her die, you won't be far behind her."*

Yes, so the legend goes. But that's all it was, a legend. Besides, he wasn't insisting the witch was his to claim her as his mate, but only to keep her with him so as to make her pay for what she did to him. That's all.

You're lying to yourself. She is yours. You admitted as much the other evening.

Luukas slammed his palms to each side of his head and began to pace the floor as the two voices warred within him. Since she'd fallen ill, he'd been able to fight down that weakness for her, and let the darkness rule inside of him. But it was getting harder and harder the more sick she became.

She could *not* be his mate. It wasn't possible. Fate would not be so cruel.

Would it?

He stopped pacing and stared down at her in alarm. Her eyes were open for the first time in days, and she was looking back at him, watching him.

MINE.

No!

There was no blame in her large, hazel eyes. No disbelief that he would do this to her. No hatred towards him.

Just a calm understanding.

"Stop looking at me like that! You *deserve* this, witch, for all that you did to me."

A gentle smile lifted the corners of her mouth and her gaze softened upon him. Her hand lifted from the bed, reaching for his, "Luukas..."

Her smile faltered. Her hand drifted back down to the bed. Her eyes glazed over as the infection triumphed over her body.

One heartbeat.

Two heartbeats.

"Keira?"

She didn't answer him or open her eyes. Her breath rattled in her chest.

"Keira?" he whispered.

Can't hurt her!

Luukas sank down onto the edge of the bed next to her.

Her lips parted, moving slightly as her eyelids twitched and then, finally, opened. He noticed for the first time that there were flecks of gold in with the green and brown of her irises. How beautiful.

She was trying to tell him something. He leaned down to hear her better, although it was more habit than necessity with his vampire hearing.

"I'm s...sorry," she breathed. "Never wanted to...hurt...you. My sister...please forgive me."

Her small hand reached for him again, and this time, he took it within his much larger one. She gave him one last attempt at a smile, and then her beautiful eyes, so bright and alive just a few days ago, fluttered closed.

"Keira?"

He couldn't breathe, the sudden pain in his chest more intense than anything he'd gone through under Leeha's command. He squeezed her small hand.

"Keira!"

Grabbing her shoulders, he shook her hard. Her head rolled backward, loose on her neck.

"No! NO!" he roared. The very walls quaked with his distress. "Don't you leave me! Don't you dare leave me!"

He shook her again, and this time, he heard the slightest groan of protest come from her limp form.

"Keira? Hang on. I demand that you stay with me. Do you hear me, witch?"

Lifting his wrist to his mouth, he sank his fangs into his veins, and pressed the open wound to her mouth.

"Drink, Keira."

The blood dripped into her slack mouth, but she didn't make any effort to swallow it.

His heart pounding, he fought down the rising panic. Pressing his wrist harder to her mouth, he shook her again with his other hand.

She lay lifeless in his arms.

"Drink, dammit! Drink! Don't you fucking leave me! I won't forgive you, witch! Do you hear me? I won't ever forgive you if you leave me!"

His harsh words must've gotten through to her. Her dry lips moved just slightly, closing on the wound, and he felt her try to suck.

"That's a good girl," he told her. "Keep drinking."

She moaned with pleasure as his lifeblood ran down her throat. Her hands rose shakily to his arm, holding him to her mouth, and she began to suck harder. Another moan escaped her, and her eyes shot open to lock onto his as she drank.

Luukas had never felt anything as satisfying or as pleasurable as he did at the moment, watching this female drink from him. Tremors wracked his body with each pull she took. He had the sudden urge to fuck her while she took his blood, to possess her completely, but he held himself back. She was too sick, too weak.

Can't hurt her.

Sweat beaded on her forehead as her fever broke, her face becoming flushed and damp. He watched as the spider's web of infection faded on her neck, the wound drying up before his eyes, until it was nothing but a slight blemish on her perfect skin.

He let her drink until he felt lightheaded, wanting to be sure she'd had enough, until he could give her no more. Gently, he pried his wrist from her swiftly strengthening hands.

"That's enough, witch," he told her tenderly, "You'll drain me dry."

She moaned in protest, but let go of his arm, licking her lips.

"Holy shit!" she exclaimed, "That stuff is like a shot of adrenaline to the heart."

He smiled faintly at her accurate description.

Her face got serious. "Why did you do that?" she asked, watching him lick the wound to heal it.

Why indeed?

"I don't know," he answered honestly.

"Well, in any case, thank you, Luukas, for saving me."

He looked away, unable to meet the truth in her eyes. "Maybe I saved you only to make your life miserable for a little while longer."

She smirked at his words.

"So, is it done then?" she asked quietly.

His eyes shot back to hers. "Is what done?"

"The bond. You've had my blood. I've had yours. We've had sex. Is it done?"

"What do you know about a bond?" he asked her suspiciously.

Pushing herself into a sitting position, she reached for her water.

"Well?" he asked impatiently.

She gave him a look over the top of her glass, setting it back on the nightstand carefully before she answered him. "I was taught many things growing up, all in secret, of course. My parents taught me everything they knew about your kind. They wanted me to be prepared, and hoped that once I became part of the coven again, I'd have the knowledge to enter into a peaceful partnership with the vampires, like it used to be."

"That doesn't answer my question," he pressed.

She quirked an eyebrow at him. "Vampires can bond to humans for life. They will know they've met their mate after they drink from them. Their instincts will kick in, or something about the blood will let the vampire know, or whatever. That part isn't exactly clear to us. Once they drink from said mate, they can never be without their blood, or the vampire will die. The human mate is given the vampire's blood in return, therefore enabling them to live as long as their vampire. The vampire gets a lifelong feeding supply and lover. The human gets the benefits of stopping the aging process, never getting sick, and having the love and protection of a vampire. Does that about sum it up?"

Luukas stood up from the bed, wandering over to the windows to think. "And you were told that this is true? Not just some old fable passed down through the years for entertainment?"

"Yes. I assumed that all of your bellowing to everyone that 'the witch is mine' was your subtle way of stating that, by some strange quirk of fate, I was indeed 'yours'. Nikulas confirmed it when we were talking the other day."

He let her words roll around in his head. After a moment, he heard her getting out of bed. "I'm going to hop in the shower if that's ok."

It wasn't really a question, and he smirked. It seemed his headstrong witch was back to her normal self.

He heard dresser drawers opening and closing as she helped herself to some clean clothes and padded barefoot into the bathroom.

Luukas waited for the dark side to return. Waited for the need for revenge to return. Waited for the voice in his head to turn hateful and demanding. Waited for it to order him to go in there and kill the witch.

He waited.

And waited.

But the voice didn't return. It didn't even whisper to him.

Tentative relief gripped him. Was it gone then?

Relaxing a bit for the first time since he'd escaped Leeha's hell, Luukas purposely flexed his power, letting it out and then snapping it back tightly to him. He'd been holding it in check as best he could since coming home, afraid he couldn't control it, afraid he would hurt someone he loved when the darkness overtook his mind. Someone like Nikulas.

Or Keira.

Did he love her? No. That wasn't possible. He felt a bond with her, sure. They'd spent years together under Leeha's sick control, with no one for company but each other, when she wasn't using her witchcraft on him. And she had helped him towards the end, as best she could.

But this entire "mating" thing, that couldn't possibly be true. He'd never heard of it actually happening in all of his more than six hundreds years of vampire life. Never. It was nothing but an old wives' tale.

Then how do you explain your feelings for this witch? This urge to keep her away from other males, and to protect her, even from yourself! How do you explain what just happened?

Keira didn't seem to have any doubts. Actually, she seemed completely fine with the idea. Didn't it scare her? Worry her in the least? Didn't she care that she could potentially be tied forever to a vampire that hated her? One that wasn't capable of treating her as he should? Couldn't protect her as he should? One who was now less than a male?

Striding over to the bathroom, he disregarded the locked door, easily breaking the latch and barging inside. The witch screeched and spun around in the shower, poking her head out from behind the curtain.

"Luukas! What are you doing? The door is locked for a *reason!*"

"Are you not concerned at all that you may be my mate? Me? The male you tortured for years? The male you can barely stand to look at?"

"Can't stand to look at? What are you talking about?"

Throwing his shoulders back, he lifted his chin, fighting the shame that filled him whenever he thought of his reflection, of the empty shell of a male that he'd become, of his stranger's eyes.

"I'm talking about the first day we came home," he forced out. "You averted your eyes from me when we were showering. Do I disgust you so much?"

"Luukas, how could you think that you disgust me? I averted my eyes because you were naked...beautifully naked, but naked nonetheless. It just shocked me, that's all. I've had sex with you since then for gods' sake. Not counting that time in the mountain when we still had clothes on. Why would I do that with someone I wasn't attracted to?"

"To save yourself?" he threw out there. "Don't lie to me, witch. I know what you see when you look at me."

He was furious, and he wasn't sure why, exactly. What did he care if he disgusted the witch? He'd have her anyway. He was a Master vampire. She would have no say over staying with him. After all, she hadn't given *him* a choice when she'd stripped him of his power and handed him over to Leeha to abuse.

He realized that she hadn't denied it again. Clenching his jaw, he raised his eyes to hers, expecting to see pity, disgust, or laughter. But what he found there surprised him. He did not see any of the things he'd expected. He saw anger, and... hunger. Hunger for him.

Yanking back the shower curtain, Keira stepped out. She didn't bother to cover herself or to turn off the water.

Water droplets ran from her wet hair, over her full breasts, down her soft belly and her smooth legs. She was still a bit thinner than he would like, but still, she was lovely. Perfect.

His cock hardened immediately at the sight of her, straining towards her against the rough fabric of his jeans. He tried to tell himself that he would react this way at the sight of any lovely, naked female. But he knew he was lying to himself. He'd never felt anything for another female that was remotely similar to what he felt for this witch.

She marched over to him, arms at her sides, completely unashamed of her nudity. Upon reaching him, she didn't hesitate, sliding her hands under his T-shirt and pulling it up over his head and down his arms, throwing it to the floor.

Running her hands up his hard stomach to his muscular chest and shoulders, she gripped his biceps and leaned forward to press a soft kiss right where his heart was. She then proceeded to press her lips to every mark and scar she could reach, peeking up at him occasionally to judge his reaction. She took her time along the raised burn scar across his abdomen. Trailing a hand around his waist, she worked her way around to the back of him. He heard her sharp intake of breath at the same time he felt her small hand on his skin, and he stiffened. His back was horrific, he knew.

"Luukas, you've healed. The lash marks are gone! Look!" Leaning over the counter, she wiped the condensation off of the mirror, grabbed him around the waist and turned him around so his back was to the mirror. "Look!"

"I'd rather look at you," he told her, his voice heavy with desire from her attentions. Scooping up her long, wet hair, he pulled it into a ponytail at the back of her neck and used it to tug her head back until she was forced to look up at him. "Take off my pants, witch. I want to shower with you."

He loosened his grip on her hair as her hands went eagerly to the waistband of his jeans. Her breasts rose and fell with her rapid breaths, and he watched them quiver as she undid his jeans, pushing them down his strong legs. He wasn't wearing anything else. He let go of her hair so she could kneel down to help him pull his feet out.

Throwing his jeans into the corner, she stayed on her knees, kissing his thighs, his stomach, teasing him like the witch she was. Holding her hair back in one hand, he held himself in the other and guided his head to her warm mouth. She flicked her tongue over him as her hands squeezed his hips, keeping him from thrusting into her mouth as he wanted. Although he could easily overpower her, he allowed her to play her game, needing her to take his mind from everything else but what she was doing to him.

She continued to taste him with small flicks of her tongue all around his head, then opening her mouth and scraping her teeth along the smooth skin.

"Ah!" Luukas threw his head back as she played with him, letting her have her way until he couldn't wait any longer to feel her around him.

"Take me in your mouth," he ordered harshly. "All the way."

Her eyes watched his face as she did so, taking him as deep as she could go before sliding him out and back in again. She smiled wickedly around his girth when her own moan of pleasure caused him to kick inside her mouth.

Both of his hands were on her head now, gently holding her hair away from face so he could watch her, so he could see her eyes when she looked up at him, and watch them darken with desire. Releasing his hip with one hand, she touched herself, pinching her own nipples as she sucked him, and then running her hand down to her clit, and back up to her breast.

Luukas' mouth went slack as he watched his little witch pleasure herself while she pleasured him. His cock began to throb. He was dangerously close to coming.

"No. Not yet. I want to be inside of you when I come." Pulling her gently away from him, he lifted her to her feet and higher, hugging her against him as he took her mouth in his.

Fuck. The feel of her soft skin against his...he'd never felt anything so good.

He continued to kiss her as he climbed into the shower with her in his arms. Sitting down under the warm spray, he sat her on his lap, her legs straddling him.

Breaking off the kiss, he studied her intently, "Are you certain you're feeling up to this, Keira? You were just so ill..."

She smiled brightly, her hands running over his muscular chest and broad shoulders greedily. "I feel more than up for this. I had to stop myself from jumping you the moment you took your wrist from me. I want you, Luukas, so much. That hasn't changed after all that's happened. If anything, I admire you more. Want you more."

How could that be? She saw him restrained and starved, screaming from the pain. "But I was weak…"

She took his face in her hands, forcing him to see the honesty in her eyes. "No! You were strong! So strong! I would never have been able to survive what you did. I am in awe of you, Luukas. You never broke. Not once. I was so proud of you, even as I hated myself for what she made me do to you."

She kissed him then. Kissed him until he forgot everything but her. Her lips, her soft skin, her scent. She surrounded him completely, claiming him as her own.

Grabbing her luscious hips, he lifted her, impaling her with one strong thrust. She cried out, and he worried that he'd hurt her. She was so tight and small. But then she used her legs to raise herself up and come down fast on him again. And again.

He allowed her to set the pace; his hoarse cries joining hers as she rode him, slowly at first, and then quickly gaining speed. His fangs ached to pierce her flesh, to taste her again. It'd only been days since he'd last had her, but it felt like so much longer.

He crushed her to him and buried his face in her neck, fighting back his orgasm, wanting to wait for her. "You smell so good. I want to taste you. Can I taste you, witch?"

Her answer was to tilt her head away, giving him better access to her throat. He growled deep as he reared back and struck her hard, so starved for her he found himself incapable of being gentle.

She cried out again and rocked her hips harder as he began to pull at her vein.

"Luukas! Ah, gods!"

Holy fuck. The taste of her sweet blood! It was different now that the infection was gone. It was impossibly better. He growled again as it spread throughout his body, strengthening every part of him, igniting every nerve ending until he felt every inch of her sliding against him.

MINE.

It was the only thought he had as he rocked her up and down, faster and faster, her full breasts bouncing against his chest, her hands clutching his hair, holding him to her throat.

"Luukas! I'm coming! Ah! I'm coming!"

As her body began to convulse in his arms, he felt her bite his shoulder hard, drawing blood.

Withdrawing his fangs from her neck, he roared as he released inside of her, his cock pulsing forcefully on and on as she drank from her bite.

He held her tight under the warm water as she lapped at his healing wound like a cat, and their breathing returned to normal, his little witch settling down to lay boneless on top of him.

With his face hidden in her neck, he breathed in her delicious scent, and attempted to ignore the hateful voice that had returned after all.

25

KEIRA

Keira awoke with a smile on her face. Yawning, she attempted to roll over so she could snuggle into the wall of hard, warm vampire lying beside her.

Except she found that she couldn't move.

Blinking in the dwindling sunlight, she craned her head around. Her arms were stretched above her head, her wrists lashed securely to the headboard with some type of material resembling a heavy scarf, or...she glanced over at the window...a torn off piece of the curtain.

Seriously?

Bending her knees, she discovered that her ankles were also tied to the bed under the covers.

She stared at the ceiling as she chewed her bottom lip, and tried to decide how to handle this latest obstacle of life with her damaged vampire.

She wasn't very concerned about her predicament. After all, she could untie herself anytime she wanted with a few chanted words. However, she decided to wait it out. He'd be waking up soon, and she didn't want to cause him any further distress by not being here when he did, when he was so obviously worried about that exact thing happening.

Something in his injured mind had led him to tie her up after she'd fallen asleep this morning. Was he afraid that she would leave? Did he just want to make sure she stayed by him as he slept? Was he afraid to be alone?

Her heart ached at the thought.

Luukas began to stir beside her, and she smiled at him when his eyes shot open.

He eyed her warily, no doubt waiting for her reaction.

"I need to use the bathroom," she informed him matter-of-factly.

Without a word, he reached up and untied her wrists, then sat up and undid her ankles, his abs and back muscles rippling under her appreciative gaze. He was looking healthier every day.

"Thank you."

Hopping out of the bed as naked as she'd fallen asleep, she headed to the bathroom as if nothing strange had occurred, and she woke up tied to the headboard every day.

When she'd finished her morning - or more precisely, her evening - rituals, she wandered out of the bedroom to find Luukas had gotten up and was now in the glass-walled office with the door closed, a stack of folders in front of him and papers in his hand. As he was preoccupied, she veered off towards the kitchen rather than bother him, tying the pajama pants and pulling down the T-shirt that had become her normal attire.

She was in the midst of whisking some eggs she'd found to scramble when the front door burst inward, the objects used to barricade it flying through the foyer and into the main room. Following closely behind them was Nikulas.

Keira smiled at him. "Good morning. Er, good evening, I guess I should say."

Nik scanned the room, and she followed his gaze over to his brother, who hadn't so much as glanced up at the intrusion. She smiled again as his blue eyes came back to her.

He returned her smile and took a seat at the bar.

"Whatcha makin'?"

"Just some scrambled eggs. Thanks for the food, by the way."

"Sure. You look better," he noted.

She poured her eggs into the frying pan she had heating up on the stovetop. "Vampire blood can do wonderful things for a dying girl."

A look of relief came over his handsome features. "That it can. What happened to your wrists?"

Glancing down at the fading red marks encircling them, she blew off his concern. "It's nothing. Your brother has taken to tying me to the bed while he sleeps."

"No shit?"

She just shrugged.

"Huh."

She concentrated on keeping her eggs from burning, the kitchen silent as she cooked. Scooping them onto a plate, she took it over to the bar and sat with Luukas' brother.

Taking a bite, she looked him over as she chewed. "So, what's up with you and my little sister?"

Nik pushed his hair back off of his face, a nervous gesture for him, she'd noticed.

"What do you mean?"

"Are you bonded to her?" Keira asked bluntly. She didn't believe in wasting time beating around the bush.

He stilled. "Have you said anything to Luukas?"

"Nope." She took another bite of her eggs.

"Please don't," he pleaded. "He doesn't need this added burden right now. He's having a hard enough time readjusting to being back."

"I won't," she promised. "But tell me, does she know about all that stuff? Did you explain it to her? More specifically, does she know that you'll die without her blood now?"

"She knows."

"And she still left?" she asked incredulously. "That doesn't sound like Emma."

"She was angry with me, after we left you there with Luukas. She was *so* angry. And besides, it's better this way. I didn't exactly try to stop her."

"Better for whom?"

Nik glanced at her sideways, chewing the inside of his cheek, but didn't answer.

"Do you love her?"

"It doesn't matter..."

"Do you love her?" she demanded.

"Yes," he whispered. "Desperately. Which is why I let her leave."

"Does she love you?"

His eyes saddened. "She said she did."

Keira finished her eggs and got up to rinse off her plate. Drying her hands on the towel lying on the counter, she leaned back against it and wondered why men always had to make everything so damn difficult.

"Then quit being a martyr and go get her, Nikulas."

He shook his head. "I can't do that. Being with me...she'd just become my personal feeding bag..." He trailed off as he noticed the expression on Keira's face.

"Sorry. I didn't mean..."

"Yes, you did," she stated. "But you're being stupid."

"I'm not being stupid," he protested indignantly.

"Yeah. You kinda are," she shot back. "The whole feeding thing aside, if you love her, and she loves you, why are you making her life miserable?"

"I'm not! I'm letting her *have* a life. A real life. The human life she was supposed to have."

"Have you asked her what life she wants to have? It is *her* life, after all."

The muscles in his jaw clenched stubbornly as he looked away.

She didn't say anymore, letting him mull over what she'd said, and hoping he'd quit being stupid.

Finally, he sucked in a quick breath and scrubbed his face with his hands, then gave her a nervous smile.

"What if she doesn't want me anymore?"

Keira walked over and leaned on the counter across from him. "Well, then you'll know," she said, returning his smile with an encouraging one of her own. "But while you're there, would you let her know that I'm ok? And that I'll call her as soon as I can?"

Nik nodded. "Sure. Let me just go update Luuk on what we've been doing since he's been gone. He looks a little lost. I'll leave first thing tomorrow night."

She patted his hand. "You do that."

Three hours later, Luukas was still in the office with Nikulas, and Keira was bored. She'd showered, done laundry, picked up what she could from the busted barricade, and read for a while. Now, she was eyeballing Luukas' closet, wondering if he'd be angry if she rearranged it.

Speaking of which, she really needed some clothes, and shoes, and her own shampoo. Maybe she could talk him into a shopping trip tomorrow night.

Or, she thought, *I could just order everything online, if I can get a hold of a credit card.*

As she stood there making her mental list of everything that she'd need, Luukas strode into the room. Squeezing past her without acknowledging her, he grabbed some boots from the closet and sat on the bed to pull them on.

"Where are you going?" she asked.

He didn't answer her, so she followed him as he strode out of the room.

"Luukas? Where are you going?"

"Out."

Pulling the busted front door closed behind him, he left the apartment.

"Out," she repeated to herself, rolling her eyes.

Why had she ever thought that a vampire male would be any different than a human one?

Blowing her hair out of her eyes, she decided that two could play that game, and headed over to the office to search for that credit card.

26

LEEHA

Leeha hesitated briefly before opening the door, struggling with her feelings about this.

But no, it had to be done. He already knew too much.

Indicating for Aiden to follow her, she pushed open the door and led him inside.

The room that greeted them was reminiscent of a saloon straight out of an old western movie. Except it was filled with vampires instead of cowboys, and it served up blood straight from the vein rather than whiskey.

As she entered, every immortal in the place stopped what they were doing and dropped to one knee before her, heads respectfully lowered.

Pleasure and pride filled her at the sight. Soon, she'd have an entire continent, perhaps an entire world, of vampires bowing before her.

Her voice rang out strong and clear, "You may rise."

They did so, standing at attention before her.

Glancing over at Aiden, she noticed his smile of greeting faltering. Ah, yes. He was not stupid, this one. He sensed something was amiss.

And he was correct.

"What have you done, Leeha?" he asked quietly. "These are Luukas' vampires that followed you when you left, yet I feel that they're...not."

She looked over the room, seeing it through his eyes. An old wooden bar ran along the left wall. Tables and chairs were spread throughout the remainder of the space, and there was even an old piano over in the corner. It made her feel like she'd gone back in time to the gold rush days in America. One would almost expect to see a gunslinger come ambling in at any moment, cowboy hat low over his eyes and pistols slung low on his hips.

Male immortals were scattered throughout the room, still at attention and reverently attuned to her. Amongst them was an array of young, beautiful humans in various stages of undress and blood loss. They lounged where they'd been tossed aside, regarding her warily.

She'd found this old, abandoned town when she'd first arrived to the area, and had quickly set her vampires to renovating it for no other reason except that she had a thing for old ghost towns.

She'd had no idea at the time how very useful it would be to her.

Later, they'd dug large tunnels through the rocky underground from her mountain residence to the town, allowing her to go back and forth between the two any time of the day or night to check on her creations.

They seemed quite happy here.

Aiden walked towards his old friends cautiously, searching their faces, and not appearing to find what he was looking for.

His expression uncharacteristically solemn, he faced Leeha again.

"These are Luukas' vampires, or they were before you led them to the dark side. Quite literally, it seems. These are the bodies you gave to the demons. Is there anything left of them at all in there?"

"Not enough to matter," she answered gleefully. "They are completely and utterly my subjects now."

Clasping his hands behind his back, Aiden wandered back her way. "Weren't they already your subjects?"

"No," she told him, "Not really. They came with me, taken in by my beauty or what have you, but they were never completely mine. I didn't create them, Luukas did. No matter how much I would've wished otherwise, they would always have a bond with him."

She turned away, admiring her handiwork. "But not anymore. Now, they are truly *my* creations."

"How did you manage to muck up the others, but not these?" he wondered aloud.

"These were the earliest ones. As I told you in the altar room, the first one was quite by accident. But once it was done, I started bringing the rest in one at a time, all with the same results."

"And how, exactly, did you go about the possession?"

"Once they are bound to the altar, I drain the vampire until he's near death. The demon can then enter their body. I reanimate them with my blood, and a human sacrifice feeds them, completing the transition."

"That's it?" he still sounded skeptical.

She pouted a bit, and grudgingly admitted, "There *is* a spell that must be used also that enables the possession."

"A witch's spell?"

She nodded.

"And you actually found some twat who was willing to be a part of this evil mess?" he asked in disbelief.

"I found something better," she gloated.

Aiden scratched his head. "So, why did it work with these vampires, but not the others? The ugly, smelly, grey things?"

Curling her arms around herself, she refused to meet his eyes. "I didn't know at first, but I now believe it has to do with the age of the vampire," she cleared her throat, "And the identity of the one who created them to begin with."

She could practically hear the gears grinding in Aiden's sharp mind as he began to pace in front of her.

"So, the ones who failed the experiment, they were new vampires that you'd created recently from humans."

"Yes," she confirmed.

"Mmm-hmmm, mmm-hmmm."

His pacing got faster and faster as he figured it out. "That's why they don't work. They're too new, and your blood isn't strong enough for the bodies to handle the possession."

She said nothing, shame filling her as he pointed out her shortcomings.

"So their body begins to decay, and they appear more like the demon's physical form, if they had one, than their own. Interesting, interesting...How long do they last before they rot completely?"

"It depends. The first ones rotted within days, but the more I create, and the stronger I get, the longer they survive. It's still not long enough, however. It seems I am insufficient as a Master vampire in that way. I can only steal a more powerful vampire's creations and turn them into my own. It's quite disheartening."

Aiden came to a halt directly in front of her and lifted her face up with a gentle finger under her chin.

"Aww, poppet. Keep your chin up. The great ones always fail before they succeed, as they say. You will too. You'll see."

He flashed her a smile, and she couldn't help but return it: his handsome face and positive attitude, as always, a balm to her weary soul.

He gave her a lusty wink. "There she is."

He swung his arm in an arc, taking in the males behind him. "So you have your own creations now. How do you keep a hoard of demons entertained, I wonder?"

She eyed her creatures lovingly. "They love all things physical, of course. Feeding, fighting, sex. They've been incorporeal for thousands of years, their spirits unable to leave that altar."

"That's it? There's no other purpose for this, other than to prove that it's possible?"

"Oh, there's a purpose," she promised, "As Luukas insists on fighting me, rejecting the future that should be ours, I'm going to take that future for myself. Soon, he will have no vampires of his own, for they will all be turned to belong to me. I will rule this entire continent, and Luukas will have no choice but to come to me and beg for my forgiveness. For without his vampires, what purpose does a Master vampire serve?"

"There's just one small flaw in your plan, poppet. He'll weaken more and more with every loss of a child, until there's nothing left of him for you to claim."

"No, he won't, because I'm not killing them. They're still there, somewhere. It's just that the demons are stronger, their possession overwhelming to the former occupants of the bodies. They are suppressed."

Leeha glanced over his shoulder, and gave a slight nod, before catching Aiden's grey eyes with own turbulent red ones. "And now we must say goodbye, my beautiful Aiden."

Confusion crossed his features, then his grey eyes filled with understanding. He touched her porcelain cheek, cocking his head to the side.

"Ah. I see. I have to admit, I'm quite gutted, poppet. I had such plans for us."

"I'm so sorry, my Aiden."

A male voice began to chant softly from the back of the room as she pulled his head down and kissed him softly on the lips.

True regret overflowed within her as Aiden's eyes rolled back in his head and he fell heavily to the floor. She caught his head before it hit the hard wood, and gently lowered it the rest of the way.

"Take him to the altar room," she ordered the cloaked figure, her voice choked with tears.

27

LUUKAS

Luukas finished pulling on his dark grey hoodie as he stepped out of the elevator into the underground parking garage, zipping it closed and pulling the hood up to conceal his face. He wasn't ready to be seen just yet.

Looking around for his brother, he spotted him over by his SUV.

"Are you sure you're ready for this?" Nik asked him as he approached.

"No," he answered honestly. "But I've got to do it sooner or later. Might as well get it over with. I can't believe you've succeeded in hiding my absence this long as it is."

"It was no easy task, my brother. But I felt it was necessary, and everyone else agreed. If the truth had gotten out, it wouldn't have done anything but create a panic. We would've had vampires banging on our door every night, wanting news, wanting to help...it was just easier this way. Of course, we assumed we'd have you back much sooner."

Getting into the drivers seat, Nik went on to tell him, "We announced that you were implementing heightened security measures on the home front to explain why visitors wouldn't be allowed to visit there anymore, but there was a lot of suspicion anyway."

Starting the car, he let it warm up a moment. "And we had our hands full. Master vamps from all over were poking around, trying to get somebody to slip up and say something. I even had Christian pretend to be you for more than one phone call. He does a dead-on imitation of you, by the way. And we'd drive around in the SUV with him dressed in your clothes. We never stopped the vehicle, and with the tinted windows it seems we pulled it off. They may have suspected something wasn't quite right, but there was never any proof."

"You did well, Nikulas. Thank you."

"No problem, man."

They left the apartments and pulled into the downtown traffic. It wasn't very heavy this time of the night, but they still hadn't gone far when they stopped at a light, and Luukas felt his brother's blue eyes boring into him. "What?"

"I was just thinking," Nik gave the road his attention again as the light turned green. "Is Keira gonna be ok, leaving her at the apartment by herself? With a busted front door? I know there's security all over the place, but..."

Luukas smirked. "She's a powerful witch, as you constantly like to remind me. She can take care of herself."

"You're not worried she'll take off?"

"How? She has no clothes of her own. No money. No phone. I doubt she'd walk barefoot through the streets of Seattle in my pajamas."

"Yeah, I guess you're right."

He needed to get off of this subject. "So, where are we going first?"

"Well," Nik suggested, "I thought we'd head down to the waterfront, cruise by some of your businesses. Let you be seen by the vamp crews. If you feel ready at any point, maybe we could stop in a few places. Not too many though, that would look too suspicious. Having you all over the place when no one's really seen you for seven years. Plus, I think we should take this one step at a time."

Luukas felt his chest tightening up with anxiety. "Yeah, we'll see how it goes."

They drove in silence after that, each caught up in their own thoughts.

Luukas wondered what Keira was doing, then just as quickly pushed her out of his head.

Or at least he tried.

Pulling his hood off, he gazed out the car window, letting his vampires see him, occasionally giving a small wave. His mind, however, was far from his reinstatement into society.

Instead, it was obsessed with a curvy, raven-haired, smart-mouthed witch.

His lips quirked as he finally gave up the fight and let her in.

She was a ballsy little thing, that was for sure, standing up to him in ways that would make grown males quake in their boots.

He remembered her back in their cell, bringing him blood and water to drink. She'd had to get so close to him, he could have easily bitten her. But she'd done it anyway.

And she hadn't tried to run when they'd gotten free, even when she'd felt certain he was going to kill her.

She still hadn't run away, even now.

Mine.

Luukas crossed his arms over his chest, fighting what everything inside of him was trying to tell him. He refused to believe it. All of this mated shit was just that, a bunch of bullshit. An old tale passed down through the years for amusement, or hope for pathetic souls that there was a chance to ease the loneliness, or whatever. It just wasn't possible.

And he would prove it.

"Pull the car over," he ordered.

"What? Here? There's nothing around here. Just a bunch of houses and the cruise ship terminals."

"I said, pull the fuck over."

"All right, all right." Nikulas pulled down a side street and stopped the car. "But where are you going?"

"I'll meet you back at the apartments." Slamming the door, he took off at vamp speed before his brother could ask any more questions.

According to the stories, once a vampire had found and drank the blood of his fated mate, he wouldn't be able to feed from anyone else.

Well, let's just see about that.

Covering his head with his hood again, he stalked the streets of Queen Anne. He'd prove that this bonded mate thing was nothing but a bunch of fucking bullshit, and then he'd end this game he'd been playing and send that little witch packing. He didn't need her.

He hadn't been walking long when he spotted an attractive, thirty-something female sitting on her porch steps, talking on her phone. She eyed him suspiciously as he approached.

"Hi," he said, trying to turn on the old charm that used to be so effortless.

She didn't answer him, tensing to flee as she interrupted the other speaker, "Hey, hey hon..."

Catching her eyes with his own, he commanded, "Tell your friend you have to go now."

"I have to go now," she said obediently.

"Now hang up the phone."

She did, laying it down on the step beside her.

"Do you live here alone?" he asked.

"No, I live here with my husband."

"Is he home?"

"No. He's working late."

"Good. Invite me in," he ordered in a low tone.

She hesitated just for a second. "Come in."

Following her inside, he locked the door behind him as she stood waiting, her heart pounding and her pulse racing, but unable to break free of his pull on her and run.

A lazy smile crossed his face, his fangs lengthening as he caught her scent. "What is your name?"

"Anna," she whispered.

"Come here, Anna."

She did as he told her, coming to stand directly in front of him. She was tall for a female, the top of her head reaching his nose, unlike his little witch, who barely came to his shoulder.

He snarled, fed up with her constant intrusion into his thoughts, and the human's eyes widened in fear.

"You will not run away, you will not scream, and once I'm done and I leave here, you will not remember me at all. Do you understand?"

"Yes," she said breathlessly.

Her dark hair was cut short, so nothing stood in the way of his feeding. Tilting her head to the side with one hand, he pulled her closer to him with the other. He took a moment to appreciate the sight of her pulsing artery, inhaling her pleasant scent again. She was tall enough that he barely had to bend forward.

His fangs scraped her warm skin, and she whimpered.

"Do not be afraid," he whispered.

Slowly, appreciatively, he sank his fangs into her throat, tasting her blood as it pooled to the surface.

He stiffened.

Her blood tasted nothing like it should. Was she ill? Was it his imagination?

Taking a small pull, he tasted her again.

Her blood tasted like it had been fermenting for years in a rotting corpse.

Quickly, he removed his fangs, spitting her blood onto the floor.

Licking his thumb, he rubbed it over her small wounds to heal them, unable to bring himself to lick them closed as he normally would.

"Are you ill? Do you have some human disease?" he asked the woman.

"No. I just had all my blood work done two weeks ago."

Luukas released her abruptly, turned, and fled from the house.

That fucking witch! She'd done something to him! Some spell...some curse!

No, he would try again. Maybe that woman *was* ill, and just didn't know it yet.

Two hours and six human females later, Luukas was back at his apartment building. He stood across the street and looked up at the top floor, watching the witch as she stood at the window as he so often did. She wouldn't be able to see him with her human eyes, but he could see her very clearly.

After a few moments, she sighed, and walked towards the kitchen until she was out of sight.

It could not be true.

She could not be his mate.

Fate would not be so cruel!

Nikulas walked out the front door and jogged across the road to join him, dodging cars as they beeped at him angrily.

"Did you find out what you needed to know?" he asked.

"It seems so," Luukas answered.

"Ya know, for a while there, I wasn't sure if your instinct for vengeance would be stronger than your instinct to protect her."

"That's still up for debate," Luukas growled.

Nik shot him an uneasy look. "I was in the lobby talking to the front desk when I saw you out here. I'm taking off for a few days."

He didn't bother to ask where his brother was going. He assumed it had something to do with the missing Hunters.

"I'll be leaving tonight."

"All right." Luukas finally tore his eyes from the window. "Be careful."

Nik smiled at him. "Always."

28

KEIRA

Keira jumped as the front door slammed shut and Luukas came striding through the foyer, not stopping until he reached her.

He was angry.

Very angry, by the looks of him.

Taking the water glass from her hand, he threw it across the kitchen, smashing it against the cabinets.

"What did you do to me?" he bellowed at her.

She scowled up at him, opening her mouth to give him a good piece of her mind for his behavior, when she caught a strange scent coming off of his clothes.

Sticking her nose right up against his chest, she took a deep whiff of his hoodie. Pulling back, she looked up at him, hurt pouring out of her eyes before it was replaced by her own anger.

Hauling back her arm, she slapped him as hard as she could.

"You fucking bastard! That's where you've been all night? With another woman?"

His eyes lit up dangerously and his lips pulled back from his fangs, his face more frightening than she'd ever seen.

Instinctually, she took a step back, but continued to rail at him.

"I've been here alone for hours, worrying about you, you son of a bitch!"

She went to slap him again, but he caught her arm before she could, holding it midair in his iron grip.

"Don't," he hissed out.

Keira had never felt such fury. Not even while in the torture cell. There she'd felt impotent, and sad, and frustrated, but nothing that compared to the white-hot fury that was burning through her at this moment.

Tears ran down her face, and she yanked her arm out of his grip to dash them away. Without another word, she walked around him and headed towards the bedroom.

Screw this.

"Don't walk away from me, witch. I asked you a question!"

She ignored him.

Stupid, stupid. She'd been so stupid. Allowing herself to care for someone who would do this to her.

But, he's been through so much. Even though he seems to be getting better, his mind can't be right. I'm sure he didn't mean to hurt you.

Oh, shut up! She told the rational side of herself. She was in no mood to be rational. He'd betrayed her! After all they'd been through together, and all they'd experienced together since. So much for the "fated mate" stories.

Bastard.

Violently yanking open a drawer, she searched for some actual clothes that wouldn't fall off of her.

She was so out of here.

"What are you doing?" Luukas asked from the bedroom doorway.

She didn't answer him. She couldn't. If she stopped, if she looked at him, she would break down. And she refused to show him how much he'd hurt her.

Little late for that, isn't it?

Oh, shut up!

You could always just zap him into the next room, or put a containment spell on him so he'd never be able to leave the apartment like that again.

SHUT UP!

"Keira! What are you doing?" he yelled. He sounded panicked.

Finding a pair of sweats with a drawstring, she threw them on the floor and pulled open another drawer to look for a heavy shirt.

She'd just yanked out a navy sweatshirt when she was gripped by the arm and spun around.

"*What* are you doing?" he asked again, his voice barely above a whisper.

She refused to look at him. "I'm packing. What the hell does it look like?"

"Packing? To go where?"

"Anywhere away from you."

He visibly recoiled at her words, and her heart clenched painfully in her chest.

"No," he insisted, his eyes unnaturally bright. "No. You're not going anywhere."

She yanked her arm away again. "Watch me."

Turning away from him, she yanked open his sock drawer, only to find herself spun back around into his arms.

"No, witch. You can't leave me," he whispered hoarsely.

She tried to push him away, tried to get away from the sweet perfume that was wafting from his clothes, but he held her tight.

"Let me go, Luukas!"

"No. I won't. I can't."

Taking her face in his large hands, he starting raining kisses on her forehead, her cheeks, her nose. He kissed her tears away.

"I'm sorry. I'm so sorry."

Her chin quivered as she tried to pull his hands away from her face.

"Keira, I'm so sorry. I'm so sorry," he repeated.

Finding her lips, he kissed her urgently, passionately, gently trying to get her to open to him.

With a sob, she wrenched her face away. "Stop! Stop it! You reek of another woman, and you expect me to kiss you? Are you insane?"

At her words, his entire body stiffened, and Keira stopped struggling.

Shit. Why had she said that word in particular?

His hands dropped to his sides.

She reached out a hand towards him. "Luukas, I didn't mean..."

"I'll go take a shower. Do not move, witch." Turning on his heel, he strode into the bathroom.

Standing there in front of the dresser, she listened until she heard the water come on.

Why had she said that?

Because it was true.

Looking down at the floor, she caught his sweatpants out of the corner of her eye, and angrily grabbed them off of the floor.

If he thought she was going to stand here like a good little girl while he washed another woman off of him before coming to her, he *was* insane.

She was dressed and out the door in record time, the credit card she'd found earlier gripped tightly in hand.

The elevator was open when she got there and she took it down to the front desk, formulating a plan to get some shoes. She just prayed it would work.

The concierge looked up in curiosity as she approached, a girl in too-large sweat clothes with her hair in a ponytail and no shoes.

She smiled easily. "Good morning! I think I left my shoes in the gym yesterday, did anyone happen to turn them in?"

He relaxed immediately. "Actually, yes. They did. Sneakers? Blue, with white laces?"

"Yes! It sounds like them."

"One moment, I'll go grab them from the back."

She held the smile on her face until he was out of sight. As soon as he was gone, she watched the elevator, her heart beating rapidly every time it began to ascend, breathing again when it didn't go to the top floor.

On her left side, the rising sun was warm where it shone in through the front windows.

Come on, come on, come on.

After what seemed an eternity, he returned with the shoes.

"Here you go, miss," he announced with a smile.

She grabbed them out of his hand. "That's them! Thank you!"

Scuttling towards the door, she heard the elevator ding behind her just as she walked out into the rare Seattle sunshine. Quickly sliding on the shoes, which were only a half-size too big, she took off towards the intersection without tying them.

Suddenly, the hair rose on her arms and neck, and she thought she heard a beast roaring from the rooftop behind her.

But maybe it was just her imagination.

Keira walked for blocks without stopping, needing to be as far away as possible, until her growling stomach and need to pee forced her to find a coffee shop. Logically, she knew he couldn't follow her while the sun was up, but she still looked back over her shoulder every few steps.

Bladder relieved and juice in hand, she was back on the street. She needed to get to the airport.

She briefly thought about getting some new clothes, but she really didn't want to owe Luukas any more than she had to when he found her. Because he *would* find her, of that she had no doubt. She wasn't stupid. Her little adventure here would end in the not so far future, probably as soon as darkness fell.

He'd had her blood, and she'd had his. He would be able to find her anywhere in the world. There was nowhere she could hide.

But maybe she could at least see her sister for a bit before he locked her away in his tower again. Maybe Nikulas would still be there and he could help her. She hoped so.

Ok. Airport, airport. She assumed by the platinum status of the credit card in her hand that she'd be able to purchase a ticket without any problems.

Walking to the edge of the sidewalk, she looked for a cab. Did they even take credit? Guess she'd find out. If not, well, she *was* a witch after all; she'd just convince him to take her there for free.

Shading her eyes, she peered down the street looking for a car with a 'taxi' sign on the top. She was so engrossed in her search that she didn't even notice the black van pull over to the curb right behind her. She didn't hear the door slide open, or see the male sitting inside in shadow, just out of reach of the sun's rays.

She didn't notice until she heard a deep voice say, "Hello, Keira."

29

LUUKAS

Luukas showered quickly but thoroughly, his mind racing nearly as fast as his heart.

It was true then. Impossible as it seemed. Keira really was his.

A comforting peace filled him at the thought.

Keira was his.

His witch.

His angel.

Now, to get things straightened out with her. He needed to let her know that nothing had happened. Needed to explain why he'd run around the city half-cocked trying to drink from others. Needed to explain that sex had never been in the equation. He'd only been trying to prove the "mate" thing wrong.

But obviously, it was he who'd been wrong.

He wrapped a towel around his waist and barged back into the bedroom, eager to rid her of her uncertainty of him, but she wasn't there.

"Keira?"

The clothes were gone from the floor.

No.

No, no, no!

He ran out to the main room, searched the other bedroom.

"Keira!" he yelled, more frantic with every passing moment.

The sun was coming up, if she'd made it outside, he wouldn't be able to follow her! She could be anywhere in the country by the time he could leave the building.

He ran over to the window, protected by the special glass, and searched the street below. It took him less than a minute to spot her charging out onto the sidewalk.

Pressing his hands to the window, he watched her rush awkwardly towards the intersection, her shoes untied.

An animalistic roar of pain tore from his chest at the sight of her running from him.

"NOOOOOOOOOOO!"

He punched the glass, not caring if it broke and killed him instantly.

Fucking sun! It was the one thing that crippled him at times like these.

He began to pace.

There had to be a way to get to her, something he could travel in.

They could get a human driver for the SUV! The back windows were tinted especially to protect ones such as him. He'd be fine as long as he stayed back there.

Nikulas would know how to get one. He wasn't leaving until tonight.

Luukas rushed back into the bedroom and threw on the first things he could find. Taking the stairs down to Nik's apartment, he beat on his brother's door, letting himself in when it wasn't immediately opened for him.

"Nikulas!"

His brother came out of his bedroom, his pajama pants and his hair equally rumpled.

"What the fuck, man? It's sleep time."

"Keira left."

"What do you mean, left? To go get food or something? She'll be ok. No need to panic."

"No. I mean she left. She left me, and I need to get her back. Now."

Nikulas stumbled his way into the kitchen, and Luukas noticed for the first time that his brother wasn't looking quite right.

"What's going on with you, Nikulas?" he demanded.

"What? Nothing, man. I'm good." He threw a bag of blood into the microwave.

Luukas joined him in the kitchen and narrowed his eyes at him, taking in his pallid appearance, bruised eyes, and sunken cheeks. The signs were subtle, but they were there.

Why had he not noticed this?

"Don't lie to me," he reprimanded him.

Nik took the blood out of the microwave and shook it up. Tearing off a corner, he chugged it down quickly, grimacing at the taste. He threw another bag in and hit the start button.

He glanced at his brother with an almost guilty expression, and then sighed, and seemed to make up his mind about something. "Emma, Keira's sister, is my mate. That's why I've been so sure the stories weren't just old wives tales. That's how I know that it's true."

Luuk frowned in confusion. "But, you let her go home, and the legend says..."

"Yeah," Nik interrupted, "I know what the legend says."

Luukas looked back and forth between Nik and the door, caught between the need to find his female, and the need to find out what was happening to his brother.

Then he remembered something.

"So, if you know what the legend says, and you know these stories are true, then without Emma's blood, you're dying?"

Nik finished chugging down his second blood bag, tossing the empty plastic into the recycle can. "It appears so."

"I don't understand." Luukas paced away and back again, rubbing his temples. "Why not just go get her?"

"Now you sound like Keira."

Grabbing his brother by the shoulders, Luukas shook him slightly. "You must go get her. Bring her here! Why did you let her leave? What the hell is wrong with you?"

Nik shrugged out of his brother's grasp. "I wanted to give her a choice."

"A choice?" Luuk asked incredulously.

"Yes, a choice," Nik reiterated. "A choice to live her life the way she was supposed to."

"She's supposed to live it with YOU!" Luukas was having a hard time keeping his calm. "Do you know where she is?"

"Yeah."

"Then go get her, Nikulas," Luukas gritted out, "Or I will go get her myself, by whatever means necessary. I'll drag her back here tied and gagged if I need to. I will not stand by and watch my only brother commit suicide. Do you understand?"

Nik raised an eyebrow. "Chill out, man. I'm heading there tonight. That's where I'm going."

Luukas took a calming breath. "Good."

Nik grinned at him. "You know, you're acting more and more like yourself everyday. And your eyes are almost back to their normal color."

"They are?" He hadn't noticed. He still avoided mirrors whenever possible. And why the hell were they talking about his fucking eyes?

"Nikulas, I need to go find Keira. Do you know where I could find a human driver?"

"You can't go out now, it's daylight."

"I can go in the SUV, the windows are tinted in the back. I just need a human to drive."

"It's still a crazy risk, man. It looks like it's shaping up to be an unusually sunny day out there. Besides, she probably just needed some air. She won't go far. She has no ID, no money. Why don't you just hang out here with me, give her some space in case she comes back on her own. If she doesn't, we can set out as soon as the sun sets. I think you're freaking out over nothing."

Luukas rubbed the back of his neck. He knew Nik was probably right. She was just angry. She'd come back in her own time and then they could sit down and talk.

He just felt so shaky without her around. She did something to his psyche, calmed him somehow. Which was weird, considering their past, but there it was.

And his instincts were burning inside of him, telling him to go after his female. He didn't know how Nikulas had lasted this long so far from Emma. No wonder he looked like shit.

Was he just overreacting? He didn't know anymore.

"Yeah, ok. But I'll go on my own, you need to go get Emma."

"Are you sure? You gonna be all right?"

No. "Yes."

Nik eyed him dubiously, but after a moment, gave a nod. "Ok. Let's get some sleep then, shall we? You can crash in Aiden's room."

Luukas went to head that way, but stopped. "Nik?"

He paused, "Hmm?"

Luukas opened his mouth to attempt to express all that he was feeling, but found he couldn't get the words out. So instead, he pulled his brother to him and wrapped him in a bear hug. "Thank you."

Nik patted him awkwardly, "Uh, you do realize that I've been a horrible brother, right?"

"No. You haven't. You weren't prepared for what happened, and that was my fault. I should've spent more time with you, kept you up to date with things, trained you for an emergency such as that. I should've listened to you in the first place and not have gone there alone. None of this would've happened. You all did as well as you could, and you've been great since I got back. With me. With Keira. And I want you to know that I appreciate it."

His brother gave him a quick squeeze and pulled away, embarrassed. "Come on, let's get some sleep."

Smacking Luukas on the shoulder, he turned and went back to his room.

Luukas watched him until he closed the door behind him, and then headed to Aiden's room.

30

LUUKAS

Luukas shot out of the elevator and into the lobby as the last rays of the sun sank below the horizon. Bursting through the front door, he lowered his head as he walked, searching for Keira's scent.

He'd woken up in a cold sweat at Nik's just a few minutes earlier. Running upstairs, he'd searched his apartment.

She hadn't come back.

Dodging pedestrians, he walked in the direction he'd seen her go this morning, following her familiar smell. It was faint, but it was there.

He followed it for many blocks, in and out of a coffee shop, and then suddenly, it just disappeared.

Luukas stopped in the middle of the sidewalk, turned back to catch it again, and followed it again more slowly, ignoring the strange looks of the people having to move around him. He lost it again in the same spot at the edge of the sidewalk.

She hadn't crossed the street. It just disappeared completely.

Had she gotten into a car? A cab?

Had someone taken her?

Fighting down the panic, he tried to think rationally. Maybe she'd just caught a cab or something.

With no money?

She could've found cash, or a credit card, when he was gone earlier. It was all over the apartment if you knew where to look, or if you were good at snooping around.

But what if she *had* been taken? What if Leeha had someone watching them, just waiting for the right opportunity?

He took a deep breath, closed his eyes, and tried to concentrate.

Relax. You can find her. Her blood is running through your veins and yours is in her. It will call to you if you just fucking listen.

Yes. He needed to stay calm. He would find her.

He stood solid as a wall, ignoring the humans as they hustled around him, blocking them out, blocking out everything. Concentrating only on his breathing and steadying his heartbeat, he reached out with his senses, and listened with every cell in his body.

It didn't take long.

There! Yes. He could feel her. She was calling to him, and now he knew where to find her.

Luukas' Hummer skidded to a halt outside of the entrance of Leeha's fortress. Slamming the door shut, he strode purposefully towards the mountain cave, following the creek to the interior.

By this time, his fear and anger were so intermingled that they radiated outward from him like sonic waves, pulsating through the air around him, fighting for dominance. The trees vibrated with it, leaves and small branches fluttering to the ground as he passed. The normally gentle ripples of the creek surged up into waves and splashed onto the bank. The very earth seemed to feel his anguish, trembling with the intensity of his feelings.

He entered the cave without breaking stride, determined to not let his emotions get the best of him. It was completely dark, with no torches lit to welcome him this time, but that didn't matter. He could see just fine.

And he knew his female was here. Her blood continued to call to him, stronger now, singing loudly in his veins. And her scent was fresh. She'd passed through here not long ago, and another was with her. A male he wasn't familiar with. Not vampire, but not quite human either.

His nostrils flared at the strange, male scent and he clenched his teeth, his protracted fangs cutting into the inside of his mouth.

How *dare* he touch what was his.

Without hesitation, he darted away from the creek and over to the tunnel that would lead him to the interior of the mountain. But upon entering the narrow passageway, his stride faltered.

A cold sweat broke out on his forehead. His heart pounded fast and hard in his chest. Closing his eyes, he swallowed hard and tried to breathe through the terror, but it was too much. The memories paralyzed him where he stood.

The pain, the hunger, the blood, the *fire*...

He was unable to go any farther.

No!

He clenched his fists at his sides. No. He would *not* accept this weakness. He was *not* a pale comparison of the male he once was. He was *not* unworthy of her.

Keira needed him.

Vehemently suppressing the horrific memories of what had happened to him in this godforsaken place, he focused only on his female, of what she must be going through.

And though he trembled with fear, he took a deep breath, and forced one foot in front of the other.

He took another deep breath, fighting for control, and took a few more steps.

Another deep breath, only this time, he could also smell her terror lingering in the air.

"KEIRA!" he roared.

Instead of trying to fight it anymore, he used the strength of his emotions to blast his way through the tunnel, widening the passageway as he passed through. Rocks and loose gravel flew outward from the path, clearing the way for the raw force of nature that he had become.

The mountain groaned and shuddered around him. Leeha would know he was here.

Good. He wanted her to know. He wanted her to hear him. Wanted her to sense the death that was coming for her. Wanted her to be afraid. Wanted her to try to run.

His lips curled up into a chilling smile. There was nowhere on this earth or beyond where she would be able to hide from him if she'd harmed one hair on his female's head. For he would find her, and when he did, there would be nothing left of her to harm anyone again.

He sped down the tunnel, not giving himself time to think, letting his rage fuel him. It possessed him, strengthened him, until *rage* was all that he was.

Reaching the cathedral-like main room, he stopped, gazing around uneasily. It was eerily dark and quiet.

His skin tingled and the hair rose on the back of his neck in warning. He searched the room warily, but saw no one else there.

Pictures of this room, of him on his knees while his power was drained from him, flashed through his mind, and he fought the urge to turn and run.

Rubbing his sweaty palms on his pants, he again forced himself to calm down, to focus. Keira's scent was stronger here - much stronger.

Dropping down into a crouch, he studied the area around him. Something had dripped onto the floor here, barely discernible among the pattern of the mosaic tiles.

It was blood.

He dipped his fingers into the fresh droplets, bringing them to his mouth to taste it, though it wasn't really necessary. He knew whose blood it was.

His lips pulled back from his fangs, a feral growl rumbling from his chest as he noticed more blood...and more still. His eyes following the path where she'd been dragged across the floor.

He stood and followed the trail to the gaping hole he'd left in the wall the last time he'd been here, and stepped into the passageway.

A lonely torch was lit twenty yards away, beckoning to him.

He hesitated, staring at that torch uneasily, a cold sweat breaking out all over his body. As he watched the flickering flame, a faint, metallic smell rose in the air around him.

The smell of blood, but not Keira's blood.

His blood.

It was so strong he looked down at himself in fear, convinced he would see his stomach slashed open and his guts hanging out.

But there was nothing. He twisted his torso around, looking everywhere. He wasn't bleeding. It was all in his head.

Wiping the sweat from his face with his forearms, he eyed up that torch again.

What the fuck are you waiting for? Quit standing here like a fucking pussy. Your female is down there somewhere.

The smell of his blood grew stronger, and he jumped as a scream echoed past him through the passage.

The voice was his own, yet he hadn't made a sound.

Squeezing his eyes shut, Luukas gripped the sides of his head.

Get it together, man. They're just fucking with you. It's all in your head. You're not helpless anymore. You're in control! You can fucking annihilate this place on a whim. Go. Get. Your. Female.

But what if he'd been right about her all along? What if she was just the lure that would enable Leeha to capture him again?

What if she was in on it as he'd suspected all along?

He snarled at the walls around him. Fuck it. Throwing his shoulders back, he took a deep breath through his nose, catching the scent of her blood again.

Rip her open! Suck her dry! Kill her! Burn her!

If that were true, if she'd been playing him all this time, then he would kill her first.

The air around him began to stir as he confronted the empty passageway, a burning rage filling him again. His fangs ached and his eyes began to glow a grey-green. A deep growl rumbled in his chest.

Yes, he would go get his female, for better or for worse.

His boots pounded down the tunnel, increasing in speed, until he broke into a jog, then a full out run, following the pull of Keira's blood. He knew where he would find her, but it didn't matter.

He ran blindly, descending farther and farther into the depths of hell. Jumping down the last stairway, he landed with a heavy thud outside of the doorway of his old cell.

What he saw inside arrested him where he stood.

Keira hung unconscious against the far wall, like a sacrifice. For him? Her delicate wrists and ankles were enclosed with silver shackles, her arms and legs spread-eagle, her head hanging down limply on her chest. Her beautiful, long, dark hair covered her face and breasts.

She was half-naked, an unfamiliar white slip of a gown ripped nearly off of her, and she was covered in blood - on her neck, her bare arms, her breasts, her thighs.

Luukas stood motionless.

Can't hurt her!!

His dark side had dreamt of this exact scenario, and now it rubbed its hands together with delight. He'd nearly believed that side of him to be gone, but it wasn't. Not at all. It rejoiced at the sight of the witch strung up as he'd been, of seeing her suffer just as he had. It wanted to wield a knife and join in, to slice her open and cackle with glee as she slowly bled out. It urged him to sink his fangs in her, and to set her afire to finish her off.

Rip her open! Suck her dry! Kill her! Burn her!

He could still see the stains of his blood on the dirt floor, now joined by the witch's; could still hear the sounds of the rats as they chewed on his wounds; could still hear his own screams echoing off of the walls.

His glowing eyes roamed over her bare legs, revealed through the slits in the gown, and up the curves of her hips and her full breasts to the top of her head.

MINE.

Can't hurt her!

The darkness howled in anger as he pushed it deep into the recesses of his mind.

He needed to get her down. Yes. Get her down now!

Forcing his legs to move, he cautiously entered the cell, glancing around warily. His head swam as he crossed over the threshold, and his lungs were unable to take a breath, but he kept going.

Halfway in, he began to shake violently, and a loud humming sounded all around him. Sweat dripped into his eyes as his fear threatened to overwhelm him. He blinked it away. Shaking his head hard, he focused on his witch.

He was only a few steps from her when he sensed another presence in the room. A malevolent presence, but it wasn't Leeha. No, it was something even worse.

The scent was familiar, and he knew immediately who was in the room. This was the male who'd brought Keira here.

With a hiss, he whipped around towards the open door.

A masculine figure stood there, concealed in a black cloak with the hood pulled up, petting a raven that was perched upon his shoulder. His aura infused the room, and Luukas realized that it wasn't only his fear of this place intensifying his terror to such a degree.

"Welcome home, vampire."

The cloaked figure lifted a hand towards him as the raven croaked in protest, and made a flicking motion.

Luukas was lifted into the air and thrown across the room like his large frame weighed no more than a spec of dust. A grunt escaped him as he slammed into the wall hard enough to knock some of the rock loose, and he slid to the floor as it fell around him, coughing on the crushed stone. He'd barely landed when he was again flying across the room to slam into the wall opposite, even harder this time.

He told himself to move! To fight back! To *do* something! But he was overwhelmed with the site of Keira, the fear of being in this cell again, and the shock of what had just happened to him. He couldn't think, couldn't move.

He could do nothing.

He had been wrong earlier. He was *not* worthy of her.

The sound of metal creaking drew his eyes up to his witch. The wooden beam she was chained to swung out from the wall seemingly of its own accord, and before he could process what was happening, he found himself sailing backwards through the air.

Silver cuffs clamped down over his wrists and ankles, the metal weakening him immediately. He found himself back to back with his witch, chained spread-eagled as she was.

The cloaked male began to chant, his voice strong and sure, and he felt himself falling into the blackness he knew so well.

31

KEIRA

Keira tried to open her eyes, tried to warn Luukas, but the cloaked one, and his evil magic, were holding her there motionless, making it appear that she had passed out.

She was the bait.

Tears ran down her cheeks when she heard her vampire falter in the doorway. She could feel his terror, and it pierced her heart.

RUN, LUUKAS! She screamed in her head.

But he didn't run. He sucked in a ragged breath, and she heard him slowly but surely making his way towards her.

The evil one entered then, the one who had grabbed her off of the street, and her heart stopped. He was powerful, that one. More powerful than she was. More powerful than Luukas. He'd swatted away her magic like it was nothing but an annoying gnat, forcing her into the van and bringing her here from Seattle.

Anger surged through her as she heard Luukas being thrown around the room like a ragdoll.

She felt a moment of relief when he slammed into her from behind and she heard the cuffs closing around him, but it swiftly fled as she felt him go slack.

A moment later, her own cuffs opened, and she could move again.

She was free.

"You bastard!" she screamed as she fell from the chains. "Release him! Release him NOW!"

She looked up as the wooden beam swung against the wall again. Luukas hung there as he had for seven years, and she let out a sob at the sight.

The cloaked one mumbled something to his raven, petting her with calming strokes, and tickled her under her feathers.

"Or you'll do what, cousin?"

Keira opened her mouth, only to snap it shut again.

"Cousin? You are *not* my cousin!" she spit out. "I have no family other than my sister."

His head lifted, just enough for her to catch a glimmer of golden eyes under the hood of his cloak. "So I guess your parents didn't tell you *everything*, then."

Her hands fisted at her sides. "What the hell are you talking about?" she demanded through gritted teeth.

But he just gave her a small, secret smile, his eyes cutting to the doorway and back to her. "That story will have to wait for another time."

Leeha swept into the room a moment later, her emerald green gown a striking contrast to her red hair and eyes.

She looks like Christmas gone horribly wrong, Keira thought snidely.

The cloaked one smirked.

*Why is he smirking? It's not like he can hear what I'm thinking...*She frowned. *Can you?*

He lifted an eyebrow.

Holy shit. Keira's skin began to crawl. What *was* this guy?

A sharp pain burst through her cheek and her head whipped around as Leeha slapped her, successfully gaining her full attention.

"You dare to bond with *my* male?" she shrieked. "You dare to try to take him from me? I can *smell* him in you," she hissed. "And you in him. How is this possible?"

She slapped Keira again, so hard she felt the bones in her cheek break

She cried out, and threw up her arms to try to protect herself.

"Answer me, witch! How is this possible? First Nikulas bonds with your sister and now Luukas bonds with *you*. You! This should not be possible!! I demand an explanation!"

Keira lowered her arms slowly. In her wrath, Leeha's eyes were nothing but swirling nightmares, trying to suck her in, and she quickly looked down at the dirt floor to avoid their pull, sneering, "Because I added a little something to that curse you made me do on all of them."

Leeha became as still as stone. "What *exactly* did you do, witch?"

Keira risked a glance at her. What the hell? The bitch was probably going to kill her anyway now that Emma was safe and couldn't be used to control her.

She hoped.

"I added a small caveat to your little curse is all. A loophole."

Leeha took a step towards her, her hand raised again.

"I wouldn't do that if I were you," the evil one said casually. "You need her. She'll be no use to you knocked out or dead."

Leeha's harsh breathing filled the room for long moments.

"Wake him up," she finally ordered. "Not completely, just enough to allow him to feel it."

"Feel what?" Keira asked, although she was afraid she already knew the answer. "Feel what?" she demanded again.

She spun around when she heard Luukas moan softly.

"Luukas?" Leeha placed a hand on his hair. "Luukas, you need to wake up, my love," Leeha told him.

His head lolled on his chest as his eyelids fluttered.

She turned her blood-eyes to the cloaked one.

"Do it," she spit out.

Panic welled in Keira's chest. "What are you doing? Leave him alone!"

"Keira?" Luukas' voice was raspy.

She turned to find him staring at her, confused.

"Keira, what are you doing?"

"It's ok. I'll get us out of here..."

She went to go to him, to reassure him, but her feet were stuck to the floor. Try as she might, she couldn't move them. Her eyes widened in horror as an unexplainable paralysis swiftly moved up her limbs, taking over her body.

That bastard!

"Do it!" Leeha shrieked.

As Keira watched helplessly, a tear appeared in Luukas' T-shirt, and he grunted in pain. Blood began to seep down his abdomen, soaking his clothes.

Looking down at himself, he began to shake violently as he raised horror filled eyes to her shocked face.

She shook her head frantically, but he didn't seem to really see her.

"It is you!" he accused. "*Why*, Keira?"

32

LUUKAS

Luukas screamed as he twisted his torso back and forth, trying to escape the pain of the blades slicing through him.

It was worse this time, so much worse. Before, it had just been Josiah and his jealous little knife, his eyes ablaze with satisfaction as he took out his insecurities on Luukas.

But now, now it was the witch, not just holding him still, but torturing him herself without ever touching him.

Rocks hurtled fast as lightening through the air, breaking his bones and bruising his skin. Daggers flew end over end to embed their blades into his organs, ripping him open on their way out again, ten and twenty at a time.

His clothes were torn, soaked through with his blood. Sweat stung his eyes until he couldn't see. His muscles and joints screamed in agony.

And the witch...the witch stood before him, laughing as she broke him.

Fuck that.

He lunged at her with a loud hiss, snapping his fangs, and felt his shoulders pop from their sockets. The cuffs around his wrists and ankles cut even further into his already torn flesh. But he didn't care.

Rip her open! Suck her dry! Kill her! Burn her!

She was the one causing all of this pain.

She was the one holding him here with her fucking spells.

She was going to die. Slowly. Painfully.

He roared in agony and frustration as he was flung back against the wall by an invisible force before he could reach her.

"AHHHHHH!!!"

Coherent thought had left him hours ago. He focused only on her lovely face as he bled, his eyes wild, his hatred for her all consuming.

"Fucking cunt!" he spat at her.

His head was knocked to the side by a force strong enough to bust open his cheek and loosen a few teeth.

He heard her laughing.

He heard her sobbing.

The madness threatened.

33

KEIRA

Keira was forced to watch as the evil one drove Luukas insane without ever harming him. His dark magic was so much more powerful than hers, that he effortlessly held her immobile in front of Luukas as she sobbed, unable to help him.

She tried to talk to him, to tell him it wasn't real, that nothing was happening to him, but he couldn't hear her.

Suddenly, Luukas' eyes widened in terror. "No! No!"

Keira fought against the hold he had on her. "What are you doing to him? Stop it! Stop it!" she screamed.

Luukas threw himself back and forth in his shackles, fighting to escape whatever it was he thought was happening to him.

His eyes flew wildly around the room as he yelled, "Help me! Help me!"

Throwing his head back into the wall, he screamed.

Keira screamed with him. "Please! Stop! Please!"

She tried to find Leeha out of the corner of her eye. "Leeha! Please! You're breaking him! Don't you see? You won't want him like this!"

Leeha strolled forward until she was just visible, her face expressionless as she observed Luukas' reactions. "Whoever said I still wanted him?"

"But, if you don't want him, why are you doing this?" Keira whispered in bewilderment.

"For the entertainment," she told her with a cold smile. "Eventually, he'll be pushed to the point that he'll use his power without even realizing he's doing so, and then he will break free - and he will kill you."

Keira stopped breathing. "But, he'll die without me."

"Yes, he will. Two birds with one stone, as they say."

And then she smelled it, like meat sizzling on a grill.

They were burning him again, or at least he would think they were.

No. No!

His horrified screams were endless now, one flowing into the next with barely a breath in between. As she watched, he threw his body from side to side violently, slamming his head back into the stone, trying to escape the nonexistent flames.

This would break him, of that Keira had no doubt. He'd barely survived it with his mind intact the first time. He wouldn't get through it again.

Leeha watched him for a few moments, jerkily tilting her head to the side in that unsettling way she had, a satisfied smile spreading across her face. "Fun as this is for me, I think I'll be leaving. It won't be long now. Good luck, witch."

Keira heard her heels click-clacking across the floor as she slithered away to safety like the coward she really was.

Blinking away her tears, she tried again to reach Luukas through the terrors of his mind.

"Luukas! Please, listen to me! It's not real! They're messing with your head! It's not real!!"

Suddenly, he stopped fighting and sagged on the chains, breathing heavily. A moment later, the temperature dropped to such a degree, Keira's breath fogged in front of her and she shivered.

Oh no.

The raven called out loudly, her voice blending with Luukas' as he bellowed madly at the ceiling. His entire body began to vibrate then, growing larger before her eyes. His muscles bulged as they strained against the chains. His skin grew taut over his bones as his face changed, becoming tighter, the bones more prominent.

Keira watched, awestruck, at the changes in him, her breath taken away by the awesome sight of Luukas at his most formidable.

The manacles on his wrists and ankles began to crack, tiny fissures appearing in the silver. A second later, they burst open, the cuffs and chains disintegrating into dust.

Luukas caught himself in a crouch as he fell, magnificent in his power. His glowing eyes lifted to hers, and his lips pulled back from his fangs in a snarl as he cocked his head at her.

Her heart pounded out of her chest as he slowly rose to his full height, his hunter's gaze never leaving her face.

"Please," she whispered to the cloaked one behind her, "Release me."

Was he even still there?

Searching Luukas' eyes, she tried to find some remnant of the male she'd grown to admire and love. But there was nothing left of him. All she saw was madness in their soulless, black depths.

She wasn't going to survive this time, and so, neither would he.

She briefly closed her eyes, accepting her fate. Maybe they would meet again in the next life.

He stalked her, taking his time, a fearsome smile sneaking across his handsome face.

On impulse, she tried to raise her arm to hold him off, and found that she could move now. Without thinking, she spun around and ran.

Using her magic against him was not an option, no matter what. She couldn't do it.

He was on her in an instant. Grabbing her by the hair, he yanked hard, and she fell back against his hard chest with a cry.

"Where do you think you're going, witch?" he hissed at her.

Tears filled her eyes as she tried to pull away from him, but he had a firm grip on her. Her eyes shot around the room frantically, looking for help, but no one else was there. Even the cloaked one was gone.

Snaking his other arm around her waist, he held her tight against him as he pulled her head to the side, exposing her neck to his view.

She felt a sharp pain and gasped in surprise as he struck without care, sinking his fangs deep within her. He began to drink with strong pulls, and she felt a tug at her loins, her body burning for him even now.

Goosebumps rose on the back of her neck when he moaned in her ear, his body hardening behind her. He splayed his hand across her lower belly and pulled her hips back towards him, and she felt his erection rubbing against her backside.

He drank for so long, she began to wonder if he was just going to drain her dry. But then a surge of hope filled her as he lifted his mouth and gently licked her wounds closed. Maybe it would be ok, maybe he would remember. Maybe he would listen to her now.

"Luukas," she breathed.

Letting go of her hair, he slid his hand around to the front of her throat, and began to squeeze.

Keira gripped his arm, trying to pull it away, but he was way too strong. Stars appeared before her eyes as she struggled to breathe, and she could feel her face heating as the blood pooled in her head.

He lifted her right off the floor, one arm around her waist and his other hand around her throat, holding her face next to his almost affectionately.

His hand tightened even as he gently kissed her temple. "Just like old times, huh? Only this time I won't stop. You won't hurt me ever again, witch."

He was eerily sane in his insanity.

No, this can't be happening! Keira thought. He wouldn't do this! He shouldn't be *capable* of doing this! She was his mate, how was he hurting her?

Unless he'd been pushed too far, beyond the point of being ruled by his instincts.

Unless she *wasn't* his, as he'd proven the night before. He'd been with others. If she were his, he would have no desire to feed from, or fuck, anyone but her.

She kicked her feet, hitting him hard in the shins, but it didn't seem to faze him. She began to struggle in earnest as she fought to remain conscious.

The sounds of her gagging seemed to irritate him, and he tightened his grip around her throat until she could feel her bones bending under the strain.

Holy shit, he was really going to kill her.

Stars appeared before her bulging eyes, and her struggles became weaker and more sporadic.

Luukas put his nose in her hair, inhaling deeply, and then rubbed his face against hers. She felt his tears on her cheek.

"I'll see you in hell, witch," he breathed in her ear. He sounded relieved, satisfied even.

The blackness descended, and Keira knew no more.

34

LUUKAS

Luukas held his arms straight out in front of him. One hand held a severed head by the neck, the long, dark hair drenched in blood. The other held a fistful of white gown, wrapped around a female's form.

Horrified, he dropped the bloody pieces of Keira's body onto the dirt floor.

He had ripped her apart.

What have I done?

Squeezing his eyes shut, he slammed his palms to either side of his head, trying to erase the sight of her, broken at his feet.

The sound of her laughing as he was beaten and sliced open...and *burned*, echoed through his head.

Or had she been crying?

No. This couldn't really be happening. It was just a dream, or a trick, or something.

Warily, he opened his eyes.

She was still there.

"NO! NOOOO!" He doubled over in pain, his arms wrapped around his midsection. "Ah, gods! What have I done?"

Falling to his knees beside her, he gathered her up into his arms, and buried his face in her stomach. "I'm so sorry, my love," he sobbed. "So sorry. So sorry. So sorry..."

He rocked to and fro, repeating the words over and over, feeling his mind begin to crack into so many pieces; it would never be whole again.

Tears ran heedlessly down his face as disjointed ideas raced through his thoughts: ideas that would save her. Gradually, one of them stuck.

Maybe he could heal her. Maybe he could put her together and give her his blood and she would heal.

Yes, his shattered mind thought, *yes. I'll heal her and she'll come back to me. She has to come back to me!*

Laying her gently on the floor again as a whole person, he heard someone enter the room and glanced up to see the cloaked one in the doorway.

"Help me!" he called to him. "Please, help me! I have to heal her...please..." Fussing with her gown, he tried to arrange it so that it covered her decently. He didn't want the other male to see her.

"Help me," he whispered hoarsely.

"She's gone, vampire. It's too late."

Luukas shook his head erratically. "No. No, it's not. You're wrong. I'll save her."

"You killed her."

His hands stilled on her gown.

"Or, did you?"

Luukas frowned. "What?" He looked up, but the evil one was gone.

He stared at the empty doorway, wondering if he'd really been there at all.

It's not going to work.

It will! It has to!

It won't. She's gone. It's what the bitch deserved.

NO! Shut up! Don't say that!

It's too late.

No. Can't hurt her!

Biting his wrist, he ripped opened the vein and pressed it to her mouth. His blood dripped into her mouth, pooling there. When the wound closed, he reopened it and pressed it back to her mouth, rubbing her throat to get her to swallow.

Sitting back on his heels, he waited...his eyes skittering around the room.

And waited...

She didn't wake up. She didn't move.

A keening cry escaped him, growing in volume as he rocked back and forth, his hands gripping his hair. He didn't feel the pain as strands came out in his fingers, didn't feel anything except for the overwhelming anguish of his loss.

He wept, clawing at his body, wanting to escape this internal suffering that was so much worse than anything he'd gone through before. He wept until there was nothing left to feel.

Finally numb, he laid down on the floor beside her, his eyelids heavy as he memorized her lovely profile.

When he felt up to it, he would take her out of this horrid place, and they would wait for the sun to rise.

He smiled. He hadn't felt the sun in over six hundred years. It would burn, but it would be quick.

A peaceful feeling came over him as he lay there beside his witch. His revenge was complete. The darkness was appeased at last. Soon, he would be with his angel again.

The angel's voice came to him through the fog.

"Luukas! You need to wake up!"

He groaned in protest. No, he didn't want to wake up. She wasn't real.

Besides, he knew what he would see when he opened his eyes, knew where he would find himself. He wasn't ready to face that just yet.

"Luukas," she pleaded softly, "Please wake up. I need you."

He wanted to help the angel, but how could he?

It was too late. He'd killed her. He'd overcome the protective instinct for his mate, just like he'd done when he'd killed his Master. That shouldn't have been possible either, but he'd...*overcome.*

"I can't help you," he whispered.

He felt her soft palm on the side of his face, and he cried out, bolting upright.

It wasn't real!

He was only imagining that she was here, wishing she were still alive so strongly that he'd felt her touch.

His witch.

His angel.

Out of the corner of his eye, he saw a flutter of white, and his breath caught in his throat.

Had she moved? No, that wasn't possible.

"Luukas, please look at me," the angel coaxed in a soft voice, like he was a frightened animal.

His stony stare never left the wall directly in front of him. "I don't want to look. Don't make me look!" he told her forcefully.

Her dress moved again, and he squeezed his eyes shut. Pulling his knees up, he crossed his arms and hid his face between them. She was haunting him now. It was no less than he deserved.

"Luukas." This time it came from directly in front of him.

"I'm so sorry!" he cried, still not looking up. "I'm so sorry I hurt you, Keira! So sorry, I..." He couldn't finish the sentence.

"Luukas, it's all right. I'm all right."

He laughed scornfully. "How can you say that? I fucking killed you! Just go away!"

The angel was silent.

Had she gone?

Good.

Except, he didn't want her to leave. He wanted her to stay with him...stay with him while they watched the sun come up and then he could join her wherever she was now.

Lifting his head, he rubbed at his swollen eyes with the heels of his hands. "I didn't mean it! Come back..." He opened his eyes.

Ah, she hadn't left; she was kneeling right in front of him. So close, he could reach out and touch her if he wanted to. He lifted his hand, and then pulled it back again, unsure. Would his touch go right through her?

Yes, it would, because she was fucking dead.

But, he could smell her hair, could smell her blood, her sweet womanly scent.

He fought down the maniacal urge to laugh.

Instead, he let his gaze roam over her long, dark hair and delicate features. He loved her hair. He wished he'd touched it more often. Her hazel eyes seemed even larger than normal, dominating her face as she stared at him with concern. He didn't move away as she reached a hand towards him, hoping beyond hope to feel her touch him again. This time, he barely flinched when her warm fingers grazed his forehead, pushing his hair out of his eyes.

But, how could she touch him?

Maybe he was already dead somehow, and they were doomed to live out their eternal lives here in this hellish place.

That would be ok. He would stay anywhere she was, if she would let him.

He took a shaky breath. "If this is Heaven, or Hell, or somewhere in between, I would like to stay. I know I don't deserve to, but I can't bear to be without you."

She frowned at him. "You're not dead, and neither am I," she told him sternly. "It wasn't real, vampire. None of it was real."

His eyes skittered around the room again before coming back to land on her. He wanted to believe her words, but he knew better.

"I saw you. I held you in my hands, in pieces..." His voice broke, and tears filled his eyes again as he held his shaking hands out between them. "I *saw* you..."

Taking his face in her hands to make him look at her, she shook her head. "No, Luukas, no. You didn't kill me. You stopped in time. You let go of me right before I passed out, and I must've fallen to the floor."

"I don't understand..."

"It was an illusion. It was all an illusion. Well, except you did feed from me and choke me," she admitted off-handedly. "But you stopped! You stopped before you really hurt me."

"An illusion? You didn't...? I saw you!" He squeezed his head in his hands as he tried to make sense of it all.

"No! It wasn't me! I swear to you! It wasn't me! The evil one, the cloaked one...I don't know who, or what, he is...he took me from Seattle. He brought me here and put me in this stupid dress, and hung me on the chains. He's powerful, Luukas. I could do *nothing* against him. Nothing! He made me stand in front of you, made you think it was me hurting you, but it wasn't! I swear on my sister's life, it wasn't! He made you think things were happening to you, but it was all an illusion. Look at yourself. Look!"

"How...?"

"Look at yourself!" she commanded.

He did as she told him, realizing for the first time that there wasn't a mark on him. "I must've healed," he rationalized, but even his clothes were dry and intact.

How could that be? Where was the blood?

A sharp pain shot through his skull as his mind tried to separate fantasy from reality. He didn't know what was real and what wasn't. It was too much!

"Luukas, I need you to get a grip here. I'm so sorry about all of this, but I need you to keep it together. Do you hear me? I can't do this alone. He's too strong."

Stars floated in front of his eyes as his head swam. His mind was trying to shut down, unable to take it all in.

"Luukas," the angel called to him. "Stay with me."

He fought the blackness. Much as he would like to surrender to its peaceful sleep, his angel needed him.

Swaying where he sat, he shook his head. "You can't be real. I saw you, Keira. I saw you...broken..."

"Look at me, vampire." She took his face in her hands again. "I'm here. I'm real. It's ok."

He studied her closely, trying to discern if she was, indeed, real. There were fading bruises on her neck. Why would they be fading before his eyes?

I gave her my blood. He answered his own question.

His eyes widened as she leaned towards him, capturing his lips with her own.

"I'm here," she whispered, kissing him again.

A small sob escaped him as he kissed her back.

Please, let this be real!

Wrapping his arms around her, he leaned back and pulled her down on top of him, feeling the weight of her body settle into his. Her soft curves crushed against him, and he hugged her tight, kissing her lips, her jaw...her beautiful eyes. He nuzzled her neck, inhaling her sweet scent.

How could I smell her if she wasn't real?

His body hardened at the feel of her, his fangs slid down and his gums ached at the scent of her, his mouth watered at the thought of tasting her. Running his hands down her back, he cupped her plump ass, grinding himself up into her softness. Her flesh was firm and supple under her thin gown, and warm, so very warm.

How could I feel her if she wasn't real?

She groaned in his ear, pulling her knees up to straddle him.

"Luukas..."

Finding the hem of her dress, he hiked it up around her hips while she balanced herself on her elbows on either side of his head. Slipping his hands underneath the silky material, he ran his palms up her smooth thighs and over her behind. One arm encircled her back, holding her close against him as his other hand reached down and found her wet folds from behind.

She gasped as he slipped a finger inside of her. Pulling it out, he replaced it with two fingers, stretching her, feeling her muscles grasp him as he tried to remove them.

He moaned into her neck as he felt her respond to him.

Sitting up with her on his lap, he never took his eyes from her face as he undid his jeans and pulled himself out. Her skin was flushed and damp, her eyes were wide and her mouth was open slightly. He glanced down at her full breasts, straining against the material of her gown, the low neckline giving him quite a view. His cock throbbed in his hand, and he groaned, wanting to be inside of her. *Needing* to be inside of her.

She lifted herself and held her gown up with one hand so he could place himself at her entrance.

As soon as he was there, he wrapped both arms around her and thrust inside.

She hid her face between his neck and shoulder with a groan, her arms wrapped around him, gripping his T-shirt.

"Look at me, Keira," he ordered fiercely. "I need to see you."

She raised her head, and he locked his eyes on hers. With his hands on her hips, he lifted her up and down. She was so tight, and so fucking wet, and real or not, he'd never felt anything like being inside of this female.

But how could she not be real? He could *feel* her! Was it all true then, what she'd said?

Breathing hard, she threw her head back as he thrust harder and faster. "Luukas...I'm going to come!" she exclaimed softly.

At her words, an animalistic growl escaped him. Quickly flipping her over onto her back, he kept an arm around her, arching her into him as he pounded into her. Sinking his fangs into her throat, his orgasm hit him fast and hard, his shout muffled against her skin. Her cries mingled with his as she joined him. He felt her pulsing around him, demanding everything from him, and he gave it to her.

He lay still for a long time, catching his breath, until he finally worked up the nerve to roll off of her, afraid of what he would see underneath him.

Afraid he really had gone mad.

But she smiled up at him, touching his face.

He kissed her palm, briefly closing his eyes in relief.

"See?" she said. "I'm really real. But Luukas..."

He'd been running his eyes, and his hand, along her body, reassuring himself that she was, in fact, still alive and unhurt, but lifted his eyes to hers at her tone.

"We really need to get out of here."

He nodded in agreement.

"Are you all right?" she asked as she got up off of the floor.

No. "Yes," he told her firmly. Getting up, he re-fastened his jeans.

She smiled and took his hand. "Then let's get the hell out of here."

He pulled her back to him when she went to walk away, and gave her a stern look.

"You're never leaving my sight again, witch," he informed her harshly.

She smiled at him happily. "I know." Then she narrowed her eyes. "The same goes for you, vampire."

Ah, yes. He had some explaining to do, but it would have to wait.

35

KEIRA

Keira followed Luukas up the stairs and through the tunnels. They moved as swiftly and as quietly as they could. They'd be able to move much faster if he carried her, but she'd insisted on walking. She wanted his hands to be free, just in case. Barefoot, she jogged behind him, trying to avoid the worst of the rocky terrain.

She kept an eye on him as they traversed the tunnels back out the way he'd come in. He seemed ok, all things considered. Was he really ok?

She wasn't sure.

No, he was strong, inside and out. He'd be fine.

She hoped.

Guilt wracked her once more. She should never have left the apartment like that. She should've known that Leeha wouldn't just let them go. It was stupid of her not to think of that. She'd made it so easy for them to get him to come here again, and she didn't understand why he was being so damn nice to her. If she were him, she would hate her.

Instead, he held her hand tightly, glancing back every now and then, like he was reassuring himself that she was truly there. She would squeeze his hand, and he'd look ahead, only to check her out again a few seconds later. She felt his uncertainty, but didn't know what else she could do to convince him she wasn't dead. It would just take time, she supposed.

And maybe some other people interacting with her in front of him.

It seemed to take much longer to find their way this time, and every time they turned a corner, she expected a gang of Leeha's monsters to be waiting for them. But they didn't see anything other than a few rats scurrying along the edge of the tunnel floor.

Luukas slowed as they approached the main cathedral room, pulling Keira up close behind him. Cautiously, he peered around the corner of the hole in the wall, listening carefully.

Out of breath, she put her face against his back, trying to muffle her heavy breathing. The muscles under her cheek suddenly tensed.

She supposed it would've been too much to ask for them to have gotten out undetected.

Straightening up, she tried to pull her hand from his, but he held on tight. She wondered who was out there, and how they were going to get by them. If it was those ugly creatures, it should be easy. She could zap the ones coming from behind while Luukas cleared the way in front of them. No problem.

Peeking around his arm, she tried to see who or what was making her vampire stiffen up like he was. She searched what she could see of the room, frowning, but no one was there.

She heard the raven at the same time she felt it: The evil presence of the cloaked one.

Flattening her back against the wall behind Luukas, her mind spun as she tried to think of another plan. It was too late to retreat. He knew they were there just as they could tell he was. There was no way they could sneak out without him knowing, and as far as she knew, the tunnel on the other side of the room was the only exit. Even if they tried to backtrack, they would be trapped.

There was no other choice. They would have to fight.

Bracing herself, she stepped up beside Luukas. When he noticed her there, he looked at her in alarm. But then he nodded once, a firm resolve stealing his features.

Together, they stepped out into the room.

The cloaked one was slouched on Leeha's throne, one jean-clad leg thrown over the arm, his raven perched on one forearm as he scratched her head with his other hand. He didn't so much as look up when they entered the room, but she knew he was aware they were there.

Giving the bird one final scratch, he exclaimed, "Finally! It took you two forever to get here." Whispering something to the raven, he lifted her to the back of the throne, where she perched with a sound of protest.

Luukas pulled Keira slightly behind him, and she let him. Because honestly? She was pretty damn scared right now.

Luukas' deep voice echoed throughout the cavernous room. "You could just let us go. That would be the wise choice."

He rose from the throne to his full height. "Wise for whom? For me?" He laughed. "No, vampire. I'm afraid I can't do that. You see, I promised Leeha that I would not let you go without a fight, in return for letting me keep something that she's recently acquired. It was a fair deal, and I never go back on my promises."

"So, where is Leeha?" Luukas asked. "Running away, like the coward she truly is?"

He just smiled. "She had...other things to attend to."

They stood their ground as he casually descended the stairs. He reminded Keira of a monk with his hooded cloak, his hands tucked up into the sleeves - an evil, black-clad monk, whose religion was something unlike anything she'd ever seen before. He had magic, like her, she could feel it in the air. But it was also something more. She couldn't put her finger on it. All she knew was that he frightened her. Frightened her more than any other being she'd ever come across before.

She was worried that Luukas wasn't up to a battle of the magnitude it would surely take for them to have *any* chance at all of escaping this one. And she already knew her magic alone was not enough to defeat him, as he'd proven to her so easily when he'd taken her off of the street. Powerful as her magic was, it was like a child's toy compared to his. He could also communicate with that raven, and read her mind, if his smirking earlier was any indication.

He stopped in the middle of the room. "So, cousin, are you going to hide behind your male? Or are you going to live up to the family name and show us what you're really made of?"

She stepped out from behind Luukas. "Why do you keep calling me 'cousin'? I'm no cousin of yours."

Crossing his arms in front of him, his tone indicating that he didn't really need to ask, he inquired, "You're Keira Moss, aren't you? Of the notorious Moss family of witches?" He answered his own question, "Of course you are. You have a sister, Emma, and both of your parents are dead." He lowered his head respectfully, "Rest In Peace Aunt and Uncle." He raised his head again. "Your family is quite well known, in spite of the fact that they ran off from our corrupt coven, or actually, because they had the balls to do just that. You come from a long line of potent witches, Keira. And believe it or not, I'm a part of that line. That," he gave a small shrug, "And more. Although I have to say, I was rather disappointed in how easy it was for me to suppress your magic when I pulled you into the van. I mean, come on! Oh, and earlier in the cell. What was that all about? You barely even put up a fight. Either one of you! What's up with that?" He seemed to genuinely want to know.

Luukas walked forward, not stopping until they were toe to toe. Slightly taller and broader, her vampire looked down at him.

"Why don't you try me now?" he challenged.

She stayed back where she was, watching, waiting for her chance to act. It wouldn't be effective if he saw it coming. He would just hold her, impotent, as he had before, and her magic would be useless. But if she could catch him at just the right time...

"What are you going to do, vampire? Hmm? The only thing I can recall you ever doing is screaming," he taunted.

A shiver ran over Keira as the temperature dropped, the air becoming eerily still, like Luukas.

The calm before the storm.

An intimidating growl made the hair stand up on her arms as he clenched his hands into fists at his sides. Without warning, he hauled back his right arm and swung, moving so fast the cloaked one had no time to react. Luukas' fist cracked into his jaw, sending him spinning to the floor.

He jumped to his feet, spitting out blood, his hood knocked askew. He pushed it off of his head impatiently, revealing dark hair that curled at his nape. Golden eyes flashed dangerously as he wiped his mouth with the back of his hand.

"So that's how we're going to play it?" He laughed then. "A master vampire, brought so low that he's resorting to a fist fight, like a couple of high school kids. Or are you just afraid?

Afraid that you're not the all-powerful being you think you are?"

He paced back and forth in front of Luukas, never taking his eyes from his foe. "Yes, I think that's exactly what it is. You're afraid, because you know you're not the male you used to be before all of this. And you know what? I think you're right. The Luukas Kreek I'd always heard about was infamous for his daring deeds, and for his great power. No one dared to go up against him. 'The most powerful Master vampire of his time', they say."

He stopped directly in front of Luukas again, sneering, "I don't see that vampire here. All I see is an insecure male, one not worthy of my cousin. I think she needs to find another mate. One who will be able to protect her. One who is worthy of her. One who is worth her time! And her love!"

Throughout all of this, Luukas had stood frozen, following the cloaked one with his eyes as he paced the floor. His lips twitching back off of his fangs and his clenched jaw the only indication that his words were affecting him.

Keira felt her blood pressure rise as he taunted Luukas. It was like he was in his head, exposing every doubt, every fear. How dare he! When he and his bitch, Leeha, were the ones who had done this to him!

Pressing her lips into a thin line, she widened her stance, planting her feet solidly on the floor.

She'd had *enough*.

Never taking her eyes from his black-cloaked form, she began to chant quietly but firmly.

It didn't take long for him to notice. Abruptly, he stopped talking, and his head whipped towards her. He looked genuinely pleased.

"Ah, cousin. You've joined the fight at last! Good thing too. Between you and me, I'm kinda worried about this one," he indicated Luukas with a tilt of his head.

In response, she chanted louder, feeling the earth's energy empower her. Suddenly, she threw out her right hand and made an upward slashing motion.

The cloaked one was thrown up into the air and then body slammed to the floor. Rolling to the side, he barely avoided the large piece of rubble from the broken wall she hurtled at the spot where his head had been. It smashed onto the floor, shards of rock flying in all directions.

The raven flapped her wings, her worried voice adding to the commotion as she paced the top of the throne.

Rising quickly to his feet again, he threw up both hands, slamming Keira into the wall behind her. "And that was your *one* chance, cousin."

Her head slammed against rock, and she felt a wetness seeping through her hair. Sliding her hands and feet until they were flush against the wall, she closed her eyes and drew on every ounce of her magic. With a shout, she broke his hold and pushed off of the wall, landing on her feet. Without pause, she ran for cover behind a large portion of the wall that was still erect.

Breathing hard, she felt the back of her head. Her hand came away bloody.

Dammit.

Luukas had better snap the hell out of it, and soon, or they were in big trouble.

36

LUUKAS

Shame filled Luukas as the cloaked one's humiliating words echoed in his head. He tried to deny the feeling, telling himself it wasn't true! He did deserve her! He *was* good enough for her! But in his heart of hearts, he couldn't deny the truth of those words, and it froze him where he stood, unable to react or defend himself.

However, as soon as Keira went flying into the wall, Luukas came alive: the words, the shame, all of it forgotten.

Mine.

Spinning on his heel, he came up behind the cloaked one as he strode past him, heading directly towards his female. With a flick of his hand, he sent him flying backwards, away from her hiding place. He landed on his back at the bottom of the stairs, and Luukas flew across the room, landing on top of him as he slid across the floor.

Fangs bared, he grabbed him by the shoulders, lifting his exposed throat to his mouth with a feral snarl.

But before he could latch onto the bastard, he was being lifted up and off of him and thrown across the room.

Out of the corner of his eye, he saw a white blur as Keira came running from her hiding place to help him.

"No! Keira! Stay back!" But she paid him no heed.

His eyes widened with fear for her. But there was no need. She was stunning in her sorcery, her hair blowing about her face, her eyes lit from within, as she floated towards the male still on the floor. Chanting words he didn't understand, she sent a barrage of weapons flying at him.

Pieces of stone she couldn't possibly lift flew through the air past her and rained from the ceiling as she gutted the place. The cloaked one was trapped at the bottom of the stairs as it piled around him, burying him underneath it all. He'd had no time to react.

She stopped about twenty feet away from the pile, her chest heaving with her exertions.

Luukas rose slowly to his feet across the room from her.

Even the raven was quiet.

"Keira," he whispered.

She turned to look at him, her eyes huge and anxious in her lovely face.

"Come here," he ordered quietly but firmly. The tunnel out of there was closer to him than her. He reached out a hand towards her. "Come here," he repeated, a little louder.

She nodded, but then turned back to the pile of rocks, a frown marring her lovely face.

He felt it just as she turned to look at him in fear.

The room began to shake as the raven took to the air. Shrieking, she flew in circles around the rubble. Dust and small rocks started to slide down the sides.

"Keira!" he bellowed.

He headed towards her, and she turned to run to him, stumbling as the tremors became stronger, throwing her off balance.

She fell to her knees, and scrambled to get back up, but before she could, the pile of stone exploded from within. With a cry, she dropped to the floor and covered her head with her arms.

Luukas ducked, barely avoiding the flying debris. Staying low, he ran towards her, desperate to reach her and get them the fuck out of there.

But he was too late.

With a roar, the cloaked one leapt from the remains of stone, landing between him and Keira. Grabbing her by the ankle, he angrily flung her upwards as if she weighed little more than a stuffed doll. She screamed as she flew through the air, flying up a hundred feet to slam into the pointed arches of the cathedral-like ceiling.

Luukas skidded to a halt as she stayed up there, splayed out like a butterfly stuck in glue.

The cloaked one spun around to face him. "Now, where were we, vampire?"

In a flash, Luukas was on him. His fists flew as he pounded on him, needing the release of physically hitting the son of a bitch. He managed to land a few good hits before he was thrown back with a motion of his opponent's hand.

Landing on his feet, he advanced again. They prowled around each other, eyeing each other up, searching for weaknesses.

Luukas was the first to attack.

Leaping through the air, he came down from above with bared fangs, determined to rip the son of a bitch's head from his body. But fast as he could move, the cloaked one was just as fast, blocking him and flinging him back through the air.

Luukas jumped to his feet, about to attack again, when a buzzing noise filled his head and a blinding pain exploded behind his eyes.

"Ahhhh!!" He slammed his hands to his head, falling to his knees. Knives were stabbing through his skull, made worse by Keira's screams from above as she hung there helpless.

Gritting his teeth, he looked up with crazed eyes to find the cloaked one quickly approaching him, his hood pulled back up to hide his face. The raven landed on his shoulder, squawking into his ear as he stormed purposely towards Luukas to impart the finishing blow.

As Luukas watched, he raised his hands, curling them towards each other like he was holding a ball in between them.

Or a head.

The pressure increased as he watched him push his hands closer together, until he thought his skull was going to implode. Falling to the side, he rolled onto his back as the cloaked one stood over him. He squeezed his eyes shut in anguish as he felt blood dripping from his ears, the buzzing in his head growing louder every second.

"Luukas!!"

Keira's scream broke through the noise and pain.

"Luukas! Get up! Get up!"

Yes, he must get up. He must help her.

Calling on the life forces of all those he had created flowing through his veins, he fought back against the constriction in his head.

He was *not* weak. He was *not* unworthy.

The mountain shuddered around them as he released the full potential of his essence, fighting off the cloaked one's black magic. Slowly, steadily, he rose to his full height. Lowering his hands from his head, he threw a small blast of power at the cloaked one, knocking him off balance. It wasn't much, but it was enough to break his concentration, and Luukas felt the pressure and noise in his head ease up immediately.

In its place, he allowed all the pent up pain and suffering he'd experienced the last seven years rise up within him. It possessed him completely, until he was little more than an animal, protecting what was his.

Debris fell from the ceiling as the slender columns leading up to the arches shook in their bases. Fissures appeared in the dark, stone walls as Luukas stalked forward, his prey firmly in his sights.

The cloaked one backed up slowly, glancing around at the crumbling cavern. When he reached the steps, he stopped, and waited for Luukas.

Suddenly, the mountain groaned loudly, shifting on its foundation. A loud booming noise came from behind Luukas, like thunder, and he turned to find the floor opening up as the ground shifted.

The crack snaked along, breaking the tiles until it crossed the entire room. It was at least twenty feet across, effectively cutting him off from the exit.

His attention diverted, the cloaked one took advantage of the opportunity to send a forceful push his way, sending him feet first over the edge of the chasm in the middle of the room. Twisting around, he barely caught the edge in time, halting his flight. Looking down, he tried to see how far down it went. He couldn't see the bottom, even with his vampire sight.

Gripping the sides with the toes of his boots, he vaulted back up over the side, springing to his feet just in time to block the large rock flying at his head.

With a snarl, he launched himself at the cloaked one, taking him down to the floor. They rolled towards the stairs, each trying to get the upper hand. Luukas found himself on the bottom when they stopped, and pain wracked his jaw as a solid punch landed there, followed by another, and another.

Although he was a bit larger, the cloaked one was powerful. Too powerful for a normal human, too powerful even for a witch. But Luukas had no time to think more of it as he threw his arms up to protect his face. Heaving his body to the side, he managed to buck him off, and they both jumped to their feet.

The cloaked one began to back away. Luukas stalked him with glowing eyes.

Pushing his hood back, he smiled as he reached the edge of the crack, blood running from his mouth and nose. "Leeha's really gonna be pissed that you broke her fortress."

Glancing up at Keira, he wished her farewell, "Until we meet again, cousin."

Then without warning, he stepped back over the edge, the raven taking flight off of his shoulder as he fell into the chasm. She swooped in a circle before following him down with a loud call.

Luukas looked up just as Keira, released from his spell, suddenly started to fall facedown towards the floor. Reacting quickly, he flew to the edge of the chasm.

She was going to fall right into it.

Backing up a few steps, he got a running start and pushed off the edge of the floor, colliding with her mid-air and taking her with him to the other side, landing on his feet. Adjusting her in his arms, he didn't stop, but took off at full vamp speed towards the exit tunnel.

He had a horrible sense of déjà vu as he ran through the mountain, his angel in his arms. Only this time, she was awake and clinging to him tightly, and the tunnel was collapsing behind him as he rushed towards the sound of the creek and the way out.

He saw light ahead. The cave opening! He was going to make it!

Wait. Light?

No, no, no! The sun was up!

He skidded to a halt just out of reach of the beams of light. Spinning around to face the direction he'd just come from, he watched with horrified eyes as the cave walls shook, and large rocks broke off from the walls and ceiling to fall into the creek with a splash.

His heart pounding, he spun back around. The SUV was too far. They'd never make it.

Fuck! Fuck!

Wait. There was an outcropping of rock not far from the entrance that they may be able to take shelter in. Question was, would he make it there before bursting into flame, for real this time? It would only take a second for him to combust.

"Luukas!" Keira yelled. "Put me down!"

He realized that she was struggling in his arms, and he held her tighter. "I'm going to try to make those rocks!" he shouted over the noise of the cave-in.

Keira followed the direction he indicated with his chin, and her eyes grew wide with fear.

"You'll never make it! No, Luukas! Put me down!"

She fought him violently until he had no choice but to put her down or hurt her. Wasting no time, she stepped around him to face the cave-in, planted her bare feet firmly in the earth, and raised her arms.

Even though she was shouting at the top of her lungs, he could barely hear her chanting above the mountain's rumbling.

He would give her exactly 20 seconds. If nothing was happening, he was grabbing her and making a run for it.

Suddenly, more rock started falling closer around them, landing just in front of Keira. Panicking, he went to grab her around the waist and take her with him, but no sooner had his hands touched her than he was shot backwards through the air and into the wall next to the entrance. A shaft of sunlight hit his arm, and he yanked it closer to his body, slapping out the flames.

Charging forward, he was again thrown away from her, crashing into the wall with a grunt.

He was getting really fucking tired of being thrown through the air.

Adrenaline rushed through his system as more rock fell around them, and he was about to go for her again when he noticed something strange.

The rock falling around them wasn't just falling randomly; it was creating a half-circle around them, a protective igloo between them and the crumbling mountain. The witch was directing the falling stone, creating a pocket right by the entrance to the cave, leaving a small opening to the outside for them to leave through once the sun went down.

Exhausted, Luukas slid down the wall to sit on the ground as far from the rays of the shining sun as he could.

When the last rock was in place around them, Keira lowered her arms and checked out her handiwork.

Looking over her shoulder at him, she gave him a radiant smile, and his breath left his lungs with a *whoosh!* at the sight.

His strong, beautiful witch.

His angel.

She was saving them.

The daylight pulled him down, and exhausted from all he'd just gone through, Luukas closed his eyes and gave in to sleep.

His last thought before he slept was of a dark-haired enchantress, with bright eyes and a seductive smile.

37

KEIRA

Keira watched Luukas sleep, his head on her lap. Gently pushing his soft hair off of his face, she let her gaze wander over his handsome features. Relaxed in slumber, he looked young, much too young to have been through all he had.

She hadn't slept much herself, only managing to doze a bit. She'd been too worried about him. Fighting back a sob, she looked out at the increasing shadows. The sun was finally setting.

She'd been crying most of the day, overcome with all that had happened now that she had time to stop and think about it. She hated crying. Her eyes burned, and she knew they must be red and swollen.

Fed up with herself and her self-thrown pity party, she swiped at the tears with the heel of her hand impatiently.

The temperature was dropping and she shivered, wishing she had the clothes back that she'd been wearing when she'd arrived here. Guess they hadn't been dramatic enough for Leeha's little production, hence the white slip of a gown she'd been wrestled into.

Luukas began to stir on her lap, interrupting her thoughts, and she bit her lip, waiting anxiously for him to wake. His eyes fluttered open, and she found herself staring into twin pools of bright silver.

Silver! Not black!

"Hey there," she whispered with a watery smile.

Lifting a hand, he gently touched her face, his startling eyes searching hers, his features creased with concern.

Suddenly, he sat up and jumped to his feet. Reaching down, he pulled Keira up beside him. "We need to get out of here."

She agreed whole-heartedly, following him out into the semi-darkness.

He helped her into the vehicle and buckled her up. Speeding over to his side, he got in and did the same. Retrieving the keys from their hiding place, he cranked the engine, threw it into reverse, turned it around, and peeled out of there.

Neither spoke until they were back on the main road.

"Luukas?"

"Hmm?" he responded, checking the rearview mirror again.

"Are you all right?" Stupid question, she knew, but she couldn't stop herself from asking it.

He glanced at her out of the corner of his eye. "Maybe. Eventually."

She stared out the front windshield. "Do you hate me?"

A few moments passed, before he quietly told her. "I did."

Did that mean he didn't anymore?

She studied his profile, but his expression gave nothing away, and she was afraid to delve any farther into that answer.

They rode in silence for a long time after that, getting through the border with no issues. Keira had so many things she wanted to say, so many questions, but she didn't want to overwhelm him. So she sat quietly, watching the scenery go by, feeling more alone and unsure than she ever had in her life.

They were traveling down an isolated stretch of I-5 when Luukas suddenly jerked the car over to the side of the road, slamming on the breaks and skidding to a halt.

Keira gripped the dashboard, her heart pounding in her chest. "What's the matter? What is it?"

Turning the engine off, he sat staring straight ahead into the darkness.

"Luukas? What's wrong?"

"I don't hate you," he finally told her, turning to look at her. "I don't hate you, Keira."

"But, how could you not...after everything..."

"I *don't* hate you. Not now, not anymore. When I saw you lying there, and I was convinced I'd given in to the darkness in my mind..." Gritting his teeth, he swallowed hard and looked straight ahead again, staring into the night. "I'd never felt such pain. *Never*," he ground out. "Nothing that you had ever done to me even came close to the torment I felt when I thought I had lost you. When I thought I had...killed...you."

A glimmer of hope blossomed in her as he spoke.

"And I realize now," he continued, his voice harsh with emotion, "That I never want to feel like that again." His eyes blazed through her as he turned to look at her intently. Lifting a hand towards her, he picked up a strand of her hair, brushing her breast with the backs of his fingers. Her breath hitched in her chest, his brief touch sending a bolt of electricity through her.

"I know I'm not a male that you would imagine yourself being with. I'm broken, Keira, and I don't know if I'll ever be whole again. But, I would like to ask you to stay...just *stay*. I know it won't be easy, but I need you. My very *soul* aches for you, even now, when you're sitting right beside me. Please, I'm asking you. Stay with me."

"Luukas, I don't know what to say..."

"Say that you will. Say that you'll stay with me. I can't promise that I'll ever be completely right again, I can't promise you anything, except that I will always take care of you the best that I can."

Tears filled her eyes again. Unbuckling her seatbelt, she hiked up her dress and crawled across the console and onto his lap. Taking his face in her hands, she kissed him soundly. His tentative smile tore at her heart, and she relished the feeling of his strong arms coming around her to hold her close.

"I don't deserve this," she confessed. "But I'll take you anyway. I love you, vampire. I've wanted to tell you for so long. I've loved you since the first moment I saw you." Her face clouded with the memory. "And I'm so sorry..." Her voice broke as she tried to voice her feelings.

He took her head firmly between his hands and forced her to look up at him. "Stop that now. I understand why you did what you did. We'll work through it."

"What if we can't?" she asked forlornly.

"We will," he declared firmly. "Because I love you also, witch. I don't ever want to be without you."

"Then you're going to need to stop running off to other women," she scolded.

His eyes burned steadily into hers. "I did not have sex with anyone that night, Keira. I was trying to prove that this 'mate' business was nothing but a bunch of bullshit."

"And what did you find out?" she asked, genuinely curious.

"I discovered that it was true, I couldn't drink from anyone else. I tried."

Jealousy burned through her at the thought of him embracing other women, whether it worked out or not was a moot point.

"Keira, look at me."

She did so, reluctantly.

"I was a fool. Mate or not, there is no one else for me, witch."

Pulling her face to him, he took her lips roughly, possessively, until she was squirming on his lap with need.

Releasing her face, he gripped her by the back of the neck with one hand, continuing to kiss her while skimming the other down over her breast. He hefted its weight in his palm, rolling the nipple between his fingers, before continuing down and around to her side to grip her hip.

Her blood pounded through her veins, and her belly clenched as she felt him growing hard underneath her backside. She ran her hands over his hard chest and shoulders, wrapping her arms around him and holding him tightly to her.

"Luukas," she managed to get out breathlessly between kisses. "We need to get home."

He growled with displeasure. "I want to take you, right now."

Her insides turned to jelly at his words, desire pooling between her thighs. Who was she to deny him after all she'd put him through?

But no, she wanted to get home to his apartment, where they would both feel safe.

"I want that too," she told him, her voice husky with desire. "But I'd rather do it at your place, where it's safe."

He pulled his head out of her neck where he'd been scraping his fangs erotically against her skin, and nodded. "Ok, yeah. Let's go home."

Lifting her back to her seat, he re-buckled her and started the engine. With one last, smoldering look at her, he pulled onto the road and headed home.

She smiled when he wouldn't release her hand, but insisted on holding it all the way there.

38

LUUKAS

They arrived back at the apartment in record time, and Luukas whipped into his parking space, barely putting the car in park before turning it off and jumping out to go retrieve his witch from the opposite seat.

Grabbing her out of her seat, he threw her over his shoulder as she squealed with delight, and hauled her effortlessly up to his apartment, closing the broken door behind them.

He really needed to get that fixed. Later.

Without breaking stride, he hightailed it straight to the bedroom, where he set her gently on her feet in front of him.

She gazed up at him with wide eyes, and for the first time since he'd known her, she seemed nervous.

"I'd really like to get cleaned up," she said.

"Why?"

"Why?" she repeated. "Look at me!"

He did. She stood barefoot, in that horrible white gown. Her hair was wild and tousled around her face and over her shoulders. Her eyes were large and bright, her skin flushed. Her full breasts heaved, about to burst from her dress at any moment. And there was a smudge of dirt on her cheek.

She was absolutely lovely.

Shaking his head no, he smiled at her shocked expression.

"No-o?" she asked.

"No," he affirmed.

And then she smiled that dazzling smile that never failed to bewitch him. "All right, but I have to get out of this damned gown."

He returned her smile. "Yes, you do." Taking a handful of material in each hand at the neckline, he promptly tore it down the middle while she giggled, pushing it off of her shoulders until she stood gloriously naked before him.

His smile faded as he slowly ran his eyes from her face to her small feet and back again. She stood unashamed of her nudity, her arms at her sides, her nipples puckering under the heat of his stare. The scent of her desire rose in the air around him, mingling with the delicious scent of her blood, and he hardened with anticipation as his fangs punched down, more eager than ever to have her.

Yanking his shirt over his head, he pulled it off and threw it to the side, enjoying the way her eyes immediately went to the muscles of his chest and abs. The tip of her tongue wet her lips as she looked her fill of him.

His breath hitched as she laid her palm over his heart. Slowly, she ran her hand over his chest, skimming his nipples, and then down his firm abs. His muscles clenched everywhere she touched him, and he dropped his head back with pleasure.

When she reached the waistline of his jeans, she slid her fingers underneath it as far as she could reach, and stroked the skin of his lower belly. His cock strained upwards from where it lay, wanting her touch, and he nearly lost it when she ran her thumb over it on the outside of his jeans.

"Enough," he growled out.

Taking her hand in his, he pulled it out of his pants and lifted it to his mouth. Turning it palm up, he kissed the center of her palm, and continued to place soft kisses down to her wrist. Lifting his eyes to her face, he watched her expression as he sank his fangs into the veins there.

Her lips parted and her eyes widened with shock, only to soften with desire when he began to drink.

His other hand curled around her hip, pulling her closer to him and fondling her plump ass. He needed to feel her skin against his.

Licking the wound closed on her wrist, he released it. Draping her arms around his neck, he leaned down and kissed her, running both hands up her back and down over her ass, slipping one between her thighs to feel her wet heat.

He moaned against her lips when she parted her legs to give him better access. Pulling her up into him, he parted her with his fingers, finding her clitoris, and flicked it gently.

She moaned, biting his lip, and tilted her hips towards him, rubbing herself against his throbbing cock.

Breaking off their kiss, he pulled away from her to undo his jeans. Reaching inside, he pulled his aching cock out.

"Touch me," he begged her hoarsely.

She complied eagerly, wrapping her hand around his thick girth. Giving him a small squeeze, she ran her hand up and down his length. He jerked in her small palm, and a drop of moisture oozed from the tip.

Dropping to her knees, she tasted it with her tongue before taking him fully into her mouth. He groaned as she did so, watching as she slid him in and out between her pink lips, and he felt himself get impossibly harder.

His hands dove into her hair to stop her, "No, witch. I want to love you." Grabbing her by the upper arms, he helped her rise and then backed her towards the bed. "I want to make you come," he told her as he lowered her onto the bed. "And then I want to push inside of your tightness, and lose myself in you until you come again."

"Ah, gods..." she whimpered.

Quickly divesting himself of his boots and jeans, he joined her on the bed, lowering himself over her.

He groaned in pleasure as he felt her arms and legs wrap around him, pulling him down to her. Lifting her hips, she rubbed herself against him, but he had something else in mind.

Lacing his fingers in hers, he held her arms down on either side of her as he kissed her neck, working his way down to her breasts.

"Luukas! Please..." she begged.

Letting go of her hands, he gripped her ribs as he nipped at her nipples, laving one with his tongue, and then the other. Going back to the first one, he sucked it into his mouth, sinking his fangs into her areola as she cried out.

Ah, the taste of her! He'd never had blood like hers. It flowed into him like an angel's essence, invigorating him, healing him; bringing him back to life.

Licking her wounds closed, he kissed his way over to her other breast as she gripped his hair, breathing hard. Pulling that nipple into his mouth as he did the first, he bit it lightly, and then flicked it with his tongue.

She arched her back as he kissed a path across her soft belly, and lower still, until he found her soft curls. Burying his nose in her, he inhaled her scent, his mouth watering, dying to taste her.

Spreading her thighs with his hands, he settled in between them. She glistened before him, wet and ready. Parting her with his fingers, he exposed her even further to his greedy gaze, growling with displeasure when she attempted to close her legs.

Before she could protest more, he ran his tongue up her silky folds, closing his eyes in pleasure.

Her hips bucked towards his mouth when he pulled away, teasing her, and he went down on her again, running his tongue between the satiny folds. Finding her clit, he flicked it with his tongue, rejoicing in the soft sounds she made. They were the most beautiful things he'd ever heard.

Skimming one hand down her inner thigh, he slid a finger deep inside of her, then back out. Continuing his assault with his tongue, he inserted two fingers, and began sliding them in and out of her, coaxing her to climax. She strained towards him, her hands in his hair. He could feel her pleasure, and it turned him on even more.

He felt her begin to tremble, and he quickened his pace with his tongue and fingers. Feeling she was on the brink, he sucked her hard bud into his mouth, and bit her. She cried out as he sank his fangs in her, her sweet blood mixing with her orgasm as she crashed over the edge, pulsing around his fingers.

He growled low in his throat. He wanted to feel her pulsing around his cock.

39

KEIRA

Keira had no time to recover before Luukas was flipping her over onto her stomach. Gripping her hips, he pulled them up and back until she lay on her elbows with her ass in the air.

He squeezed her cheeks, kneading them in his large palms. Sliding towards the center, he inserted both thumbs inside of her, and she pushed her hips back towards him, wanting more.

His thumbs disappeared, and then she felt him pushing at her entrance.

Desire clenched low in her belly again. Gripping her hips, he thrust deep inside with a moan of pleasure, his size making her cry out.

"Keira?"

"Don't stop!" she cried.

He didn't.

With a loud groan, he began to move, thrusting in and out of her. He was so large; he filled her completely, touching her womb. She'd never felt so completely possessed by another person.

"I want you to come again. I'm not going to last long," he gritted through his teeth.

Reaching down, she touched herself, rubbing her clit as he pounded into her from behind. Not stopping, he leaned down over her, and sank his fangs into the muscle between her shoulder and her neck.

Keira cried out, pulses of desire shooting out from her core as she came.

Wrapping his arms around her, he pulled her upright as he slammed into her, his mouth at her neck. Each draw he took sent bolts of heat through her, her orgasm going on and on.

With a roar, he threw his head back, and she felt him pulsing inside of her as he pushed himself in to the hilt.

Collapsing onto the bed, he pulled her down with him, tucking her up against the front of him and curling around her.

They lay there for a long time as he lazily ran his hand up her thigh, over her hip, and back again.

"So, um." Keira peered back over her shoulder at him. "Do you think I could get that shower now?"

She yelped when he smacked her on the ass.

"In a bit, witch. I want to love you again first."

"Again?" she squeaked.

"Yes. Again," he confirmed.

A week and a half later, Keira was in the kitchen making a bite to eat. Looking over towards the office, she smiled to see Luukas scowling over something or another having to do with his many businesses.

It was good to see him scowl. It was when he stood at the window for hours on end that she became concerned.

At those times, she would put down whatever she was doing, and distract him by whatever means necessary.

Sometimes, he would look down at her, and the darkness would flash in his eyes. But she would smile, and touch him, and talk to him about nonsensical things. He would blink, and she would see the darkness in him fading, then he would pick her up and take her into the bedroom. He would make love to her desperately, losing himself in her, and it would calm him again.

As for her, she practiced her craft when he was working, and worried about her sister. They hadn't heard anything from Nik since he'd left. Of course, it would help if Luukas would get the phones fixed.

Suddenly, the front door crashed open, and Nikulas came flying into the room. Spotting Keira in the kitchen, he strolled over to the stools and took a seat.

"What's up?" he asked casually.

She noticed he looked even hotter than he had before. Healthier. That could only mean...

"Where's my sister?" she demanded.

"Right here!"

Emma stood at the end of the counter, smiling a ridiculous smile.

"Emma..." Keira breathed. Dropping her salad tongs on the counter, she ran to her sister as tears streamed down her face.

They hugged each other, both of them crying and laughing at the same time.

40

LUUKAS

Luukas strolled out of the office, joining Nikulas at the counter. "How am I supposed to get anything done with all of this commotion out here?"

Nik smacked him on the shoulder. "Hey, bro. How're things?"

"I think they're going to be okay," he told him seriously.

"Good. You look good."

"As do you, little brother." He glanced over at the two girls as they hugged and cried. They were practically jumping around the kitchen. "I take it that's Emma?"

Nikulas' face lit up. "Yup. That's my Emma. She's moving in with me." He turned back to his brother. "How're things with you and Keira?"

Luukas imagined his face must look very similar to his little brother's as he looked over at his witch. "Things are good. I only tie her to the bed every other night or so, and I might get the phones replaced soon."

Nik's lips twitched. "Cool."

At that moment, the little redhead marched up to Luukas and poked him on the shoulder.

As he turned to face her, he caught Nik's look of alarm, and noticed him stiffening in panic.

He found himself face to face with a small female who had her sister's hazel eyes. It was slightly disconcerting. Luckily, her eyes were about the only resemblance.

He smiled down at her. "Hello, Emma. I don't think we've been formally introduced. My name is Luukas." He offered her his hand, and after a moment's hesitation, she took it.

"Hello, Luukas. It's nice to meet you. If you ever hurt my sister, I will stake you myself."

"Emma!" Keira protested.

He gave her a nod. "Understood."

"Good." And then she threw her arms around his neck and hugged him tight.

Nikulas stood up from his stool so fast, it fell over onto the floor. A low growl emanated from his chest. "Emma, come here."

Luukas tried not to laugh as she rolled her eyes, then turned to his brother with a sweet smile. He liked her already.

"Em, are you hungry?"

Emma joined her sister in the kitchen, where they proceeded to catch up on the last seven years between happy tears and more hugs.

The sun was rising when Luukas finally kicked everyone out, promising that they'd get together that night to discuss rescuing the others. He locked the repaired front door firmly behind them.

Keira watched her sister leave longingly.

"She'll be right downstairs," he reassured her. "You'll see her tonight."

"I know," she told him with a sad smile.

"Come to bed with me now," he demanded.

There was a naughty twinkle in her eye as she said, "Oh, I don't know. I think I might stay out here and read for a while."

Bending down, he threw her over his shoulder and headed towards the bedroom, her giggles muffled in his shirt. "That's not acceptable, witch."

Throwing her onto the bed, he yanked off her yoga pants that she'd ordered online.

He had to admit, he thoroughly enjoyed watching her strut around in those pants, but he enjoyed watching her strut around naked even more.

Grabbing her shirt, he ripped it down the middle.

She sighed. "I'm going to have to order more shirts."

"Order all the shirts you want." He grinned at her. "I'll rip them all off."

She grinned back at him, and he became serious as he stared at her, still amazed that she was actually here with him.

Stripping off his clothes, he lay down beside her and propped his head up on one hand. He ran his other hand over her soft skin, touching her face, her neck, her soft breasts, her belly; watching her hungrily as she arched into his hand.

His silver-grey eyes were fierce when they met hers.

"*Mine*," he growled out.

She touched his face. "Yes, Luukas. Yours."

With a moan of surrender, he took her lips with his.

EPILOGUE

THE MOUNTAINS OF WESTERN CANADA

"Why is he not rising?" Leeha's blood-red eyes darted anxiously over the tall, beautiful male lying lifeless on the stone altar.

The air was cold in the underground room; nearly as still as the vampire she kept watch over. She waited for some sign of life from the one on the stone. The one whose life had just been forever altered.

As she waited, her expressive eyes were unusually vacant, the horrors that normally swirled within the eerie orbs still, belying the depth of her emotions. To those who did not know her, it gave her the appearance of being somewhat sane.

But to the male that watched her from the other side of the altar, it was unnerving, for he had gotten to know her quite well over the past few months.

Her eyes scanned the ashen face over and over again, searching for the slightest sign of life...the tiniest twitch...but there was nothing. He appeared as hard and cold as the stone he lay upon.

The mountain above them rumbled ominously as hundreds of layers of rock and earth resettled after the recent battle that had taken place in the large cavern above. All of the earthen rooms her vampires had loyally burrowed out were caving in, reforming her beloved mountain home into something unrecognizable to her.

Her lovely mouth curled up into a sneer. The fight between the master vampire, Luukas, and the dark warlock who now leaned casually against the wall not ten feet away had not ended as she would have wished. However, she had needed the warlock to abandon the fight and return to her here.

Another rumble shook the small room, stronger this time. Dust floated down from the stone ceiling, and she shielded the prostrate male's face with her hands.

She, herself, paid the tremors no mind. They didn't matter. He was safe down here. And as soon as this was done, she could build another fortress, a better one; one that was above ground and didn't have this heavy, rancid smell of decaying earth.

She bent closer to his face. Was he even breathing?

A raven called out in a low, angry tone from her perch on the warlock's shoulder, upsetting the stillness in the room, vocalizing her master's displeasure that she should dare question his power. Even if only in her mind.

"He will," he answered her silent question. "Give him a moment." His voice was low and calm as he soothed the bird's ruffled feathers. "You should go retrieve the human from his cell. He'll need to feed once he's awake."

She appeared to not have heard him, instead redirecting her focus to the vampire's chest. Unzipping his ever-present hoodie with pale, shaking hands, she exposed his thin T-shirt. Studying the hard muscle beneath the white cotton, she let out an unsteady breath when she noticed a slight rise and fall. She closed her eyes and sent up a quick thank-you to the gods. His breaths were erratic, but they were there.

Leeha leaned closer to the vampire's face, her long, blood red hair falling forward to blend with his shorter, darker locks. His color was gradually returning, his olive-toned skin even slightly ruddy now, thanks to the blood she'd given him.

But he was so still. She shook her head slightly. Something must have gone wrong with the spell. He should be waking up by now.

Impatient with waiting, she straightened to her full height. She smoothed her hair back off of her face and ran her hands down the front of her whispery, indigo gown, smoothing imaginary wrinkles out of habit. Nervously, she began to pace at erratic speeds from one end of the small cavern to the other, wringing her white hands in front of her. Shadows danced on the walls as she passed, her jerky movements disturbing the torches burning along the walls.

She glanced sideways at the cloaked one still standing serenely on the other side of the altar. The hood of his black garment was pulled low over his face, hiding his features other than his strong, clean-shaven jaw and sculpted lips.

He stood calmly, petting his stupid bird, rather unconcerned whether or not the male on the table had survived his dark magic. His expression...what she could see of it...was only one of idle curiosity as to whether or not it had worked this time.

She should have *demanded* that he use Shea for this particular demon possession. That had been the plan all along, as she was the only one of Luukas' vampires that Leeha considered easily disposable.

If *that* vampire was the one on the altar, and the process went awry, she would remove her head without hesitation. She'd always hated that haughty bitch anyway. She was the only female who'd ever been allowed into Luukas' inner circle, stealing Leeha's rightful place at the master vampire's side.

However, her dark warlock over there had taken one look at the lovely vampire upon her arrival and informed Leeha that she was not to be used for a possession. Ever. He'd then hidden her away somewhere deep within the mountain where no others could enter, thanks to his boundary spell. Or perhaps he had set her free? No one knew. And being that only Luukas' vampires were strong enough to survive the entities living within them, they were left with little choice but to use the one they had available.

It should be that bitch, Shea, on this altar. Not her beloved Aiden.

She shot hostile glances at the cloaked one, and her eyes began to come alive again, nightmares coming to life within the irises, but then she forced herself to take a deep breath.

It was done. There was nothing to do for it now. She needed this particular demon, here, in their world, to help her control the others she'd already acquired for her army, some of whom were testing their limits a little too much.

Sacrifices had to be made for the greater good.

She stopped pacing near Aiden's hip, gathering up his lifeless hand in her own smaller one. He should have awoken by now! None of the others had taken this long to become reanimated once the demon was inside.

The raven studied her with one beady, black eye.

"I don't know why you're hovering like this," its master said quietly. "He's not there anymore. You know this."

She ignored him. They didn't know that for certain. Maybe her Aiden *was* still in there...somewhere. He was one of Luukas' council and a Hunter. He was strong. Stronger than the others. But was he strong enough to fight his way up through the possession?

My Aiden.

She laughed at herself. He wasn't really hers, no more than she was his, yet she'd always held a strong affection for him. Maybe it was because he was the only one who'd ever treated her like a true female, and desired her as one, without fear or ulterior motives.

She caught a slight movement from the corner of her eye. Blinking back the moisture pooling there, a rare show of emotion for her, she released his hand and moved closer again to his head.

As she watched, his eyelids flickered. Once. Twice. Her breath caught in her throat and she leaned in closer, willing them to open with everything inside of her.

"I suggest you back away now," the cloaked one ordered, his tone brooking no argument. "He's waking up, and he's not going to be happy with us."

Begrudgingly, she stepped back a few paces. Her hands fisted at her sides as she watched the completion of the spell with what could only be described as fascination.

His legs and arms began to jerk sporadically, and his chest rose on a fitful, deep breath. A low moan rumbled in his throat on the exhale. After a few more deep breaths, the spasms began to ease, and he bent his knees and then straightened his powerful legs, stretching like a large cat. They flopped back onto the altar, and he did it again, with more control this time. He made fists with his hands, and opened and closed his jaw, his tongue moving around in his mouth. It paused its movements as the tip of it came into contact with one of his extended fangs.

Instantly, he fell still, and his bloodshot eyes snapped open.

Leeha inched forward, staring into the familiar grey irises.

"Aiden?" she whispered, unable to keep the wistfulness from her voice.

She jumped back just in time as he burst up off of the altar with a roar that shook the room, landing solidly on his booted feet directly in front of her. More dirt and dust drifted down from the ceiling, dancing gracefully in the air as he confronted the one who had awakened him.

"What have you done?" he ground out at her from between clenched teeth.

Burying her regret deep within herself, she steeled her spine, narrowed her eyes at him, and held her ground.

"Are you not pleased, Waano?"

"*Why* have you awakened me?" he asked, his voice deceptively soft now.

Taking a deep breath, she braced herself and stepped closer to him, focusing her eyes on his. Desperately, she searched their depths for any sign of her lost love.

But all she saw were smoky shadows churning within the murky grey depths. It was a stranger staring back at her. A stranger who looked, smelled, and sounded like Aiden, right up to the slight dimple in his chin, but Aiden was not there.

She took another sharp breath, hardening her heart against her silly, wishful thinking. Aiden was gone. Mentally shaking herself, she got back to the situation at hand. Showing any signs of weakness was not an option with this one.

"I, we," she corrected, gesturing towards the cloaked one. "Woke you because we need you."

Aiden...or the creature that now possessed his body...glanced over his shoulder at the cloaked one, looking him up and down.

The creature scoffed.

"This one that hides behind his robes? He cares not for your plans, female. He is in this for his own gain. You are just too stupid to see it."

Leeha's nostrils flared at the insult, but she chose to ignore it, for now, and moved on to another tactic. Smiling provocatively, she pled her case.

"I am truly sorry that we disregarded your wishes, Waano. I know you did not wish to be brought into this world, but I felt that I had no other choice. I need you to help me. The others are getting too restless. I've began to dispatch them around the world to prepare, hoping it would keep them busy enough to be satisfied until it is time, but some of them are getting tired of waiting. They are wreaking havoc with the humans, drawing attention to themselves, and the more freedom they have, the more difficult they are finding it to obey me." She spread her arms wide in a supplemental gesture. "I'm losing control of them, and as much as I hate to admit it, I need your help. You are their elder, their master. They will listen to you."

His eyes were disconcerting as they came back to hers from where they'd wandered while she spoke, checking out his new physical form. They bored through her, straight to her demented soul.

"And what makes you think that *I* care about your plans? Maybe you should have left the others where they were, caught in that dimension between worlds, bound to this horrid altar." His lips lifted into a snarl. "Maybe they were there for a reason. What right did you have to bring them here? What right did you have to do this to *me*, when I expressly ordered you *not* to do it?"

He took a step closer to her, his lips pulled back from his exposed fangs. "Witless simpleton," he spit at her. "You cannot control them. You cannot control *me*. Tell me why I shouldn't just kill you right now?"

Leeha stared up at him fearlessly, her lips curving slightly. Why indeed? Maybe he needed a slight reminder of what it is like to have a physical form.

Reaching out, she placed her palm flat against his hard chest, feeling the muscle beneath his shirt jump at her touch. Her smile widened knowingly.

She could still have her Aiden, even if it was only his body.

"Tell me, would you really have preferred to remain as you were? No better than a ghost? Anchored to this room of dirt and rock? To this altar?" She scraped her nails lightly over his shirt as they made their way down the ridges of his tight stomach, stopping to tease playfully along the waistline of his jeans. Her tongue flickered out to wet her lips as she heard his heart speed up at her touch.

He wrapped his hand around her wrist and gave a slight tug. She leaned forward eagerly, pressing her full breasts against the hard muscles of his chest, uncaring that they had an audience.

Lowering his head to her neck, he moaned throatily as he inhaled her scent deep within him. Running his nose along the ridge of her jaw to her ear, he whispered, "You are a *fool.*"

With a quick twist of his hand, the delicate bones in her wrist snapped cleanly in two.

She cried out in shock and pain as he flung her to the floor.

"I want nothing to do with you, or your ridiculous plan. You'll never succeed!" he scoffed. "The only thing that will come from it will be to get your kind slaughtered, like animals. The humans are too many. You'll never control them all." He lowered his voice. "And no, I will not help you." He turned to the other male. "Now, release me. I want to go back to my world."

The cloaked one crossed his arms in front of his chest. Turning his head slightly, he whispered something to the raven on his shoulder. She chattered back at him in response, and then took flight, disappearing down one of the tunnels. Raising his head, his golden eyes came into view from within the shadows of his hood, their brilliance piercing through the dim light of the room.

"I'm afraid I can't do that."

"What do you mean 'you *can't* do that'?" Waano mocked him. His voice dropped menacingly. "*You* put me into this body, now *you* take me out."

Leeha pushed herself up to a standing position, her wrist already beginning to heal. Regaining her composure, she slithered around in front of him and gazed up at the creature, bloody triumph shining from her crazed eyes.

"He can't do it, even if he wanted to, because it takes more than one witch to complete the spell that will put you back. You see, most demons don't want to return to their own world. They like it here. They like the pleasures of having a physical body. They like to fight, and eat, and drink, and fuck. So, it takes a stronger power to remove you from that body. A power that no one witch possesses, no matter how powerful he is, or how dark his magic."

The creature glared down at her, his teeth clenched, his fangs bared in his anger. He shot a dangerous look at the cloaked one. "Is this true, warlock?"

The cloaked one nodded once.

He returned his gaze to Leeha, his eyes narrowing at her.

"Then get more witches," he demanded.

"Well now, that's a good idea," the cloaked one answered for her. "However, they wouldn't do much good without the spell. And as we only have the first part of it, the part that brings you here, to round them up and bring them here would be nothing but a waste of everyone's time."

Leeha watched him warily, this one who looked so much like her Aiden, but wasn't.

Abruptly, he threw his head back and laughed out loud.

"You think you have me right where you want me, don't you?" he sneered. "You think I'll just capitulate and do what you want of me now." He laughed again, the sound filled with disdain. "Stupid, weak vampire. I do nothing that I don't want to do. And I do *not* want to be here."

Her smile faded as her mind raced. He was proving to be more stubborn than she thought.

Leeha opened her mouth to speak, to try again to convince him to help her, but she never got the chance.

Though he never so much as touched her, she suddenly found herself thrown violently to the ceiling of the cavern. She let out an angry shriek as her backside slammed hard into the rough texture of the rock. Though she struggled, she couldn't break the invisible force holding her there.

The creature she'd spawned craned his head back and shouted up at her, "I will *not* be your puppet! I will *not* be this body for you! This...*slave*."

Her eyes grew wide as he threw his arms out to either side, gathering all of his energy within himself. Closing his eyes, he clenched his fists, smiling as he appeared to become...more.

His eyes flashed open, and he raised a hand towards her. She began to struggle anew against her invisible bonds.

He was going to kill her.

She shrieked in fear and anger as a blast of energy came from the other side of the room, but it didn't come anywhere near her. It blazed across the room, throwing Aiden...no, not Aiden...throwing *Waano*, face first into the wall in front of him. He hit so hard, he indented the stone, and it crumbled like powder around him.

Waano pushed off of the wall with a roar, twisting in mid-air and landing in a crouch to face the cloaked one.

He stood calmly in the same spot he'd been the entire time, one hand stretched towards the creature.

Waano regarded him for a moment, seeming to weigh his options, and then slowly straightened to his full height. With a last angry glance up at Leeha where she hung suspended, he bared his fangs with a hiss; A promise to her that this was not over.

And then he was gone.

Thank you for reading! The next book in the Deathless Night series is
A Vampire Possessed
Keep reading for a sneak peek!
Find out if Aiden is able to overcome the demon inside of him with some help from a cheeky witch.

ABOUT THE AUTHOR

L.E. Wilson writes romance starring intense alpha males and the women who are fearless enough to love them just as they are. In her novels you'll find smoking hot scenes, a touch of suspense, some humor, a bit of gore, and multifaceted characters, all working together to combine her lifelong obsession with the paranormal and her love of romance.

Her writing career came about the usual way: on a dare from her loving husband. Little did she know just one casual suggestion would open a box of worms (or words as the case may be) that would forever change her life.

On a Personal Note:

"I love to hear from my readers! Contact me anytime at le@lewilsonauthor.com."